Caroline on My Mind

Tara Ryan

Above Average Press

ISBN 978-1-967758-10-4 (Paperback) 978-1-967758-09-8 (eBook)

In memory of Sweetpea, who inspired the feisty and funny Norma Jean.

Chapter One

Jennings Lee couldn't find her underwear. And her shift started in twenty minutes. A groan emanated from the rumpled sheets on the king-size bed. *Screw the underwear.* She pulled her dress down toward her knees and grabbed her boots from under a chair. The fluffy white comforter fell to the floor as the man in the bed sat up, rubbing his eyes. She was out the door of the hotel room before he could open them.

She couldn't believe she'd stayed all night with a stranger. That was definitely not the plan. She'd just closed her eyes for a minute, then it was morning. No telling what kind of mess would be waiting for her at home, but she didn't have time to go let Norma Jean out now. *Stupid, stupid, stupid.*

Dinging and cheering rose from the casino floor. Jennings grasped the railing and peered down, trying to orient herself. The door to the room opened behind her and she took off to the left. She couldn't handle a morning-after confrontation. Especially not with—she checked her phone—seventeen minutes until her shift started. Six hotels away.

Inside the elevator, she braced herself against the wall for the slanted descent and slipped on her knee-high boots. The three-inch heels would make for a tough jog up The Strip but would be better than running barefoot.

She headed for the taxi stand at the front entrance of The Luxor. A quick calculation determined that she had $18 and some change in her checking account. Unless she moved money from her bankroll. Again. As she jumped in a cab and asked for the Bellagio, she realized this was why she couldn't build up a proper bankroll and quit waitressing for good. Her money management skills sucked. Hell, her life management skills sucked. Thirty-eight years old, and still living from pathetic tips, to paycheck, to selling her crap on Craigslist.

Her phone chirped and a text popped up.

Elena

> Where r u?

Six minutes, and she was stuck in the back of cab that smelled distinctly like three-day-old strawberry yogurt.

> On my way. Cover for me. And no, I don't want to talk about it.

Jennings leaned back against scratchy pleather, worn from a parade of revelers and overseas tourists looking for the magic of Vegas. She felt like the scarred and torn seat cover. Used up, ragged, and one beer away from being puked on.

"Ma'am? We're here."

Ma'am? She checked her reflection in the mirror on the driver's visor. *Damn. I'm too old for this.* Her phone chirped again, but she ignored it as she swiped her debit card in the reader attached to the seat in front of her. She could almost hear the whoosh of her last few dollars departing. "Thanks." The tip officially took her balance to zero, but she wasn't about to stiff a fellow service person eking out a living in this God-forsaken desert.

As she dashed across the pavement to the lobby, one of the bellhops called out. "Yo, Jennings. When we gonna have a repeat?" She turned in time to see him slap his co-worker on the back. "Now that's one show I'd like to see in syndication."

She really needed to assess her life choices, just as soon as the hamster wheel slowed down. "Sorry, Julio. They cancelled your cable after you couldn't get your TV turned on." Jennings heard him hiss as she spun on her pointy-toed boot and strode through the front door of the Bellagio. She headed straight to the locker room deep in the bowels of the casino. *Please let me have underwear in my locker. Please. Please.*

Just as she was about to slip inside the room, Vinnie appeared. "Lee."

Jennings tugged on the bottom of her dress. Her boss always had a way of making her feel exposed, but at this moment she may as well have a flashing sign around her neck: *A business man from Chicago is taking my hipsters home as a souvenir.*

Vinnie made a big show of checking his clipboard and fake Rolex. "It's 11:07 and you aren't even in your uniform."

"Won't happen again, Mr. Moreno." The man was ten years younger than her, yet he insisted all of "my girls address me with the proper respect."

He tapped a Montblanc (likely fake as well) against the clipboard and leered at her chest. "This could go in your permanent record, you know. Or..." A bead of sweat snaked across his shiny head as his gaze traveled the rest of the way down her body.

Twenty minutes in his office and the incident report would disappear. She needed this job until she had enough money to make a go of playing poker professionally. And there was no telling how many marks she had on her file. Sometimes if she was running good at the table, she wasn't the promptest employee. She wasn't built for a life of punching a clock, but none of her other efforts seemed to pan out.

Vinnie shifted his bulk. More drops of sweat traced down his face to the roll of pale flesh between his chin and the collar of his gold shirt. And try as she might, Jennings couldn't miss the tent in his pressed pants.

She swallowed the bile rising in her throat. "I'm late, and I understand that you have to keep records of these things." Pressing her back against the door, she edged further away from him. "I'm going to change and get out on the floor. Pronto." Jennings nodded her head and forced a smile.

She watched her boss's ego deflate, along with his pants. Vinnie lowered the clipboard and scowled. "And no chat breaks, Lee."

Five minutes later, Jennings entered the poker room, her short black skirt and fishnet stockings the only things between her bottom and a cool breeze. She'd be adding underwear to her emergency kit tomorrow.

"Cocktails? Water?" She parroted the questions as she strode between the lower-limit tables. The blinds were a dollar, and so were the tips. Another consequence of her tardiness—she got stuck with the crappy tables. Elena waved at her from Bobby's Room, the highest-limit game in Vegas. "We need to talk," she mouthed. Jennings shook her head as she made her way to the bar. Elena always talked about the same thing. About how it was time for Jennings to settle down. To stop waking up in strange hotel rooms.

Jennings couldn't argue with that one anymore. The morning had been a harsh reality check. *As of today, no more men.*

***

Mitch Kline surveyed the poker area from the side nearest Bobby's Room. He didn't follow professional poker much, but even he recognized the famous faces around the table inside. The waitress hovering over that table was Latina. The other two women serving the crowded room were no-goes as well. One was clearly in her sixties, and the other didn't look old enough to drink alcohol, let alone serve it.

He started to turn away when a woman squeezed past him bearing a tray full of drinks. His gaze followed her short skirt across the room and when she bent over to hand a bottle of water to a player, he swore he saw rounded, fishnet-covered flesh.

"Hey, Buster. No loitering." The Latina from Bobby's room faced off with him, a fire lit in her dark eyes.

Mitch raised his hands in surrender and nodded across the room to the woman with the bad dye job and no panties. "She a friend of yours?"

The waitress slapped her hands against his chest and pressed. "It's not that kind of place, Mister. You head downtown if you're shopping for something."

It wouldn't do him any good to get kicked out. He bit back laughter at the petite woman straining against him. "It's Mitch, not Mister, and I intend no disrespect. Just thought I knew her from somewhere. No biggie." He turned to walk away. Three, two...

"Where're you from?"

Mitch kept the satisfaction off his face as he turned back. "North Carolina."

She appeared to consider his answer. Then her brow smoothed and she glanced back across the room. "Jennings doesn't talk about where she's from, but sometimes I think I hear a bit of Southern twang." She swung her head back in his direction. "You're not here to give her a hard time, are you?" She crossed her arms over her chest and widened her stance, making it clear she was prepared for a fight.

He leaned closer and checked her nametag. "Can I trust you with a secret, Elena?"

She gave the sign of the cross. "On my *gran abuela's* grave, you can."

His mouth twitched up. If he wasn't on a job, he'd enjoy getting to know this spitfire a lot better. "A friend of mine is trying to find his sister. And I think that's her."

***

Mitch had been playing Texas Hold'em at a $1/$2 table for the last hour, and the most he could get out of Jennings was directions to the can. He didn't get it. Most women were powerless to his charm. Look how quickly Elena had cracked.

It didn't help that every time Jennings came near him, all he could think about was reaching up that short skirt and grabbing her bare ass. Why couldn't the woman wear panties?

He drained the rest of his scotch as she approached the table again. He needed to switch to water soon, or he'd be snoozing at the table instead of convincing Jennings to get in his truck and go back to Asheville with him. Mitch still wasn't sure how he was going to pull that off. She wouldn't even chitchat with him—it wasn't likely she'd be ready to take a road trip.

Why did I agree to this job? It wasn't a hard answer. Benny had been one of the few people who stuck by Mitch during "the incident." So, when he asked Mitch to find the sister he hadn't seen in over twenty years, "no" wasn't an option.

"Cocktails? Water?" Jennings sounded as bored as she looked. She smiled as she took the players' orders, but it was obvious her mind was far away from the Vegas Strip. Mitch wondered if she was thinking about the life she'd run away from when she was sixteen.

For someone who didn't want to be found, Caroline Jennings Lee hadn't tried very hard. A simple check of tax records had located a work card in Vegas, and a few phone calls narrowed his search to the poker room at the Bellagio. She hadn't even legally changed her name, was just using her middle one, which was her mother's maiden name.

Benny remembered her as a blonde with bright blue eyes. The blond roots were obvious under the messy mop of brown hair and her eyes were brown, but when she blinked, Mitch could see a sliver of blue behind the colored contacts. Besides, the resemblance between brother and sister was evident in the curve of her nose and the smattering of freckles her heavy makeup couldn't disguise.

Jennings made her way around to his side of the table and he switched tactics. "Excuse me, miss?"

She tugged the bottom of her skirt and then crouched beside him. "Yes?"

Mitch tipped his cards up so she could see them. "I'm wondering if you think I should slow play this hand or bet it hard."

Her eyes lit with a smile. "One player to a hand, sir. Can I get you another scotch?"

"Nah, I think I'll switch to coffee. Black is fine." He folded his hand, the deuce-eight of clubs, and flashed a smile at her.

Before she left the table, she grazed the back of his shoulder and when he turned, he could've sworn she winked at him.

***

"What's wrong with me, Elena?" Jennings stretched out on a bench in the locker room while her friend changed clothes. "I swore off men eight hours ago. Why did I write my number on that guy's coffee cup?"

Elena smiled; her eyebrows raised. She looked smug, and Jennings couldn't figure out why. Usually, her friend would be chattering on about *not* meeting up with strangers and pleading with Jennings to find a good man, like Martin. But Jennings wasn't about to give her heart to anyone. *If you don't get attached, it won't hurt when they leave.*

"I could change my number." It wouldn't be the first time.

"Maybe this guy will be different." Elena closed her locker and pulled Jennings to her feet. "Don't change your number. It's *destino*. I can feel it."

Jennings rolled her eyes.

"You know I have the gift, *chica*. It was passed down from my *gran abuela*. Only the most perceptive and spiritual—"

"'Receive the gift.' Yeah, I know. Usually when you're talking about my destiny, it involves a split-level in Henderson and a dentist named Roger."

Elena pouted. "He was a nice guy. And Martin said he really liked you."

Jennings hooked her arm in Elena's and pulled her out of the locker room. "Considering his ex-wife was almost three hundred pounds, I'm not surprised."

"Oh, Jennings, I just want you to be happy. Maybe this Mitch guy will be exactly what you need."

"Excuse me?" She stopped. "Mitch? I don't even know the guy's name... Wait a minute, this is a set-up!" Jennings jerked her arm out of Elena's.

"No, that's not it, Jen—"

"Oh, and I fell right into it. You can always count on slutty Jennings to make a pass at the hot guy." She turned and stomped toward the exit.

The tap-shuffle-tap of Elena's kitten heels chased after her. "Jennings! Wait. He just wants to talk to you. It's not a set-up."

The door swooshed behind Jennings, and she was in a cab before Elena could catch up.

Chapter Two

The cab dropped Jennings off in front her building. The ride took a chunk out of the tips she'd made, but avoiding Elena at that moment had been more important than saving money. She hadn't been home in over twenty-four hours, and she dreaded what she would find inside her apartment. The window beside the front door hinted at the disaster awaiting her. The cheap horizontal blinds were torn straight down the middle, and inconceivably, a roll of toilet paper was wedged under one side. But if Norma Jean had managed to get under the bathroom sink, maybe she'd finally learned how to use the facilities.

Jennings turned her key in the lock and took a deep breath before stepping inside. *Squish.* Closing her eyes and gritting her teeth, she fumbled for the light. *My lifestyle is complete shit.* Before she could get the light on, Norma Jean, seemingly propelled out of thin air, slammed into the side of her head and grappled to get a foothold, or rather, clawhold, as she slid down Jennings's body. The noises emanating from the little dog reminded her of the commotion when the cute little Gizmo morphed into a heinous Gremlin.

She flicked the light on, and as she suspected, the beast had destroyed the apartment. Norma Jean's transformation from lovable lap dog to spawn of Satan occurred whenever she was left alone for more than ten hours. Her lifestyle didn't make her the best pet owner.

Jennings lifted her foot out of the putrid pile and slipped off her shoe. She carefully picked her way across the living room, dodging puddles, dog toys, a diaphragm (where had she found that?), and what appeared to be a regurgitated Victoria Secret thong. *Why did she only eat my expensive underwear?*

She collapsed onto the vintage sofa she had found in the same alley as Norma Jean. It creaked under her weight, and a spring poked her in the back. Apparently, she was under attack from both her alley "treasures." A ball of fur launched into her lap and covered her face with kisses. She'd take stinky dog breath over strange man/stale beer any day. Jennings cuddled the dog close and stroked her patchy hair. The vet's best guess was that Norma Jean was a Pomeranian/Rat Terrier/Pit Bull Mix. And he'd said her hair would grow back in about two months. That was four years ago. The truth was, she not only sounded and acted like a Gremlin—she looked like one too. Tenants of the complex crossed to the other side of the street whenever Jennings and Norma Jean went for a walk. One guy had explained he wasn't scared she'd hurt him, but that he might catch something from the "mangy mutt."

Norma Jean jumped down and stood by her leash, which was hanging from the top of a floor lamp. Jennings couldn't imagine how the twenty-pound dog could pull off such feats of disarray, but she wished she could afford a nanny cam to prove that Norma Jean could fly.

As Jennings rose from the couch, her phone chirped, signaling a new voice mail. She'd ignored Elena's calls since leaving the Bellagio, and after walking Norma Jean and cleaning up the mess, she wouldn't have any energy left to deal with her friend's matchmaking. So what if the guy was hot? So what if he'd made her laugh in the middle of one of the most humiliating, underwear-less shifts of her life? So what if Jennings had decided, of her own accord, to give him her number? It was a setup, and Jennings had sworn off men.

***

Mitch hadn't been to Vegas since his mother's sixth wedding. Or was it the seventh? Both had been officiated by Elvis. Regardless, enough time had passed that he'd forgotten about the hordes of foreigners, drinks taller than his waist, and the ease of scoring "Girls! Girls! Girls!"

He crumpled yet another flyer and tossed it into a trash can. The amount of paper used to sell women in Vegas must account for at least half the deforestation of Central America.

Mitch had never encountered a dry spell long enough to justify paying for sex. Based on the stock holdings of his mother's husbands, he supposed marriage was just another form of paying for it. That was not a trap *he* intended to fall into. Marriage didn't equal happiness. If it did, his mother wouldn't trade her men up faster than her Caddys.

Ahead, a pair of showgirls posed for pictures outside the Flamingo. Their tight bodies were barely covered with strategically-placed feathers and sequins. But for some reason, all he could think about was a certain fishnet-covered ass.

He pulled his phone out and stared at it for a second. Call or text? It shouldn't be a difficult decision. A woman, he'd text. For work, only a phone call would do. Somehow with Jennings, the line was blurring. And he needed to bring it into focus real quick, or he risked losing his best friend. Sliding the phone back into his pocket, he decided to clear his mind. He knew precisely where to go.

***

Her bankroll was so low, Jennings was stuck playing the .50/$1 game at MGM. The table was well-stocked with poker virgins who didn't know the difference between a blind and a raise. But there was one guy who obviously knew what he was doing, and he was working the table like Elton John seduces a piano.

She decided to play the role of helpless, pouty fish and see if she could catch the shark unaware.

For the next few hands, Jennings hammed it up, huffing, squealing, and asking the guy next to her, "What's a flush again?" Then the dealer flicked her the perfect hand for her ploy. Jack-ten of diamonds. She made saucer eyes when she looked down at her cards and immediately started playing with her chips, purposefully fumbling them. The shark at the other end of the table guffawed when she raised the pot. He called and sat back with the confidence of a rooster presiding over his hen house.

When the dealer turned over the first three cards, Jennings jumped as if she'd been scalded. But the ace-queen-nine flop couldn't have been more perfect. She had an open-ended straight draw, and chances were Cocky down there had an ace. She checked and held her breath in a show of nervousness. Cocky also checked, and she was certain he had an ace. When the turn was a king, she peered at her cards to make it seem like she was double checking the king in her hand. She hesitantly set a small bet across the line, as if a dangerous crocodile was circling the pot. The jerk laughed again and pushed half his stack into the middle.

Jennings made a big show of counting her chips, peeking at her cards and studying Cocky. Then she checked the time, shrugged her shoulders and pushed all her chips in.

"Call." The word was out of his mouth before she got her chips over the line.

He confidently flipped over the ace-deuce of hearts and crossed his arms over his chest. Jennings was tempted to slow roll, but it wasn't her style, so she slapped her cards on the table, revealing her straight.

He doubled over as if someone had punched him in the nuts. *Take that, Chicago businessman. Take that, ruggedly handsome Mitch.* Take that, every man who'd ever crossed her path.

She stacked her chips, said goodbye, and moved over to a $1/$2 table. Now that she was done with men, she could focus on poker.

***

Mitch lined the shot up, and as he drew the club back, his phone rang. The group of men behind him grumbled, so he grabbed his ball off the tee and stepped to the side to let them play through.

He tapped his earpiece. "Yeah?"

"Don't bite my head off. It's like 11 a.m. there. You should be up by now." Benny had long ago secured the title of most logical friend.

"I'm not sleeping, I'm golfing."

Benny tsked. "Unless my sister is a golf pro, that's not a justifiable expense, Mr. Kline."

Mitch stabbed a mound of dirt with his driver. "Are you my accountant now?"

"No, but I am your client."

"I told you I'm not taking your money. Consider it best man duties." He sighted down the green, studying the hole.

"Best men pick up the tuxes, not the groom's sister in Vegas." Benny sighed. "You're a PI. You find people. I'm paying you."

The foursome moved to the next hole and Mitch stepped up to take his shot again. "In that case, I've known your sister for less than twenty-four hours and she's already driven me to golf. So, yes, this is a justifiable expense."

"You found her?" Benny's voice dropped to a whisper. "You found Caroline?"

"Yeah, I found her, B. She looks like you. Except hotter."

"Mitch, please tell me you didn't sleep with my sister."

He swung the driver back and sliced a wide arc. The ball sailed over a sand trap and rolled to a stop on the green. "She barely spoke to me."

Benny growled. "That hasn't stopped you before."

"No, B. I didn't sleep with your sister." Mitch slung the bag of clubs over his shoulder and took the path down to the green. "I told you, no sex in Vegas. Hard and fast rule."

"Why do I not feel reassured?"

Mitch pulled the putter from his bag. "B, relax. I got this under control. Your sister and I will be in Asheville in a week, tops."

Benny practically squealed. "You told her about the wedding, and she agreed to come?"

"Like I said, under control." Mitch tapped the ball and it sailed past the hole. Not a good sign.

***

She was up almost two hundred bucks and had just ordered a late lunch when Mitch sat down at her table. Jennings cursed under her breath. It was easier to swear off men when there wasn't a hot one sitting five feet away. "How the hell'd you find me?"

Mitch slid two bills to the dealer and raised an eyebrow at Jennings. "Lucky, I guess." A delicious dimple appeared beneath the stubble on his left cheek as he winked at the dealer. Marla, who'd been dealing at the MGM as long as Jennings had been playing poker, should've been immune to his charms, but it was becoming obvious that the force was strong with this hunk of hot damn.

"So, you charmed Elena. Too bad for you she's married." Jennings checked her cards and flicked them into the muck.

"She's a smart woman. You should listen to her." He tossed a few chips over the line and settled back in his seat.

Jennings glared at him, but cinched her mouth shut. She knew better than to talk to a player in a hand. It was basic poker etiquette.

Everyone folded to Mitch's raise, and he raked in a small pot, flashing a grin at Jennings as he pulled the chips toward him.

The heat started in the arches of her feet and seared up her legs, settling in a pool of unwelcome desire between her thighs. If he could do that with a smile, what the hell would happen if he touched her? Jennings glanced down at her stack. She'd done well for the day, and she knew this sort of distraction wasn't good for her game. But her lunch hadn't arrived yet, and she didn't want to give Mitch the satisfaction of thinking he'd rattled her. She grunted and peeked down at her hole cards. Snowmen. She raised the pot with the pair of eights and sat back to watch how the other players responded to her action. She'd have to ignore the dampness in her panties.

Mitch checked his cards as the action came to him and then looked up. His stare bore into her and he licked his lips.

Jennings had lived in the desert for almost twenty years, but she'd never felt so hot in her life. And it wasn't the pressure of the game. *No men. No men. No more empty, unsatisfying, hot, animalistic sex.*

"Get a room." The player to Mitch's left tapped the felt.

She wanted to crawl under the table and never come out. Mitch just guffawed and folded his cards.

As soon as the hand was over, Jennings stacked her chips, grabbed her purse, and rose from the table. "Sorry, everyone. Gotta get to work." Let Mitch stalk her at the Bellagio. She wasn't on again until Tuesday. And hopefully Elena wasn't twisted enough to give out her address.

On her way to the cashier, the waitress passed by with her food. Jennings set a $10 chip on the tray and grabbed the sandwich from the basket. "Thanks, Sunny. Distract seat three for me until I can get out of here, 'kay?"

"A sticky one, huh?" The redhead glanced over at the table and whistled. "Well, if you insist. Server code and all."

Jennings chanced one more look back at the table. Mitch was staring at her, arms crossed over his broad chest, smug smile on his face. "That one's trouble, Sunny. Mark my words."

***

Mitch knew Jennings wasn't scheduled to work for two more days. So, he'd obviously gotten to her. He'd play a few more hands, and then he'd head over to her apartment. She couldn't avoid him forever.

He was an excellent student of human nature, and he could tell she was close to bending under the weight of his charm.

But there were limits, of course. She wasn't some random woman, and this wasn't a normal case. She was Benny's big sister. And they were in Vegas. No sex in Vegas. He'd learned that lesson the hard way. His phone rang. He stepped away from the table and pressed talk. "Hey, Mom. What's up?"

"What's that noise? Where are you?" Betsy Kline's whine transcended the din of ringing slot machines and cheering players. "Are you in Vegas?"

"I'm on a job, Mom."

"I can't believe you'd go to Las Vegas and not invite your poor, lonely mother."

Mitch rolled his eyes and wandered out of the poker room. An advertisement for a performer with duct tape over his mouth filled one wall, promising a rousing good time. Only in Vegas. *If Jennings couldn't control that smart mouth of hers, maybe he'd employ a similar tactic for the road trip.*

"Mitchell! Are you listening to me?" His mother's squeal snapped him out of picturing other ways to shut up Jennings.

"I'm listening. What do you mean you're lonely? What about Gary?"

Her silence was enough of an answer. His mother was folding on another one. Mitch couldn't understand why she didn't give up on marriage altogether.

"I'm working, Mom. Missing person. Not a vacation." So, his job included perks like golf and gambling. It was still work. Jennings Lee was definitely work.

"Hm. Maybe you'll stop by on your way back? Unless you suddenly started flying?"

Betsy Kline might be fickle about love, but she was shrewd about most things. She knew full well Mitch hadn't flown, and that he'd have to pass right through Memphis on the way back. Just like she knew that the right combination of guilt, persistence, and lawyers would guarantee her half of her latest victim's net worth. The poor schlubs never saw it coming. "It depends on how agreeable this person is once I find them." The less information Betsy had, the better.

"Fine. I'll just be sitting here. Alone."

Mitch hadn't seen his mother's latest abode, not that it mattered. Like her husbands, her houses all blurred together. Heavily-brocaded this, plastic-covered that, all topped off with a Victorian flair. Whatever this house looked like, Betsy was just passing through en route to her next conquest. "Bye, Mom."

He needed to stop answering his phone.

Chapter Three

Jennings had managed to restore her apartment to its pre-tantrum state, and she wasn't about to risk another run-in with the Gremlin so, as soon as she got home, she leashed Norma Jean up and they headed out for a leisurely stroll.

They meandered along their usual route, Norma Jean's retractable leash allowing her to jump across the concrete drainage ditch to the patch of hard-packed dirt and occasional sprig of grass on the other side. In Vegas, all the grass was reserved for golf courses.

As they came upon the scenic overlook highlighting the dumpsters, Mitch appeared from around the corner of the building like a mirage amongst the drought-resistant plantings. Despite her exasperation at his knowing where she lived, she wanted to drink up the sight of him.

The pale-yellow polo shirt straining across his first-rate chest featured a familiar logo. The Grove Park Inn was known worldwide for its top-rate golf course. Jennings wondered how recently he'd been to Asheville. His brown twill pants were more working class than country club, and his battered sneakers wouldn't have been permitted on the hallowed grass of any golf course she knew. His cheeks sported two days stubble, and his hair was past needing a haircut. But it was the rough and ragged part of Mitch that tempted her. If he was completely put together, he'd be easy to resist.

"The Strip is six blocks that way." She pointed south as she brushed past him, allowing herself a sample of the bicep testing the limits of his taut sleeve.

"I'm more of an off-the-beaten-path sort of guy." His grin reached all the way to his eyes. Not easy to fake. He crouched down to greet Norma Jean who, as usual, was a complete attention whore. "Is this one of those Mexican hairless things?"

Jennings jerked the leash and scowled. "She has hair." *Just not her full share.* She quickened the pace back to her apartment, dragging Norma Jean behind her.

Mitch sprinted past her and jumped between her and her front door. "Hey, sorry, I didn't mean to insult your dog." He flashed her another grin, accompanied by that damn dimple.

"I suppose most women are overcome by that dazzling smile and your mediocre good looks, but I'm not most women." She crossed her arms over her chest and feigned boredom.

"Mediocre, huh?" He tapped his finger at the juncture of his sexy scruff and an untrimmed sideburn.

All she had to do was take two steps forward and she'd be pressed against that hard body. She closed her eyes and imagined squeezing his tight butt.

When she felt his breath against her cheek and his hand snake around her waist, she forgot her "no men" pledge and sank into him. Her hands grazed up his back, the hard plastic of the leash bumping along his vertebrae. Her free hand continued up to his hair and as she twined it in her fingers, she was grateful he hadn't cut it.

His lips traced a path up her neck to the sensitive spot behind her ear and his tongue darted out to deliver a jolt of tingles down her spine. She moved forward, trapping him between her yearning body and the front door. His hands crushed her hips against his and found their way under her shirt, skimming along her back as if wakeboarding along the top of a wave.

The thin cotton of his pants did nothing to disguise his arousal, and her body responded without her permission. Her panties dampened for the second time that day, and her nipples felt as if they would pierce straight through her bra and t-shirt.

She never brought men to her apartment, but he was here, and she wanted this *now*. While she fumbled with the key attached to Norma Jean's leash, Mitch continued his exploration of her neck and the cleavage peeking out the top of her shirt. She pushed the door open and the three of them fell in a tangle of bodies and tongues on the floor. When Norma Jean wedged her compact body between theirs, Jennings unbuckled the leash and gave the dog a push, propelling her out of the way. She refocused her attention on the intoxicating man on her foyer floor, but as she lingered above him, deciding where to attack first, he held up a hand to block her descent.

"I'm sorry, I can't. B would never forgive me." His hungry eyes countered his words.

The statement had more effect than a bucket of ice. "Of course. You're fucking married." She rocked back on her heels, shaking her head, remembering why men were never a winning proposition.

Mitch laughed, which made Jennings want to hit him even more. Instead, she stood and pointed to the open door. "Get out."

He rose to sitting and swiped a hand across his forehead. "Jennings, wait. B isn't my wife."

Girlfriend, whatever. "Get out."

"He's your brother."

She couldn't move. Couldn't breathe. She thought about Benny every day, but with the word hanging out there, in the air between them, it was like her brother was real again. Not merely a memory of a freckle-faced kid following her around. "Get. Out."

Mitch sighed but got to his feet and, after patting Norma Jean on the head, exited the apartment.

Jennings closed the door behind him and then slid down it, collapsing on the floor. She didn't realize she was crying until Norma Jean climbed on her lap and started licking the tears off her cheeks.

***

I couldn't have handled that any worse. Mitch kicked his front tire and swore. It was this forsaken city. Las Vegas caused temporary insanity. He opened the door to his truck and flopped across the bench seat. 1) *As soon as I found her, I should've called B and had him fly out here and approach her. 2) I never should've thought about her ass.* Which was her fault—for not wearing panties that first day. Maybe she went commando at work to rack up more tips, because she'd definitely had panties on today. And Mitch had seriously considered ripping them off.

His phone rang and a check of the display revealed the last person he wanted to talk to right now. "Yo, B. What's up?" *Yo?* When had he ever said, "Yo?"

"I'm dying here, man. I've got to talk to her." Benny didn't comment on Mitch's odd greeting. "Is she happy? Or mad? Or indifferent? That'd be the worst. Tell me she's not indifferent."

"B, chill. You'll freak her out even more than she already is." As soon as Mitch said the words, he wished he could wind them back into his mouth.

"What do you mean, she's freaking out?" Benny took a breath, but only to refuel. "You slept with her. Mitch! It was the one thing I asked. I didn't tell you not to gamble, or to fly instead of driving. All I asked is that you not sleep with my sister."

Mitch exhaled hard enough to make his air freshener dance. "I didn't sleep with her, B." *More like a near miss.* "She's rattled about me finding her. I mean,

Encyclopedia Brown could've found her, but she'd made an effort to be someone else, so I'm sure it's a little shocking."

"It's been twenty-two years, Mitch. Maybe it's too late."

If the tears forming in Jennings's eyes as he walked out of her apartment were any indication, Mitch doubted it was too late. "She needs time to process, B. When she sees you, it's gonna be the best day of her life." *As soon as she gets over the hurt and anger.*

Benny sighed. "Thanks, man. I can never repay you for this."

"Yeah, I'm shootin' for the Best Man award. Later, B." Mitch ended the call and closed his eyes. This would have been so much easier if Caroline Lee, aka Jennings, looked more like her brother, and less like a woman whose sex appeal shone through her dishwater brown hair and heavy makeup.

The Vegas sun pounded against his knees. He probably looked like an idiot, half-laying in his truck with the door open. *I'll get up as soon as I figure out a plan.*

"How do you know my brother?" Her shadow slid over his smoldering kneecaps.

Mitch propped himself up on his elbows. Jennings stood framed in the open door of the truck, arms crossed over her chest, eyes rimmed in red. Her hair had fallen from her ponytail and hung in limp strands. She flicked one out of her eyes.

"Go on. Explain yourself. This is your chance." Her stance and the daggers shooting from her eyes told him it was his *only* chance.

He pulled himself to sitting and cleared his throat. "I met Benny my second day in Asheville. He was playing Hackey sack on the common at UNCA. He's not the most coordinated guy ever." Mitch couldn't help but laugh at the memory.

A smile tugged at the corner of Jennings's mouth. "He never was."

Reassured, he slid across the seat, offering her a place to sit down. She tucked herself behind the steering wheel and faced him. The sun was even hotter through the passenger-side window, but he wasn't about to disrupt this tentative connection. "The sack hit me in the head as I was heading to the library. Benny insisted on buying me a beer. I insisted he give up Hackey sack."

"So, you went to school together?" She leaned back against the driver's door; the lines of her face relaxed.

"No." Mitch laughed. "I went to Life U."

Jennings nodded, and he got the impression she'd done her time as well.

He continued. "I was on campus looking for a missing co-ed. Turned out she was on an extended bender, so it was a quick case. But Benny and I, we've been friends ever since."

"So, you're a detective?"

"A PI. Most of the time, I'm following around cheating bastards, but occasionally I get to actually investigate." She was so close, and Mitch's thoughts veered back to the taste of her skin.

She bit her bottom lip. "Like tracking me down?"

Rambo. Ken Griffey, Jr. Tomato Soup. Bea Arthur. He took a deep breath and focused on her question and not her mouth. "It took him years to tell me he had a sister. He's such a positive, upbeat guy, but every so often, it's like someone turns his dimmer down. That's when he's thinking about you. He's missed you." He didn't want to guilt her—hell, based on what he knew, he'd have taken off, too. A ten-year-old shouldn't have to raise her little brother. As soon as Benny was safely in foster care, Mitch would've gone looking for freedom.

A tear slid down her cheek, and without thinking about it, he leaned forward to wipe it away. Their eyes locked and he realized she wasn't wearing her brown contacts. The blue of her iris was tinged darker around the edges of the pupil.

She shuddered, and her sorrow took up all the air in the cab. She'd lived without a family for over twenty years. As vapid and materialistic as Betsy was, Mitch couldn't imagine a life without his mother. She wasn't always great at showing it, but he knew she loved him.

Mitch pushed the hair out of Jennings's face and kissed her left temple, then her right. As he lowered his mouth to hers, she braced her hands against his chest and heaved. Caught off guard, he flew back, knocking his head on the door frame. "What the hell?"

"I don't need your pity. I've managed just fine on my own." She reached behind her and pulled the door handle, practically tumbling out of the truck.

He reached up to rub the knot forming on his head and watched through the windshield as Jennings tore across the parking lot. *Why do I have such a knack for finding these women? Damn Las Vegas.*

Sliding behind the steering wheel, Mitch started the truck and squealed out of the parking lot. He wasn't about to stick around where he wasn't wanted. He didn't need to be taught that lesson twice.

Chapter Four

Jennings arrived for her shift twenty minutes early. Life had moved in slow motion since she found out Benny was looking for her. It was as if her consciousness needed to catch up with the notion that he wasn't just a fond memory. A simple task, like making toast, took her focused effort and left her feeling spent. Not able to risk losing her job, she'd started getting ready at eight for her eleven o'clock shift. Now, she sat on the bench in the locker room, staring at the black apron in her hands, unable to convince her arms to tie it around her waist.

The door flew open, and Elena burst into the room. "Damn, *Chica*, you had me worried. I've been calling you for two days." She stopped and waved her hands in front of Jennings's face. "Hello?"

Elena's voice sounded distant, echoing and bouncing off the walls of the small room. Jennings heard the words, but she couldn't bring herself to respond.

"Are you hung over? Sick? What is it? I'll tell Vinnie to piss off." She crouched in front of Jennings. Her voice softened. "Mitch told me about your brother." Her hands cupped her friend's knees. "*Chica*, please. Talk to me."

Jennings licked her lips in preparation for speaking. She hadn't uttered a word since the confrontation with Mitch. "Cocktails? Water?" She rose from the bench, knocking Elena to the floor, and tied the apron around her waist. "I'm taking Bobby's Room." Her life was far from perfect, but it was rarely complicated. She didn't get attached to people, and Elena had crept up on her. Coffee, a drink after work, then dinner and exchanging life stories. Well, the version that Jennings told. Now, her friend knew about the brother she'd abandoned. Would she judge her? Or worse, pity her?

She wandered aimlessly, killing time until she could clock in. In the lobby, a family was checking in, the distracted father at registration, the anxious mother working a strand of pearls at her throat, a boy, about eight, staring up in wonder at the *Fiori di Como*, the blown-glass chandelier by Dale Chihuly that took up the entire ceiling. The boy had a mop of blond hair and a handful of freckles on his cheeks. Jennings sucked in a breath and bit back the lump in her throat. It'd been lodged there since her world imploded. *Benny.*

Stooping beside the boy, she craned her neck up at the ceiling. "I think it looks like a bunch of jellyfish."

"But jellyfish are clear." He cocked his head toward her.

She forced a smile. "Enjoy your stay." Pressing the back of her hand to her mouth, she dashed back into the bowels of the building and flew into the nearest bathroom. The sob broke as soon as she was through the door. She braced herself against the counter and let the tears spill into the sink. It was how Benny was cemented in her mind—curious, contemplative, with an unwavering sense of eight-year-old logic. She didn't want to risk that memory. Reality rarely measured up.

The door opened, but Jennings didn't look up. She stiffened when arms encircled her shoulders.

"*Carina*, I can't imagine what you must be feeling." Elena spoke softly and the rich tone of her accent soothed Jennings. "I don't know why you've been hiding from your life, but no matter what, I am your friend."

Jennings turned and tentatively reached her arms around the other woman.

Elena pulled her tight into an embrace. She stroked her hair and whispered something in Spanish.

For the first time in over twenty years, Jennings didn't feel alone.

Once the tears subsided, she stepped back and reached for a tissue. A glance in the mirror confirmed that her makeup had fled the scene, leaving behind a trail of black gunk. She dabbed helplessly at her face, then shrugged her shoulders in defeat.

"Come on, let's get you fixed up. Because if we don't get out on the floor, Vinnie is going to fix us good." Elena steered Jennings toward the door. "But between us, I think we could take him."

Jennings erupted in laughter. Apparently, Elena wasn't going away, come hell or high water, and maybe having someone on her side wasn't so scary after all.

***

Their shift was ending and, mercifully, Vinnie hadn't said a word to either of them for starting late. Jennings had a suspicion their boss was a little scared of Elena. And with good reason. When the Latina fire sparked in her eyes, she was a force to be reckoned with. She often reminded him of her ability to hex those who wronged her. Regardless of why, Jennings was grateful for one less hassle.

Then Mitch showed up.

Jennings searched for an escape route, but he stood between her and the way out. There were only two tables playing in the high-limit room that day, and at the second one she found her savior. Well, at least a diversion.

Joey "The Nuts" Hopkins was a pro who had been hitting on Jennings for as long as she'd worked at the Bellagio. She may have slept with her share of men, but she never went home with one of her regulars. Men passing through were less likely to get attached.

After checking to be sure he wasn't in a hand, Jennings leaned down and whispered in his ear, "You wanna take a quick break?" She added a subtle peck behind his ear for extra effect.

His eyes widened bigger than the $25 chips in front of him. He shoved his chair back and practically fell out of it in his haste to rise. "Hell, yeah."

Jennings grabbed Joey's arm and pulled him down toward the booking room—and away from Mitch.

As soon as they rounded the partition surrounding the poker area, she pushed him up against it and leaned in next to his head in order to keep an eye on her least favorite private eye.

"Oh, baby, I've been waiting for you to change your mind." His hands slid up under her skirt and grabbed two handfuls of her rear. "Give me a few minutes, and I'll get Vinnie to hook us up with a room."

The mention of her boss's name sliced into her consciousness. This couldn't end well. Either she left Joey hanging, which would definitely create an "unsatisfied customer," or she followed through, which meant sleeping with The Nuts. She should really think things through.

Mitch squinted in her direction; his brow furrowed.

She buried her face in Joey's neck, trying not to gag on his musky scent. When she looked back up, Mitch was across the room, deep in conversation with Elena. As soon as she saw him leave, she pushed back from The Nuts.

"Joey, I think I've let my desire get the best of me. This is a bad idea." She channeled her inner Marilyn and ran a finger playfully down the side of his face. "I could get in real big trouble for messing around with a customer, ya know?" Somehow Marilyn morphed into Betty Boop.

"Nah, Jennings, me and Vinnie are tight. I can smooth it over, no problem." He tugged at her hips, trying to move her back into his embrace.

Jennings stepped further back. "I don't think I can take the chance. I gotta have this job, ya know?" Betty, or Marilyn, someone besides Jennings, twirled a lock of hair in her finger. "But maybe if I saw you out somewhere..." She arched her eyebrows and slid even further away.

"Yeah, yeah, that's good. I could give you a private lesson. Anytime." The Nuts shifted from foot to foot and pulled the crotch of his jeans down.

She winked and hopped up the two steps leading to the poker room. Then made a beeline for Elena.

"What was *he* doing here?"

Elena handed a player a bottle of water and took the chip he offered as a tip. Sliding it in her apron pocket, she backed away from the table. "He wanted to talk to you." She placed a milkshake in another player's cup holder. "He's not a bad guy, Jennings."

She leaned close to Elena and kept her voice low. "He tried to get me in the sack to get close to me."

Elena shrugged. "And you've never used sex to get something you wanted?" Her tray loaded with empty glasses, she headed to the back.

Jennings trailed behind her, vacillating between indignation and shame.

When they were at the back of the bar, Elena set the tray down and slid a business card out of her pocket. "He gave me this."

It was a simple card, printed on white card stock, with the capital letters "MK" inside a circle. *Mitch Kline, Investigations.* On the back, he had scribbled "Benny" and a phone number.

"He said you should call your brother."

Jennings traced her finger over the scrawled writing. She half expected it to shock her or burn her skin "I..." A sob that she didn't even know was there broke through.

Elena placed a hand on her arm. "Wait for me in the locker room. I'll finish up your tables."

She wasn't sure what she'd done to deserve a friend like her, but Jennings was relieved not to have to go through this alone.

***

It was out of his hands. She had Benny's number, and now it was up to her. Mitch stuffed his clothes into a duffel bag and searched the room for anything he might have forgotten. He wasn't a family therapist, dammit. His job was to find people. Find them cheating, find them hiding out, find them up to no good.

Jennings was a big girl. She could take care of herself. And if she couldn't, there was certainly a line of men waiting to take care of her. Mitch didn't wait in line.

He'd stepped into the bathroom to collect his toothbrush when the phone rang.

"You've been gone for over a week, Mitch. Tell me you've got good news, man."

He'd been putting Benny off for days now. He owed it to him to tell him what was really going on. "I gave her your number. But I don't know if she'll call. I screwed up, B."

"I'm getting married in less than two weeks. Aimee is freaking out about the caterers and her dress and her bouquet. I'm freaking out because my side of the aisle will be empty. Caroline's my only family, Mitch. So help me, if you slept with my sister, and scared her away, I will never forgive you."

"Trust me, B. Your sister has no interest in sleeping with me." *She'd rather screw a schmuck poker player with money to spare.*

"Well then, you shouldn't have any problem convincing her that I miss her. No ulterior motives. I just want my sister at my wedding." Benny sounded like a little kid begging to stay up half an hour longer.

Mitch hadn't hesitated when Benny had asked him to track down his sister. Of course, he hadn't known she was going to be a pain in his ass. But Benny had been there for Mitch after the shit hit the fan with Carla, and he'd do anything for the guy.

Unzipping the duffel, Mitch tossed his clothes back in the dresser drawers. He didn't know how he'd accomplish it, but he wasn't leaving Las Vegas without Caroline Jennings Lee.

Chapter Five

Is it weird to stalk your little brother on Facebook?

Jennings scrolled through the page of pictures. It was surreal to see Benny all grown up. He was no longer the freckle-faced little boy who followed her everywhere. The tow-headed tot who'd curl up in her lap while she read him *Charlotte's Web*. He was a man. From his photos, a confident man who was content with his life. What if leaving was the best thing she could have done for him?

She fingered Mitch's business card as a tear slid down her cheek. She'd spent the last twenty-two years forgetting her past. Benny was the only good thing. The only thing she hadn't let go of. So why couldn't she call him?

She knew why. Fear. She was terrified that the whole thing would go up in smoke—like every other good thing in her life—and then even her memories would be spoiled.

Norma Jean started barking, and the doorbell rang. Jennings peeked through the ripped blinds beside the door to find Mitch standing on her doorstep.

Crap. She looked down at the shirt she'd thrown on after work. The torn tee stretched tight across her chest and barely covered her navy pinstriped hipsters. She'd gathered her hair up in a hasty ponytail and was munching on a roll of cookie dough for dinner. "Be right there." Wiping the tear off her cheek, she darted into her bedroom and grabbed the nearest bottoms, a pair of running shorts circa 2010. *That should complete the look.* She pulled them up on her way to throw the cookie dough back in the fridge. A quick glance in the mirror by the front door confirmed her fears. She was a mess. But Mitch was the last person she was worried about impressing.

She threw open the door and Norma Jean launched herself from the arm of the sofa. Mitch caught the little dog like a football and scratched her between the ears while she licked him hello. Obviously, Norma Jean's judgment meter was on the fritz.

Jennings crossed her arms over her chest and blocked him from entering the apartment. "What do you want?"

Mitch set Norma Jean down and held his hands up in surrender. "I'm here for Benny. I promise I'll behave."

She didn't trust him, or herself, for that matter. But she had grown desperate for information about her brother, and until she could muster up the nerve to call him herself, Mitch was her best option. Her only option. She stepped aside and pointed at a chair near the television. "You sit there. And stay."

"Yes, ma'am." He ducked his head and made a wide swath around her. As he settled in the chair, Norma Jean, the traitor, jumped in his lap and curled into a ball. Mitch stroked her patchy coat but kept his wary eyes on Jennings.

"Is Benny happy?" She tucked her feet underneath herself as she plopped on the couch. "I need to know that he's okay."

Mitch bobbed his head. "B has his act together. He's practically a saint."

Could our lives have turned out any more differently? Jennings bit her lip. "Go on."

"He's told me a little about when you guys were kids. About going into foster care. He was lucky, found a great family who did right by him. That's why his job is so important to him."

"His job? What does he do?" She sat up straighter and leaned forward.

His eyes darted to the laptop open next to her. "I figured you knew."

Benny's Facebook profile taunted her from the screen. She slapped the computer closed. "I barely looked at it, I mean…"

"He's a social worker. He places foster kids in good homes."

Jennings realized she wasn't breathing. *A social worker?* She squeezed her eyes shut. She could still picture the woman in the boxy cardigan with her grey hair in a bun at the base of her neck. The woman in the white minivan who dropped her off at the group home and drove away with Benny. The woman who had taken away the only good thing left in Jennings's life.

The tears started before she could do anything to stop them. She opened her eyes, and Mitch was kneeling in front her. Defeated, she tumbled forward into his embrace. He sat back on the floor, pulled her into his lap, and encircled her with strong arms. She clung to him, as if she were teetering on the edge of the Grand Canyon, and only Mitch could pull her back up. She sobbed into the crook of his neck, soaking his shirt with her tears, grasping at his shoulders, his back, anything she could hold on to.

She had no idea how long they stayed that way, but eventually the tears ran out. And they remained. Her head on his shoulder. His hand tracing small circles on her back.

"You were supposed to stay in the chair."

"You were supposed to be easier to resist."

***

Mitch checked his image in the mirror for the fourth time that morning. It was ridiculous that he was nervous. He was having breakfast with a client. It wasn't a date. Certainly not a date with a woman he was becoming increasingly attached to. He drew a hand through his hair, wishing he had time to get a trim. Leaning closer to the mirror, he turned his head and squinted. *Is that grey?* He'd known Jennings for a total of five days, and he already had grey hair. He was barely thirty-seven.

The door to his room swooshed shut behind him as he headed to the lobby to meet Jennings. She was chatting with the hostess at the small bistro. Her hair was braided, with errant curls escaping around her face. She wore a short purple sundress and a pair of sparkly flip flops. And when she threw her head back to laugh at something the hostess said, Mitch's breath caught in his chest.

I am in so much trouble.

He approached the women and cleared his throat.

Jennings swung around, a smile lighting her entire face. "Good morning."

"Morning." His tongue stuck to the roof of his mouth, causing him to stutter like a preteen on his first date.

The hostess gestured into the dining room, and they followed her to a small table near a bubbling fountain.

Regaining his voice, Mitch peered at Jennings over the menu. "Do you know her well?"

"Who?" She studied her options while one hand fiddled with the end of her braid.

"The hostess."

She slid the plastic-coated paper down and grinned over the top of it. "No. Just met her. Nice girl." She started to look back at the menu but stopped. "Why? You interested?" A teasing gleam lit her eye. "I can get her number for you."

Mitch laughed. "Nah, that's okay. She's a little young for me. Besides, it'd break a strict rule."

"There are rules, huh?"

"Only about the really important stuff."

She set the menu down and leaned forward, setting her chin in her hand. "Do tell."

As the gleam turned into a sparkle and her smile grew wider, Mitch started having serious doubts about his rule. "No," he decided to edit it for her sake, "dating in Vegas."

"What do you have against Vegas?"

"I love Vegas. What I don't love is the 'anything goes' mentality. It's too easy to get sucked in."

A waitress appeared and took their orders, and Jennings leaned back in her chair. "So, you got burned, huh?"

How had they gotten into this conversation? He hadn't been in a relationship serious enough to tell any woman about "the incident," and yet here they were a breath away from the most humiliating moment of his life. He needed to redirect. "Benny's getting married."

Jennings sat straight up in the chair, her easy demeanor morphing into anxiety. "Married?"

"Yeah, in less than two weeks." He'd asked her to breakfast to tell her, but the plan had been to ease into it. From the shock on her face, he'd failed.

"Two weeks?" Her hand clamped around the arm of the chair, her knuckles turning white.

He scooted his chair around the small table until he was next to her. Taking her hand, he rubbed his thumb over her fingers. "Jennings, look at me." She turned slowly, meeting his gaze. "It's not a bad thing. Aimee's a great girl, and Benny is really happy. But he doesn't want to get married unless you're there. That's why I came to find you."

She sucked in a breath, her body jarring with the effort. "He's not eight anymore."

"No. Although, get him in front of a PlayStation and he sure turns into a kid." He laughed and was relieved when her shoulders relaxed.

"Two weeks." It was more a statement than a question, her gaze focused somewhere in the distance—or possibly the past.

"I'm leaving tomorrow. I can take you back."

***

"Vinnie, I have a family emergency. My brother is sick and needs a kidney. I'm his only hope." Jennings sniffled and dabbed her eyes with a tissue, then looked up at Elena. "Is it too much?"

Elena's dark eyes twinkled. "Screw Vinnie. This is your *familia*."

"I may have to—if I want to keep my job."

"Are you so sure you do?"

Jennings laughed. "Don't worry, I'm not going to do anything with Vinnie. I'm not that desperate."

"No, *Chica*. I mean are you sure you want to keep your job?"

"Oh." She sank back onto the bench, her fishnets clutched in her left hand. "I don't know. What else would I do?"

Elena sat beside her and wrapped an arm around her shoulders. "You can do anything you want, *Carina*."

They leaned their heads together and sat in silence until Vinnie pounded his fist on the locker room door. "Lee, Jordan, get out on the floor now, or there's gonna be a serious scar on your record."

Jennings sat up, balled up the stockings, and chucked them into her locker. She stomped across the room, unconcerned about her state of undress. Throwing open the door, she smiled in satisfaction as her boss stumbled backward. "Screw my record, Vinnie. I quit."

***

The next day, sitting on her living room floor surrounded by boxes, Jennings felt less confident about her snap decision. *I should not make major life changes when I'm hormonal.* Norma Jean perked up from where she was curled up on the sofa and, seconds later, the doorbell rang.

Her heart raced, but Jennings had no idea whether it was the prospect of going back to Asheville and Benny, or the road trip with Mitch. She'd seriously considered dipping into her bankroll for a plane ticket, but with no job, and zero prospects or plans, she'd need every penny.

Soon, she'd be getting into a car with a man she was dangerously attracted to and setting out across the country. She figured it would take about four days. Her initial trip from Asheville to Vegas had taken nearly two years, but it had hardly been a straight shot. There was no time to dwell on the past, however, when the present, and immediate future, was staring her in the face—or rather, ringing her doorbell.

She rose and opened the door. Mitch wore a plaid shirt, unbuttoned to reveal a snug white tee. Jennings had been conjuring images of his form since she'd met him, and this shirt left no doubts. His jeans, faded from wear, hugged him in all the right places. *I cannot be alone with this man for four days.*

It was true that her attitude toward sex could best be described as cavalier, but she selected her partners specifically. Specifically, she would never see them again.

Mitch was her brother's best friend. Not likely that she could sleep with him and never see him again if she planned to have a relationship with Benny. She could not screw this reunion up by succumbing to a purely sexual desire. *But this isn't just about sex.* "Yes it is!"

"What is?" He looked over his shoulder.

Ah, hell. Jennings cast about for an explanation. "A beautiful day."

He narrowed his eyes. "I didn't say otherwise." He looked past her into the kitchen. "Are you okay?"

"Absolutely. No doubt. Uh-huh!" She nodded and grinned.

As Mitch stepped into the living room, his eyes widened. "What's with all the boxes? You do realize I only have the one truck?"

She laughed and pointed at two suitcases near the door. "That's what I'm taking. These," she gestured at the boxes, "are going to Elena's. She's going to store them in her garage until I get back."

"You're giving up your apartment?"

"Let's see. I quit my job, I'm leaving for an undetermined period of time, and I have no idea what I'll do when I return." Jennings counted the items off on her fingers. "So, yeah, I gave up the apartment."

Mitch sank onto the couch, and Norma Jean jumped into his lap. "I guess my showing up was life changing."

"Don't give yourself too much credit, buddy." She hoisted one of the suitcases and plucked her dog from his lap. "Now take me to my brother."

He rose, grabbed the other suitcase, and followed her out the door. "Are we dropping Norma Jean off somewhere?"

"No. She's coming with us." Jennings headed for the parking lot.

"Whoa. I mean, I like the mutt and all, but four days in a truck with her?"

She slowly turned around. "This is not open for discussion."

"Oh, I don't need to discuss it. We'll drop her off at Elena's." He grazed past her and flung her suitcase into the bed of the truck.

Jennings stood in shock. She wasn't used to men challenging her. In fact, she preferred the agreeable types when she wanted some male company. The cocky, commanding guys repelled her. The present heat in her belly was rage, she was sure. She stomped to the passenger side of the truck and flung the door open—or more accurately, off.

The door hung from the body of the truck by a lone wire that did not look sufficient to bear its weight.

"Are you worried that my little dog is going to mess up your fancy truck?"

Mitch's eyes blazed, the intensity flying over the bed of the truck and heating up the rest of her body. His chest rose and fell rhythmically, his muscles pulling the thin t-shirt tight with each breath. He started around the back of the truck, his steps calm and his stare unwavering.

Jennings took one step back, and clutched Norma Jean tighter to her chest. The dog resisted and squirmed until she was freed from the constricting embrace. She pranced over to Mitch and gave a little bark before rolling onto her back.

He stopped and stared down at Norma Jean, who was blocking his way. After contemplating the small dog for a few seconds, Mitch stepped over her and reached for the door hanging off its hinges. He righted it and slammed it several times until it stuck. Then he turned to Jennings. "Two rules." He held up two fingers. "1) We don't use this door. 2) If Norma Jean has to pee, you're going to have to hold her out the window, 'cuz I don't stop for anyone." He grabbed her other suitcase and carefully placed it in the back of the truck. Then he covered the bags with a blue plastic tarp.

Heading back to the driver's side, Mitch opened the door. Norma Jean bounded around the truck and leapt onto the bench seat. Her tail wagging, she sniffed the interior of her temporary home.

"You coming?" A hint of a smile lit Mitch's eyes. At least Jennings hoped it was a smile. "Or am I transporting vermin across state lines for no reason?"

Jennings circled the truck, gauging his face, his body language. Running her hand along the vehicle's dented, scraped body, she inquired, "Will this piece of junk even make it across the country?" She stopped in front of him, studying his eyes, holding her breath in suspense of his next mood.

He shrugged, spun her around and pushed her into the cab of the truck by cupping her rear. "Guess we'll find out."

Chapter Six

Norma Jean was proving to be excellent company, which was a good thing, since Jennings slept through most of Arizona. The little dog had inserted herself between Mitch and the steering wheel before they'd left Vegas. Once he determined how to steer around her, he found he rather enjoyed a warm lap and the occasional kiss—as long as he was careful not to breathe in through his nose when she let one rip.

Static interrupted Johnny Cash's "I Walk the Line." Mitch spun the radio dial, settling on "Every Little Thing She Does is Magic" by the Police.

"Finally. Some decent music." Jennings sat up, pulled down the visor, and fussed with her hair in the mirror.

"You got a problem with The Man in Black? Besides, I thought you were sleeping."

She flipped the visor back up, but it fell into her lap. She waved it at him. "What's going to fall off next? The engine?"

Mitch reached forward and adjusted the radio dial to Patsy Kline crooning about "Leavin' on Your Mind." Maybe Jennings would take the hint.

"Oh, that was real mature." She stuck her tongue out at him.

He snickered at the irony but kept his eyes on the road and the radio on the country station.

Jennings huffed and crossed her arms over her chest. "Where are we, anyway?"

"We should be in New Mexico soon."

"If I'd flown, I'd be there by now."

Barren land stretched out all around them, and the sky was streaked with red as the sun set in the rearview mirror. He couldn't very well leave her and her smart mouth in the middle of the desert. "No one forced you to ride with me."

"Does this flight offer meal service, or do I have to eat Norma Jean's kibble?"

"I would've stopped for lunch in Flagstaff, but you were busy sawing logs."

She rummaged through the bag at her feet. "Probably sounded better than this crap."

The woman had a lot of nerve, insulting a legend like Waylon Jennings. He flicked the radio off.

"Aha." She jerked her head up, hitting the glove box, which promptly fell open. Or rather, apart. Jennings turned, a granola bar in one hand and the plastic door in the other. "Can I request a last meal?"

"This truck will get us to Asheville just fine. It's me you have to worry about." He grabbed the door to the glove box from her and threw it over the seat.

"Honestly, I'm only testy because I'm hungry." She rolled her head. "And I've got a crick in my neck from sleeping funny."

They were passing an exit, so Mitch made a split-second decision to get off and give them some air. He pulled into a truck stop and put the Ford in park. "Jennings, I've known you nearly a week and you've been testy the entire time. Maybe you should eat more." He unbuckled her seatbelt and turned her to face the window. Brushing her hair aside, he pressed his thumbs into the soft flesh of her neck.

She moaned and squirmed under his grasp.

"Well, hold still." He kneaded her shoulders, trying hard not to stare at the line of her neck, and even harder not to lean down and taste it.

"You can listen to anything you want as long as you never stop doing that." She was practically purring.

His body ached with the desire to lay her down and do things his truck hadn't witnessed since high school. He tried to recall why he shouldn't. They weren't in Vegas anymore.

"Does Benny listen to country music, too?"

Benny. That's the reason. Logic pressed past the yearning and Mitch lowered his hands. "No. He's more of a rock 'n roll guy."

"Good. Our parents would roll over in their graves if they thought he'd gone country." She faced forward and stretched, her perfect breasts arching up into the air.

Mitch flung his door open, and he and Norma Jean tumbled out. He'd forgotten all about the little dog on his lap. "Your parents were big music fans?" He waited while she scooted across the seat and stepped out of the truck.

"Oh, yeah. Met at Woodstock as teenagers." Jennings snapped Norma Jean's leash on and walked her away from the truck. When Mitch caught up with her, she continued. "I spent my first seven years living in the van with them going from festival to festival. When Mom got pregnant with Benny, we parked the van behind Granny's. That was their idea of putting down roots."

"You don't strike me as a hippie."

She laughed, and the setting sun framed her silhouette, lighting a fire around her. "Our parents were hippies. After spending a lot of years on the road, I appreciate a warm bed and a hot shower." Norma Jean's business complete, they walked back to the truck. "But they instilled in me a love of great music."

"I know Benny's named after the Elton John song." Mitch opened the truck door and Norma Jean jumped inside. Jennings moved past him to unhook the leash, and he trapped her in the small space of the open door. He leaned in close and inhaled her sweet, tangy smell. She smelled good enough to eat. "What song are you named after, Caroline?"

She blinked rapidly but didn't break the stare. "No one's called me that in twenty-two years."

Mitch watched as she bit her lower lip and the perfect bow of her upper one quivered. He forgot about all the reasons why not and grazed his lips across hers to still the trembling. Her mouth parted and she wound her arms around his waist, pressing her soft, feminine body against his. He drank in the smell, taste, and feel of her. A man could get drunk off Caroline Jennings Lee.

They broke the kiss, and breathless, Mitch studied her eyes and savored her flavor. "It's Neil Diamond, isn't it? *Sweet Caroline*."

"Yeah, I never could quite live up to that song." She ducked under his arm and strode toward the diner.

***

The man was bad news. Either he'd get what he wanted and disappear, or he'd make her fall for him and disappear. No good ever came from getting overly involved. And if he kept kissing her like that, there was sure to be "involvement."

Jennings pushed through the door of the truck stop, into a land of southwestern décor. Maybe she could buy Benny a dreamcatcher as a wedding gift. *Hey, buddy, haven't seen you in twenty-two years. Have some feathers and string.*

The bell jingled as the door opened again, and Jennings could tell it was Mitch by the shiver that raced up her back. It was either desire, or a premonition of evil. Based on her track record with men, it was the latter.

She entered the attached diner and chose a stool at the long counter. That way she wouldn't have to stare at him through dinner.

He sat next to her, his arm touching hers, his leg pressed against hers. Staring at him would have been better. At least in a booth, there'd have been a table between them. She focused on the menu and tried to ignore her quickened pulse and quivering legs.

"Whatcha eatin'?" The man who banged through the swinging doors from the kitchen looked like he'd been plucked straight out of a Kansas cornfield. Under his grease-stained apron, he wore overalls and a flannel shirt and even had what appeared to be hay sticking out his back pocket.

Jennings searched the restaurant for other staff, but it appeared Earl, according to his name badge, ran the whole show. She stole a glance at Mitch, who seemingly unconcerned, studied the menu.

"What do you recommend?" He slid the menu across the counter, ready to take the farmer/cook/waiter's suggestion.

Earl grabbed a knife from a basket of silverware and picked at his teeth. "The brisket's fall off the bone happy, but the chicken pot pie will remind ya of ya mama. I grew the peas and carrots myself."

Jennings stared out the window at the desert that stretched as far as the eye could see. *Where'd he grow vegetables? On cactus stumps?*

"The pot pie it is, then. Although my mama never made a pie in her life. Or dinner, for that matter." Mitch nudged her with his arm and laughed at his own joke. "Whatcha eatin', Jennings?"

"I'll have the grilled cheese." How scary could bread and cheese possibly be?

Tossing the knife back into the basket, Earl slammed through the swinging doors singing "Ring of Fire."

What is it with these men and Johnny Cash? Jennings thumped her forehead on the counter and wondered where the closest airport was.

"Grilled cheese?"

Jennings turned her head to the side and glared at Mitch, but he continued.

"Who comes to a fine American diner and orders grilled cheese?"

Fine American diner? Something skittered across the floor behind the counter. "Maybe I'll wait in the truck with Norma Jean." She buried her face in her crossed arms and tried to remember what else she had to eat in her bag. Kibble wasn't looking so bad.

Mitch grabbed her shoulders again and kneaded at the tension there.

She tried to resist but found herself melting under his fingers. "How much further before we stop for the night?" The massage moved down her back, the muscles on either side of her spine relaxing under his expert touch.

"You anxious to get to a hotel?" His breath on her neck sent rockets of pleasure straight to her core.

Earl banged back through the swinging doors and Mitch dropped his hands. Jennings immediately missed their warmth. "One clucking pie and a hot cheese." Earl slid the plates across the counter.

Jennings had to admit the food smelled wonderful. And nothing on her plate moved. "Thanks."

"Looks great, Earl." Mitch stabbed his pot pie and steam erupted through the holes left by the fork. He speared a perfect bite of chicken, crust and veggies. Then he caught Jennings staring. "Regretting your decision?"

Chicken pot pie. She hadn't eaten it since her granny died. She bit into the grilled cheese, a staple from the years after, when it was just Benny and her. Though she'd helped Granny in the garden, and even pounded dough for whatever she was baking, Jennings had never been allowed to turn on the oven.

Mitch dug through his pot pie like he hadn't eaten in days. She'd barely finished half her sandwich when his fork clanged one last time against the empty dish. He ogled her plate, which she slid further from his reach. "You going to eat those fries?"

She tucked the basket in the crook of her arm. "Yes." She stuck a fry in her mouth for good measure.

He licked his lips, but he wasn't looking at the fries anymore.

"Darn, boy. You cleaned that plate bare."

Jennings hadn't noticed Earl come back to the counter.

He refilled their drinks and picked up the empty dish. "You considerin' somethin' sweet?"

Mitch kept his gaze on Jennings and nodded. "I am. But we need to get to Albuquerque tonight."

She crammed the rest of her sandwich in her mouth and faced forward—away from the intense stare that made her squirm on her stool. Out of the corner of her eye, she saw Mitch throw a few bills on the table. She chewed faster, reaching for her purse. She didn't expect him to pay her way.

His hand stopped her from reaching into her bag. "It's grilled cheese. I got it."

Jennings swallowed the giant mash of cheese and bread and turned her head. When had he gotten so close? His hand twined around her wrist, his thumb skipping over her flesh, sending pulses of electricity up her arm. She'd experienced plenty of desire. After all, she had a string of one-night stands on her conscience. But no man had ever produced electricity with a mere touch. Talk about playing with fire.

Mitch leaned closer, and Jennings held her breath, waiting for another kiss that would turn her bones to Jello. Then his arm snaked around her and grabbed a handful of fries.

"Hey!" She swatted at his retreating hand, but he held it high overhead, dropping a fry into his waiting mouth.

He shrugged his shoulders and grinned, chomping another fry. "I paid for them."

***

Getting Jennings hot and bothered was becoming a habit. A habit Mitch didn't mind keeping. The only hazardous side effect was that too often, he got just as hot and bothered.

She was still mock-pouting about the fry thing, but her shoulders relaxed as soon as they got back on the road. All that kneading had done its job. The last rays of sunlight disappeared behind them, and Albuquerque was only forty miles away. Which meant Mitch had forty miles to figure out how he was going to share a hotel room with Jennings Lee. And keep his friendship with Benny intact.

Thirty-nine miles later, it became clear he'd have to pop for two rooms. With a steel door between them. Maybe he'd let Benny reimburse his expenses after all.

He pulled off the exit and Jennings stretched. "Are we stopping?"

Mitch wondered how she'd sleep that night since she'd slept most of the day. Then he thought of alternatives to sleeping. *UFOs, John Candy, Bea Arthur.* "Yeah, we covered a lot of ground today. Time to get some shuteye." He turned into the first decent hotel he saw and pulled up to the registration area. "Be right back."

Several dozen people milled about in the lobby, but the reception desk was deserted. He rang the bell and then leaned over the counter to see if anyone was working.

"Need something?" The elderly woman spoke from behind him.

He whirled around. "Yeah, a couple rooms, please."

"Nope." She turned back toward the crowd.

Nice customer service. "Excuse me." He waited for her to face him again. "Can you get someone who can help me?"

She pursed her lips and clicked her tongue. "Son, you don't listen too well. There. Are. No. Rooms."

He stood in shock as the woman disappeared into the crowd of people. Slowly, he plodded back to the truck. When he started the engine and pulled back onto the main road, Jennings opened her hands in a questioning gesture.

"No rooms."

It was the same at the next four hotels. Apparently, a national insurance convention was in town. At the last hotel before another hundred miles of desert, he got lucky. Or not.

He returned to the truck, pulled into a parking place around the building and held up a key card. "I'll sleep in the truck."

"Mitch."

Sliding out of the truck, he waited for Jennings and Norma Jean to get out. "Really, I don't mind."

She moved close to him, her blue eyes pleading. "And I don't mind if you come in the room."

He stepped away, pulling the tarp back and grabbing her suitcases. He tried not to watch her silhouette in the light from the hallway. Instead, he pictured Benny drinking a beer and throwing horseshoes in the backyard. Jennings disappeared into the room, and Mitch trudged behind lugging the suitcases. He had to drop off the bags and get out. Clean break. No goodnights.

The room was dimly lit, the only light coming from a lamp on the desk. Jennings was stretched across one bed on her stomach, her feet in the air. Norma Jean was curled up on the pillow of the other bed.

"See, there's two beds. No reason to sleep in a truck." She clicked the remote and the theme from *Cops* filled the room.

The song taunted him, asking what he would do. Mitch wasn't sticking around to answer. He dropped the bags and backed out of the room.

Chapter Seven

Jennings was usually the one to flee hotel rooms. As she lay there trying to figure out how Mitch had turned off so quickly, she realized it stung.

She flicked through the channels, pausing briefly on a reality show about taxidermy. *That's how I feel—gutted.* Okay, that was a tad melodramatic, but she wasn't used to rejection. With Mitch's hot breath on her neck and strong hands on her back, she'd been willing to risk the potential long-term disaster and focus on the immediate pleasurable possibilities.

On the screen, a large, tattooed man raised a machete-looking knife over his head, a poor, dead buck sprawled on the slab before him. Jennings clicked the TV off before she had to witness the post-mortem dismemberment. She jumped off the bed and shook her arms. *Dead animals—one way to curb my lust.* Stripping her shirt over her head, she headed toward the bathroom. She kicked the shower up as hot as it would go and tossed the rest of her clothes in a heap in front of the vanity.

Seven minutes later, the hot water had gone the way of the dodo, and the remaining tension in her shoulders had followed it down the drain. She stepped out of the shower and grabbed a towel off the shelf above the toilet. Rubbing at her sopping hair, Jennings stepped back into the room to grab a brush out of her cosmetic bag.

"The truck doesn't have cable."

The scene flashed across her vision, her startled mind absorbing it in bits and pieces. Mitch stretched across one of the beds petting Norma Jean, who was sprawled on her back like a playboy centerfold. A rerun of *The Office* on the TV. And herself. Naked and dripping wet.

She bolted back into the tiny bathroom, her breath coming in short bursts, her knees threatening to buckle under her. Sinking down onto the seat of the toilet, Jennings lowered her still wet head between her legs and tried to pretend she was alone, and that Mitch and Steve Carell hadn't just seen her bits and pieces.

Someone knocked on the door. It probably wasn't Steve.

"Sorry if I scared you. I knocked, but when you didn't answer, I used the extra key."

A chill hit her damp skin, so she grabbed another towel and wound it around her body. *If I stay here long enough, he'll go away.*

"Honest, Jennings, I didn't see anything. Well, much. And what I might have seen you should absolutely not be embarrassed about. I mean, wow."

A smile crept past her humiliation, and she realized that if he'd stayed in the damn room to begin with, he probably would have seen it all anyway. She swiped at her hair a few times with the brush, made sure the towel was secure across her chest, and pulled the door open.

Mitch leaned against the dresser; his interest obvious against the worn denim of his jeans. "I should go back to the truck."

"We have two perfectly good beds right here." She stepped forward, planted her feet between his and leaned closer. "No reason to spend the night in a truck."

Mitch gulped, his Adam's apple plunging, and tried to lean further back, but he had nowhere to escape. Jennings pressed her still-damp body against his hard, lean frame. She could feel the roughness of the denim through the thin towel, and his quickening heartbeat through the soft cotton of his t-shirt.

Winding one arm around his neck, Jennings leaned in even closer, right next to his ear. "You can stay in your bed, and I'll stay in mine." She took a step backward but halted when he grabbed the front of the towel, jerked it loose, and crushed her against him. The towel dropped to the floor as his hot mouth overtook hers, strong arms circling her, and his breath growing ragged. When she sank against him, he relaxed into the kiss and his grip loosened, his hands exploring her back, her sides, her butt. Her skin turned to fire everywhere he touched. He straightened, and tugged, pulling her legs up and around his waist. His mouth trailed down her neck, exploring her collarbone, her breasts, her fully awakened nipples. Jennings arched her neck backward, savoring the feel of his mouth on her skin, the firmness of his hands on her.

He stumbled forward, his head buried in her chest, and they fell onto the closest bed. He drew back, but she kept her legs wrapped around his waist, holding him captive. "You're not going back to the truck, dammit."

His laugh was rich and deep, and sent jolts of pleasure straight to her heart. Startled, Jennings dropped her legs. He tore his plaid shirt off and whipped the white tee over his head. *God, he has a beautiful chest.* He leaned closer, a lazy grin tugging at his mouth, that covert dimple appearing in his left cheek. And her heartbeat skipped again. *No, dammit! Stop that.* As his tongue trailed between her breasts and down her stomach, he murmured her name. Her heart swelled with pleasure, completely overshadowing the physical ecstasy she was supposed to be focused on. *This is really, really bad.*

"Um, Mitch." Jennings heard her voice crack, her breath caught somewhere near the source of discomfort.

"Mmmhmm." He didn't look up from his encampment near her belly button, his tongue continuing its lazy exploration.

She pressed against his shoulders. She had to stop his sweet noises, and the way his hands were trailing down her body, claiming her, cherishing her. She had to stop him, or her heart was going to explode right out of her chest. "Mitch!" Jennings shoved him hard, knocking him backward and off the bed. She slid off after him and leapt over the half-naked, startled, sexy-as-hell man on the floor and sprinted for the safety of the bathroom.

Sex and emotion weren't allowed in the same room, let alone the same bed. And Mitch wasn't going to get on a plane and disappear tomorrow. Sex with him definitely did not qualify as safe, no matter how many contraceptive devices were involved.

***

Mitch sat on the floor wondering what the hell had happened. She'd had all the signs of a woman ready to take it to the next level—perky nipples, goose bumps along the line his tongue had followed, and as he'd neared his destination, the scent of desire. Hell, she'd been the one pressed up against him in nothing but a hand towel.

Rising off the floor, he adjusted his jeans in a futile attempt to allow room for the problem Jennings had created and then abruptly abandoned.

She'd taken off on her own at sixteen, so he figured she'd have issues, but this woman gave more mixed signals than the people of Babel.

He should've stayed in the truck.

His phone rang, and relieved for the distraction, he answered it without even checking the caller id.

"How's New Mexico?" The rocks in Harry's voice suggested he was still smoking three packs a day. Despite the diagnosis.

"How the hell do you do that?" Mitch hadn't told anyone where they were stopping for the night.

Harry laughed, which quickly morphed into a coughing fit. Clearing his throat, he answered, "I'm a PI for Christ's sake. If I didn't know where you were I'd have to quit my goddamn job."

The doctor had been trying to get Harry to retire for over a year. Ever since they found the first spots on his lungs. Mitch had offered to help tie up his loose cases and close the office, but the man who'd taught him the business wasn't going gently into orthopedic shoes and the early-bird special. "Seems it'd be easier to call and ask where I am."

"Easier is rarely better. Besides, I heard you were headed this way, needed to know how close you were."

Betsy. "On the way back to Asheville with a Found. Not a lot of wiggle room on time."

"What I got won't take more than a day or so, but it's real important." Harry coughed again, hard enough to dislodge a lung. "I wouldn't ask otherwise."

"Yeah, I know." Harry didn't ask for help. And Mitch didn't tell Harry no. "We'll be there in a couple days." Mitch glanced at the bathroom door. "Any chance you won't tell Betsy I'm stopping?" Things were already rough with Jennings. Introducing his mother into the mix would be like adding lighter fluid to a string of lit firecrackers.

"Can't help you there, son. Betsy Kline knows more than I do."

Mitch slid the phone back in his pocket. *Harry admitting he needs help. World must be coming to an end.*

He debated trying to talk some sense into Jennings, but he wasn't sure what sensible was at this point. One hot night wasn't worth his friendship with Benny. And even more sobering, he was pretty sure it wouldn't be one hot night. There was something about this woman. Something he felt deep in his gut. Something he hadn't felt since Carla. And look how that had turned out. Sensible was going back to the truck.

***

Jennings heard Mitch talking on the phone, but the room had been quiet for what seemed like a long time. Not like there was a clock in this two-star bathroom. Securing another towel across her chest, she opened the bathroom door and peeked into the room. Norma Jean sat staring at the door, Mitch nowhere in sight. Releasing her breath, Jennings flopped down on the closest bed. The one she and Mitch had been rolling around on. Her hormones had gotten her into a lot of less-than-appropriate situations over the years, but tonight desire had mixed with something intense, and scary.

It was because of Benny. Knowing he was looking for her, that she was going back to Asheville, going to see him—it put a crack in the carefully erected wall around her heart. And Mitch might as well be wielding a chisel. The way he stared at her, the way his hands claimed her, the way his kiss shook her all the way to her toes. Jennings hadn't been hurt in over twenty years. But she remembered. She'd never forget the pain of losing every single person she loved. And while she couldn't keep people from dying—or leaving—she could keep herself from loving. Then when they left, it wouldn't hurt.

Chapter Eight

Jennings seemed more stable, and he knew his mother would watch her like a vulture guarding carrion, so Mitch left to meet Harry. The office where he'd cut his teeth on investigating was located on a side street in the Historic District. The frosted glass door with chipped lettering was straight out of a 40's noir flick. Inside, the battered desk and chairs were the same as that day twenty years ago when Mitch had slipped in the door, a cocky kid thinking he knew how the world worked.

Harry was on the phone, so he waved Mitch toward a chair. Instead, Mitch paced the tight office, noting small details that hinted at the twenty-first century outside the door. The laptop computer on the corner of the desk, the fax machine balanced on top of the gunmetal filing cabinet, the digital camera tucked in the pocket of an open briefcase. Harry didn't adopt new technology easily. He was straight up old school.

Mitch kept one ear on Harry's side of the conversation. It was a PI habit that was impossible to break. When he heard Harry refer to The Beetle, Mitch swore softly under his breath and considered bolting right then. If this favor involved that hole in the wall, it probably also involved Jason, and likely Carla too. The only two people on the planet he could do with never laying eyes on again.

As soon as Harry hung up the phone, Mitch turned on him. "Tell me this isn't about Jason."

Harry sighed and leaned back in his chair. The flesh hung loosely on his face. His hairline had receded so far, it'd disappeared entirely, and he probably weighed about 110 pounds soaking wet. "I considered handling it myself."

"Hell, Harry. You've got to let this go." He sunk into the chair in front of Harry's desk. It creaked under his weight. "When did you see the doctor last?"

"Carla came to see me." Harry'd been a boxer in his younger days, and he could duck a jab better than anyone.

Mitch closed his eyes, counted to twenty, and wondered if his mentor still kept a flask in his bottom drawer. "What if I told you I was in love?"

"That sure would make things easier, but somehow I doubt it."

He didn't know what the hell he felt for Jennings, but having a girlfriend would be awfully convenient right now. It might save him from Carla's vortex for once.

"It shouldn't take long. Just poke around and see if Jason's doing the same." Another coughing fit took over, nearly vibrating Harry right out of the chair.

Mitch didn't doubt that Jason was stepping out on Carla, but in the grand scheme of things, he couldn't figure out why it mattered. The guy was a crook, had been since they were kids. Mitch had been lucky to get away before he'd gotten in too deep, but Jason had honed his deviant behavior over the years. "She chose him. Twice." As far as he was concerned, Carla had made her bed.

Recovered, Harry took a swig out of a coffee cup. "She's family, Mitch."

He knew Harry would always have a soft spot for his sister's little girl. No matter how many times she screwed up. If it wasn't for Carla, Mitch never would have met Harry, who'd been the only father figure he'd ever had. So, as much as he wanted to walk out the door, grab Jennings and drive straight to Asheville, he stayed in the chair.

"Two days. Tops." The job, or the cancer, or both, had aged Harry beyond recognition. Mitch had always thought the old man was invincible. Harry caught his eye, sat up straighter. "I'm fine. Stop looking at me like I'm gonna die."

"Benny's wedding is in a week. I've got to be home."

"You'll be there." He pulled a yellow legal pad from beneath a pile of papers. "Now, who's the girl?"

***

Jennings had laid down to rest after Mitch left, but the light coming through the lacy curtains was dawn, not dusk. She'd slept straight through.

She swung her feet over the side of the bed and massaged her temples. Her stomach churned, the result of Betsy Kline's peppermint tea and no dinner. She cracked the door open and peered down a dark hall. Silence. Betsy and Mitch likely weren't up yet. *Would it make me a bad guest to pillage the cupboards for food?* She tiptoed down the carpeted hallway, toward what she assumed would be the kitchen. Instead, she ended up in what some might call a den, and others might call a shrine.

The King was alive. His memory, at least. Every surface in the room was covered with Elvis kitsch. Statues, dolls, even Elvis fabric on the sofa. And the pièce de résistance, a giant velvet painting on the far wall.

Laughter bubbled up in her throat and escaped before she could stop it. She half expected "Hound Dog" to start playing from the speakers mounted in the four corners of the room.

"Shh. You'll wake Betsy." Mitch's arms snaked around her middle and his warm breath tickled her ear.

She sucked in a breath. He held tight, his body solid against her back, and then he started moving backward, taking her with him. Before she could react, he pulled her inside his bedroom, shut the door, spun her around, and pressed her against the wall.

"You really don't want to wake my mother up before eight on a Sunday morning. Saturday is the only day she spikes her tea." He trailed kisses down her neck and along her collarbone. "You were asleep when I got back last night." The kisses moved up the other side of her neck. "I hoped you'd wake up."

"Mitch..." She wasn't sure what had him feeling amorous, but his mouth felt so hot, so good on her skin, she wasn't about to complain.

He pulled back, locked gazes with her, but his hands remained on her hips. "Are you going to tell me to stop?"

"No, but..." She braced her hands against his hard chest, bumping down the planes of his stomach, itching to strip that shirt over his head.

He lowered his mouth to her neck again. "But what?"

"I thought your mama didn't like rock 'n roll."

He jerked back, dropping his hands, and she immediately missed their heat. "What?"

She nodded her head in the direction of the shrine. "Elvis."

His hands returned to her hips, and he smiled in the delicious way that made her toes curl. "Elvis isn't rock 'n roll. He's a deity." Hunger replaced the laughter in his eyes, and he moved in to kiss her.

Fire ripped through her body. She shoved her hand under his shirt, pressing him closer, and exploring his taut, smooth back. The kiss deepened, and Jennings let herself enjoy it, really enjoy it, and not analyze what it meant or where it would lead.

Without breaking the kiss, Mitch lifted her and carried her toward the bed. When he lowered her onto it, she got tangled up in the rumpled covers. She kicked her feet, trying to get free of the sheets.

He hovered above her, a sly grin on his face, seemingly enjoying the show. "Let me help." She stopped moving, he lifted her legs, and ripped the covers completely off the bed. "Better?"

"Almost." She sat up and reached for him, yanking his shirt off as she pulled him down with her. She loved the weight of him, how every ripple pressed into her, especially the rod poking against her thigh.

He kissed her again and, reaching his hands around her, rolled their locked bodies to the foot of the bed. Their bodies molded together like a twisted pretzel and tiny fires erupted everywhere their flesh touched. She broke the kiss, and straddled him, her fingers splayed across his chest, savoring the contact and taking her time to study the delicious man beneath her. He hadn't shaved since they'd left Vegas, and the stubble on his chin had become soft and sexy. His hair was mussed, whether from sleep, or her hands in it, she wasn't sure. Somehow, when Mitch kissed her, everything blurred.

His hands braced her hips, his fingers pressing into her flesh, signaling his eagerness. But he didn't push.

Outside, the sun was rising, and the sprinklers started on the lawn. The day was waking, and soon his mother would as well. *Screw it.* Jennings ripped her shirt off and threw it across the room. She lowered her head, her hair falling past her face and brushing Mitch's shoulder. Just as her lips made contact with the sensitive area behind his ear, the door flew open.

"Mitchell, breakfast." Betsy's singsong announcement was quickly followed by a loud gasp. "Oh, gracious!" The door slammed.

Jennings buried her head in Mitch's shoulder. His mother had just gotten a front row view of her green lace bra, and the tramp stamp she still regretted from her first week in Vegas. The prim Southern lady would likely evict her for such debauchery.

Mitch twitched underneath her.

"I am so sorry. Your mother must be mortified." She rolled to the side and started to sit up.

He grabbed her and pulled her back on top of him. "I've walked in on my mother doing far worse."

"Betsy Kline? With her tea and Victorian sofa?"

"When I was growing up, we were more a couch on the porch kind of family."

She pushed up on one arm and stared at him. She'd seen this house and assumed he'd had a hifalutin' childhood. The sofa on her granny's porch had been *the* spot on a warm summer evening. The fireflies would dip into their valley at dusk and put on a show that'd put the Times Square fireworks to shame.

She hadn't thought about that house in more years than she could count.

"Jennings?" His hand cupped her jaw, his thumb stroking against her cheek. She focused on him, searched his eyes to see what else he might understand about her past. "Where'd you go just then?"

"Home." The word felt foreign on her lips. It'd been so long since she associated anything with it. She'd hopped from one apartment to another every couple of years, never feeling settled. In moments of weakness, she'd imagined what it would be like to go back to Asheville. To find Benny. But it'd seemed impossible. Knowing that maybe he was better off without her.

Mitch sat up, sweeping her legs across his lap, cradling her close. "I'm going to get you there." He held her tight, and for a moment, she could almost believe he'd keep her safe.

She allowed herself to pretend that it could be. Just for a moment.

***

The mood had shifted from hot and steamy to sweet and tender, and Mitch wanted to resist how good that felt. Trying to protect a woman had gotten him into trouble more than once. He still didn't know what Jennings was scared of, but he wanted to dive into that crack in her independent veneer and take care of her. She wouldn't admit she needed help, that he was sure of. He'd have to tread lightly. Sneak in the back way.

How different she was from Carla, who used helplessness as a ploy to manipulate. Jennings acted tougher than any woman he'd met, but in moments like this, with her arms twined tightly around his neck and her face buried in the crook of his shoulder, he knew deep down she was terrified of something.

Thinking about Carla reminded him of the lunchtime meeting with Harry. Was Jennings too vulnerable right now to help him with his ruse? Or was she vulnerable enough that she'd say yes?

He stroked her hair and, from this perspective, noticed the morning sun reflecting off the rich gold at the crown of her head. Why had she ever chosen to cover that up with drab brown? He planted a kiss on her temple. "Jennings?"

"Hmm?" She snuggled even closer to him, and his heart rate picked up.

This is so bad. Of all the women to develop feelings for, why did it have to be Benny's off-limits sister? *If B doesn't want me to sleep with her, I'm guessing he doesn't want me to fall in love with her either.* He relaxed his hold on her and tried to focus on what needed to be done. "I need your help with a case."

She pulled back to look at him. "Me? What could I possibly do?"

He shifted on the bed and grabbed her to keep her from falling. "There's some history with this case, and it would really help if I wasn't, um, available." He stared at a landscape that hung over the dresser. Asking a woman to pretend to be his girlfriend was worse than asking for real.

"Available? How can you take the case if you aren't avail...oh."

"I know it's asking a lot," he forced himself to look in her eyes, "so I understand if—"

"I'll do it."

His heart skipped a beat, and he tried to remind himself that she was only agreeing to a pretend relationship. "Really? You don't mind?"

She leaned forward and kissed him lightly on the lips. Then she hopped off his lap, grabbed her shirt, and started toward the door. She swung to face him, her hand on the knob. "I don't mind one bit. But I won't pass for a decent girlfriend in these day-old clothes. I need to change. But first, a shower."

With the taste of her still on his lips, thinking about her in the shower was almost more than Mitch could bear. But he forced himself to stay on the bed and watched her leave the room. Getting up with a hard-on would've made a scene anyway.

Chapter Nine

They arrived at the restaurant early, and as they waited out front for Harry and Carla, Mitch grappled with first-date jitters. Not that it was a first date. Or a date at all. Jennings sat beside him on a wrought-iron bench, stunning in a simple pink sundress. The sides of her hair were pulled back and fastened with a clip and, somehow, the style made her two-tone hair work. Stretching his arm over the back of the bench, he slid closer to her and drank in her soft, feminine scent. The combination of his mother's lavender soap and something fruity kicked up his heart rate. He fought the urge to lean down and nibble on her bare shoulder.

"So how long have we been dating?" She angled her body in his direction, a hint of green lace peeking from under the neckline of her dress. The memory of her in only that bra made the warm spring day unbearable.

Jackie Robinson had 734 career RBIs. His first game was on April 15, 1947, against the Boston Braves. Mitch took a deep breath and stared across the parking lot, away from the lace. "I'm not sure we have to go into specifics."

Jennings placed her hand on his thigh, and he was surprised it didn't sear straight through the denim. "Well, if you want it to be believable, we need to be on the same page."

The same page? Mitch wanted to throw the whole damn book out the window and get the hell out of Memphis. Of course, Asheville wouldn't be much easier because Benny would be breathing down their necks the whole time. As it was, he was calling daily to check on their progress.

Mitch heard the engine of the Lincoln Harry had driven for the last thirty years a block away. "Let's keep things general. You know, we've been dating a while, everything's great, all that."

Jennings withdrew her hand, and Mitch regretted not taking it while it was there. "I'm going to run to the bathroom before they get here." She was inside the restaurant before he could respond. Maybe she was nervous too.

Harry swung the boat into a parking space. They had agreed to meet at 11:30, so the lunch crowd was still thin. The passenger door swung open, and Mitch's stomach dropped to his feet.

Long, slender legs ending in dangerously high heels exited the vehicle, and he was transfixed by the curve of her calves as the car door closed. When Carla moved toward him, his gaze followed the curve up her thigh to the short, black skirt that left nothing to the imagination—of course, he'd seen it all, touched every inch. A red halter barely contained breasts that hadn't been around the last time he'd seen her. He'd liked her 34C's, but she'd always talked about going bigger. Apparently, Jason had taken care of that.

Her black hair was cut short, in a pixie style that ramped up her already overt sexual energy. She had that provocative, just-out-of-bed look and, immediately, he was taken back to their first time—in the back of his old Ford truck. Carla may have been thinking about the same thing because her gaze flickered to his truck, and when it returned to him, there was a definite hunger in her eyes that had nothing to do with lunch.

It was happening again. Like unsettled weather producing a twister, this woman could destroy everything in her path. A throbbing started behind his right temple, and he struggled to remember the plan. He'd had a plan, right?

"Oh, Mitchell." Carla purred his name, and her hand trembled when she placed it on his arm. "I'm so glad you're here." She pressed close to him, her big, green eyes telegraphing fear. "I know Jason's cheating on me, and once you prove it, I'm done." Her fingers trailed up his chest, around his neck, and snaked into his hair. "I'm done with him."

Mitch stood stock still.

"Carla," Harry shifted from foot to foot, obviously uncomfortable with the erotic scene, "we should get inside."

She didn't release her grip, or her cobra stare. "You go on in and get us a table, Uncle Harry."

Harry didn't budge.

"Mitch?" Jennings's voice shook, and the uncertainty in it snapped him out of his trance.

He didn't want Carla, he wanted Jennings. Of course, that wasn't the plan either. They were only pretending to be in love. "There you are." He disengaged from Carla's grasp, stepped toward Jennings, hooked his arm around her waist, and kissed her with more force than was necessary. But right now, she was his lifeline. He pulled back and stared into her bright blue eyes. "I missed you." He dropped his voice so only she could hear. "Please don't leave me."

Her brow furrowed, but she reached up and caressed his cheek, gently kissed his lips. "I'm not going anywhere."

"Excuse me!" Carla stomped her heel against the pavement.

Reluctantly facing his ex-girlfriend, well, ex-fiancée technically, Mitch recalled all of the toxic things about Carla. When she didn't get her way, there was hell to pay. That was Jason's problem now, not his. He squeezed Jennings closer to his side. "Carla, this is my girlfriend, Jennings Lee."

Carla's attractive features morphed into an ugliness that couldn't be replicated by the most extensive Hollywood make-up. The cliché "if looks could kill" popped into his head. He stepped in front of Jennings. Maybe putting her in the middle of this wasn't the best idea after all.

Harry took Carla by the arm and practically dragged her through the front door of the restaurant. "Let's get a table."

Mitch was grateful for Harry's intervention. He turned to Jennings, gripping her shoulders tightly. "I'm so sorry I dragged you into this. Maybe we should reconsider the plan."

"Babe, I've dealt with far scarier chicks than that. I've lived in Vegas for twenty years. It's a showgirl-eat-stripper kind of world."

Had she been either? He glanced down at her tight sundress. The dress he'd already figured out how to remove at the first opportunity. He tried to picture her in feathers and sequins, or hell, in nothing but a G-string. *Screw Carla, screw the case.* "Let's get out of here."

Jennings laughed, and her face lit up brighter than the noon sun. "I've always dreamed my fake boyfriend would have a killer sense of humor."

"You assume I'm kidding."

"You don't strike me as the kind of guy who avoids his problems. You're hauling *me* across the country, after all."

Mitch moved his hands down to her waist and pulled her closer. "Me wanting to leave has less to do with the psycho inside and more to do with wanting to get you out of this dress." But getting away from Carla definitely held appeal as well.

"Your mama probably already thinks I'm a Vegas floozy here to corrupt her little boy."

The closer they got to North Carolina, the more Southern Jennings became. Her speech had developed a lyrical quality that settled into Mitch's bones. "Trust me, my mama knows I'm past corrupting. She exposed me to debauchery at a very early age." He stroked his thumbs across the ribbon that circled her waist. If they got out of here, he could show her just how corrupt he was.

Jennings stepped closer, reducing the distance between them to two layers of very thin fabric. "I'm getting the impression that your mama wasn't always the proper Southern lady she appears to be."

"You've got that right." They were talking about his mother, but their hands and eyes were having a completely different conversation. He leaned down, grazed her lips, and slid his hands up her back to press her even tighter against him.

"Mitchell Kline! Get your dimpled ass in here right now!" Carla slammed the door, causing the plastic open sign to bounce to the floor.

Jennings snickered, and Mitch turned back to her.

"So, your ass is dimpled, too, huh?" Her mouth quivered.

He steered her toward the door, anxious to get this meeting over with as quickly as possible. "I have *one* dimple in my ass, thank you."

***

Mitch's ex-girlfriend was beautiful by most people's standards. But Jennings lived in Vegas, and she could spot a boob job from fifty paces. Hell, a three-year-old could tell those ta-ta's weren't real. The woman was nipped, tucked and inflated in all the right places. And Jennings would guess she wasn't even forty yet.

All her years in Vegas, a city that thrived on gambling and beautiful women, Jennings had never worried about having a perfect body. Weight wasn't an issue when you didn't have enough money to buy groceries. And it hadn't really mattered after she left the stage a decade ago. She'd decided a long time ago to age gracefully. There certainly wasn't anyone she needed to impress.

Carla had put the nasty away for now and was working a poor-pitiful-me whine. Something about her husband cheating on her, but Jennings wasn't paying much attention. She was focused on the lazy patterns Mitch traced across her thigh. Obviously, this pretending thing was a disaster in the making, but she'd deal with the consequences later. She wondered if the stall in the bathroom was big enough for the two of them.

She leaned into Mitch's shoulder, partially for Carla's benefit, but mostly because he was making her weak. They could lay down and get to business right there in the booth, but Jennings didn't think the after-church crowd would appreciate the show. Sliding her hand across his thigh, she located her target. When she undid the button of his jeans, his hand stilled. He slid his gaze to her, a question in his eyes.

She smiled. She'd finished eating, and everyone else at the table was talking about some creep named Jason. Jennings wanted a little entertainment. When she unzipped Mitch's fly, he shifted closer to the table. Her hand met bare flesh and knowing that he was going commando caused her nipples to pebble. She remembered that first day she'd met him, just over a week ago—the day she'd lost her panties. Right now, she'd be willing to lose them again.

"Jennings, what do you do?" Carla's question shocked her out of her naughty fantasy, and she pulled her hand back.

"Um," she mumbled as she tried to assemble her wits. The truth was the presentable section of her resume was blank. "I play poker professionally. But I'm between tournaments right now." Hell, it was a pretend relationship, she could have a pretend career.

Carla's black-rimmed eyes glared at her. "Poker, huh? That's so masculine." The word came out in a hiss.

Mitch's arm circled her back and he kissed her bare shoulder. "Jennings is 100% woman, and an excellent poker player. That's how we met, actually."

"Oh, really? I didn't think you'd go back to Vegas in this lifetime, Mitchell." She looked triumphant, and Jennings had to wonder why.

His grip on her loosened, and all of the bluster drained out of his posture. This woman held some sort of power over Mitch, and Jennings wanted to pop Carla's arrogant bubble. And those balloon tits.

"Goodness, I don't know why you'd say that. Mitch didn't seem to have any issues with Vegas when he seduced me right at the poker table. If I remember correctly, we were told to get a room. Right, honey?" She stuck her hand back in his crotch for encouragement.

He locked his gaze with hers, and they were the only two people in the room. "That's exactly what happened, *baby*."

"And then you tackled me before we even got in the front door." She smiled at the memory and realized that pretending wasn't necessary.

He hooked his finger under her chin and chuckled. "If I remember correctly, *you* were on top of *me*." His head lowered, and the kiss, combined with his dick throbbing in her hand, nearly sent her into orbit.

"We're eating!" Carla slammed her fists on the table, rattling all the plates.

Jennings and Mitch pulled apart, doused with a burst of reality. A zipping sound came from under the table, and Mitch swigged half his water.

Harry buried his head in his hands, and Jennings wondered how much he knew. Did Mitch tell him they were pretending? Or was he simply uncomfortable with the excessive PDA? Beside him, Carla quivered with fury. Jennings expected steam to shoot out of her ears. *I wonder if it's jealousy because she wants Mitch, or if she's just used to being the center of attention.* But the woman didn't faze her. She dealt with drama on a daily basis in Vegas.

Finally, Mitch cleared his throat and rubbed his hands together. "You guys will have to forgive us." He glanced at her and smiled like a fox caught in the hen house. "New love and all that." He turned back to face Harry and Carla. "So, I'll head down to the Green Beetle tonight and *reconnect* with ol' Jason. Find out what there is to know." He tugged at the fabric over his crotch and shifted in his seat.

It was good to know that she wasn't the only one turned on by their charade. Although what scared her the most was the moment it had shifted from sham to reality.

Chapter Ten

Mitch threw a few bills on the table and grabbed Jennings by the arm. "Okay, well it was great to catch up with you, Carla." He stepped out of the booth, pulling Jennings along with him. "Harry, I'll be in touch."

"Um, I guess we're leaving. Bye." Jennings waved with her other hand.

"Uncle Harry," Carla whined, "I think Mitchell should have to talk directly to me since it's my case." She obviously realized pleading with Mitch would get her nowhere.

He almost stuck around to hear Harry's reply, but Jennings was pressed against his back, and his arousal had reached crisis proportions. He wondered how she'd feel about sex in the back of his truck. It'd been good enough for Carla.

No, that wouldn't do. He'd known Jennings a little more than a week, and he already knew she had more character in her pinky finger than Carla possessed in her entire synthetically altered body. Something simmered under the surface of Jennings's hard, self-sufficient exterior, and Mitch wanted to chip away until he discovered what it was.

But first, they needed to resolve the giant matter of the electricity between them. Outside, he threw open the door to the truck and pointed.

"Where are we going?" She stood beside the door, arms crossed, in typical stubborn Jennings fashion.

He could feel the Neanderthal creeping in, but he resisted the urge to throw her in the truck and take care of matters in the parking lot of a chain restaurant. It was Sunday after all, and his mother hadn't raised a brute. "We need to finish what you started in there." He took a breath, gestured toward the open door in a more congenial manner. "Please."

The corners of her mouth quirked up, but she kept quiet as she climbed into the truck and slid across the seat.

Mitch didn't completely trust her compliance, but he hopped in the truck and peeled out of the parking lot anyway.

Jennings finally spoke as they pulled into his mother's neighborhood.

He braced himself for an argument.

"I'm all for finishing what we started, but after this morning, I'm keeping my clothes on in your mama's house."

Betsy. He hadn't really thought out this plan, but in his defense, all the blood flow in his body was concentrated below his waist. He checked his mirror and executed a perfect three-point turn. Racking his brain, he tried to think where he could take her. All they really needed was a bed and about thirty minutes alone. His gaze shifted over to her legs, where the pink dress had bunched up, revealing a significant portion of thigh. *Make that an hour.* A hotel was the obvious choice, but this trip had already cost him close to a grand, and he wasn't exactly living the high life. Hell, he still drove the truck he bought when he was sixteen. Of course, that was mostly for sentimental reasons—reasons less appealing by the day. Maybe it was time to try something new.

Money seemed like an asinine reason to delay their mutual gratification. Maybe he should let Benny pay him for services rendered. *Okay, that thought is wrong on too many levels to count.*

He pulled his phone out of his pocket and pressed the speed dial. Harry answered on the second ring. "Are you alone?"

"Yeah, I dumped Carla off with her mother. I swear that girl is going to send me to an early grave. She's the reason I never had kids."

"You never had kids because you couldn't find a woman who'd put up with your ornery ass." Mitch pulled to the side of the road.

Harry grumbled. "Looked like you and that broad were getting ready to make some babies right there at the lunch table."

Mitch wasn't sure about making babies, but he definitely wanted to be alone with Jennings. "Yeah, about that. I'm doing a favor for you, so it seems fair is fair."

"Do you really want to play the who-owes-who game?"

He considered all the times Harry had saved his hide. Yeah, he probably shouldn't give his mentor a chance to tally the score card. "Okay, it's not a favor so much as a simple act of kindness."

"No one's getting laid in my bed except me."

Curiosity won out. "You getting any action these days?"

Jennings snickered and spun on the seat to face him.

"Rubbing it in won't help your case, son."

With her back against the passenger door, she stretched her legs across the seat, and her bare toes traced a path up his thigh.

Her attention helped focus him on the task at hand.

"Sorry, Harry, just asking, not rubbing. Anyway, I was hoping you'd take Mom out for a nice dinner. Get her out of the house for a while this evening."

Pink-tipped toes circled his crotch.

"Or rather, this afternoon. As soon as possible." He gulped and tried not to follow the long line of her legs up to the hem of her dress. Where he could easily slip his fingers...

"If you're so hard up, boy, why don't you take her to a motel?" Harry laughed, but Mitch could hear the teasing in his tone.

Unable to resist any longer, he slid his hand up her calf, over her knee, along her thigh…and stared into her eyes. "She's too special for a motel, Harry."

Jennings flinched, and her eyes widened.

He halted his movement up her leg, but left his hand on her thigh, his thumb circling her knee.

"You do have it bad for this one, don't you?" Harry's tone softened.

"Yes, I do."

She sat shock still, blinking like a baby fawn seeing first light.

He wanted to wrap his arms around her and tell her not to be scared. That whatever someone had done to hurt her, he'd never be that way.

Goosebumps popped up along her legs. He tucked the phone between his shoulder and ear and used both hands to rub them.

"I'll call Betsy and see if I can set something up." Harry coughed and then cleared his throat. "But I make no promises. Your mother is the most stubborn woman to walk God's green earth, so if she don't feel like it, there won't be no swaying her."

"I know, Harry. Thanks."

"Uh-huh. With all the messes I've yanked you out of, you're gonna owe me for the rest of your days, boy, so you best be ready to pay up."

Jennings had relaxed somewhat, and he reached out a hand to her.

"You have my eternal servitude, Harry. Bye." He let the phone fall to the seat.

She tucked her hand in his, and he pulled, sliding her across the seat until she bumped up against him. There was still fear in her eyes, but she didn't resist when he wrapped his arms around her and kissed her temple.

"Who hurt you, Jennings?"

***

She liked the feel of his arms, but not his questions. Hooking her leg over his, she slid her hand up his thigh. Distracting men with sex was a sure-fire way to shut them up. They'd been heading that direction anyway.

Mitch sucked in a breath when her hand reached his crotch.

"A hotel is fine, really." Hotels were her comfort zone. Jennings brushed her lips against the sensitive spot behind his ear. His hands moved up her back, twined in her hair. He pulled her head back gently and trailed his tongue along the curve of her neck.

He spoke against her throat. "This truck is getting ready to be fine, if you keep up with what you're doing. Although I imagine the neighborhood association would have a problem with that."

She pressed harder against the fabric of his pants. His mouth opened, and he sucked in the soft flesh of her neck. No one had given her a hickey since high school, and she'd forgotten how sensual it was. Bunching up the front of his shirt, she leaned back, pulling him on top of her. "Screw the association."

He struggled to get out from under the steering wheel. "I had someone else in mind." Mitch freed himself, and fell on top of her, nearly knocking the wind from her lungs. "Sorry." He pushed up on one elbow and stared down at her. His other hand pushed the hair out of her face and lingered on her cheek. "You are really beautiful."

"*You* are really horny." Why did men feel the need to get all sentimental when they were already getting what they wanted?

His face got serious, which was better than the sappy look from a few seconds ago. Then he pushed all the way up, off her.

She missed his weight, his heat, his hardness.

"You're too good for a motel room, and for an old pickup truck." He ran his hand across his forehead, where the hair was damp. "Jennings, you're too good for any kind of fling."

She struggled to remember a time when sex had been anything else. Maybe with Jack—but she guessed under the bleachers didn't count as romantic. It had just seemed that way at the time because she'd loved him. Or so she thought. What the hell does a sixteen-year-old know about love? Certainly not enough to stay away from it.

Mitch stared at her, studying her, and she missed the lust in his eyes. Lust she knew how to handle. She sat up, pulled her skirt over her knees, reached down and slid her sandals back on. "Don't you have a case to solve?"

He stared at her a beat longer, then turned away, started the truck, and swung back toward his mother's house.

Chapter Eleven

itch awoke Monday with a hard-on and a hangover. After the incident in the truck, Jennings had retreated to her room and ignored him the rest of the evening. They were finally alone, and he wouldn't have minded the not talking, but the two doors between them made sex difficult. His mother and Harry came back around ten, happy and laughing about some classic movie. Mitch had grabbed his keys and told Betsy not to wait up.

Three hours at the Green Beetle and Jason hadn't shown. Mitch was frustrated, confused, and more than a little pissed off. Six shots didn't dull his irritation, just made it stupid to drive, so he'd had to take an Uber back to his mother's house.

Now, it was morning, he was still frustrated as hell, confused, and royally pissed off. His head pounded, and his truck was all the way downtown.

He pulled on a pair of shorts and had the sense to berate his erection so he could safely leave the bedroom.

Betsy and Jennings sat at the small kitchen table, talking animatedly—that is, until he entered the room. The smell of coffee penetrated his crap mood and, after pouring a cup, he ventured civility. "Morning, ladies." He dipped his head, took a careful sip of the hot brew, and sat in the vacant chair.

Neither woman acknowledged him. *I know I'm horny, but did I grow actual horns?* Jennings buttered a slice of toast and took a delicate bite, then wiped her mouth with a white linen napkin. How long had he been sleeping? Long enough for Betsy to brainwash her into a proper Southern lass? Two days ago, Jennings was drinking milk from a shared carton and had powdered sugar coating her breasts. Mitch remembered, because he wanted to lick it off.

"I had to leave the truck downtown last night. Do you think you can run us down there later, Mother?" He stared at the piece of bacon lying on his mother's plate, untouched. His stomach warned him to stick to toast.

"Sorry, Mitchell, but we have other plans." She rose from the table with her plate and scraped the remains of her breakfast into the garbage. Including the perfectly good strip of bacon.

"We?"

She rinsed her plate in the sink and then returned to the table to take Jennings's plate, which still had an entire fried egg and half a piece of toast on it. "We're going to Graceland." Betsy smiled at Jennings like she was her long-lost daughter. "No boys allowed."

They shared a chuckle, and Jennings rose, setting her napkin on the table. "Thanks so much for breakfast, Betsy. I'll finish getting ready." Without so much as a glance at Mitch, she swept out of the room.

Mitch stared at the empty table and then at his mother, who stood by the sink. "Do I at least get breakfast?"

Betsy turned to him, hands on her hips. Her polka-dot dress and red apron reminded him of June Cleaver. Like they'd ever had a *Leave to Beaver* kind of life. "Boys who stay out late drinking can make their own breakfast." She untied her apron, hung it on a hook and swirled out of the kitchen.

What just happened? Did I really get scolded like a twelve-year-old? I was working, dammit! He lowered his head to the table and allowed the cool surface to appease his pounding head. *Jennings is pissed off that I value her too much to simply screw her, and my mother has turned into a Stepford wife—only she's missing the husband.* Maybe if he went back to bed, he could wake up to a world that made sense.

***

Two hours later, he was the same amount of confused, but his head hurt less, and he decided he could face the day. One thing he had figured out was how to track down Jason. But before he saw him, he needed to do some research. And he knew exactly where to find it.

He pressed the speed dial button for Harry and popped two pieces of bread in the toaster. He could make his own breakfast. He wasn't helpless.

"Boy, I think you're about out of favors."

He hadn't even asked him yet. *Why is everyone so ornery this morning?* "I could be calling to set up golf."

Harry coughed and wheezed. "No one with any sense plays golf in the afternoon."

"It's only ten o'clock. We could get nine holes in before lunch." Mitch opened the refrigerator, pulled out cheese, ham, and a green pepper. An omelet would hit the spot. Now that he could eat.

"Do I look like a fool, son? You want me to drive my ass out to Germantown and get you."

How does he do that? He reached back into the fridge and grabbed the container of eggs. It felt awfully light. "Shit," he mumbled. There was one egg left.

"I told you I have my ways."

"Not that, Harry. But talking to Betsy doesn't count as detective work." A one-egg omelet hardly counted as an appetizer, much less a meal.

"I haven't talked to your mother since I dropped her off last night. A favor for which I am still owed, mind you."

Mitch flopped down in a chair, defeated. "Yeah, taking my mother out is a real trial for you, Harry." His toast popped up. "You've always carried a torch for her." Which he'd never understood. His mother treated men like staff. Or ATMs.

Harry grumbled, and another coughing fit took over.

"Don't get all choked up, man. She likes you, too." He didn't mention that Harry's P&L wasn't up to his mother's standards. Not bothering with butter, he bit into the piece of toast.

"I saw your truck near The Beetle on my way to work this morning." Harry smoothly changed the subject and cleared his throat again. "Did you talk to Jason?"

"No. In fact, I didn't see any of his guys. But I figure he's probably got a whole new crew of runners." He filled a glass with water from the tap. "Is Charter Vance still on the crime beat?"

Harry laughed, a big, booming sound that forced Mitch to pull the phone away from his ear. "Yeah, what else would he be qualified to do?"

The two men had never gotten along. Harry was convinced that Charter was no better than the criminals he was so fond of writing about. Of course, Harry didn't trust foreigners, and Charter was from New England.

"So, are you going to pick me up, or do I have to call a cab?" Mitch crammed the rest of the toast in his mouth.

"Be ready in twenty. And get us an eleven-fifteen tee time."

***

"Mitch the Snitch." Charter Vance rose from his desk, flipped the police scanner off, and extended his hand. "What's it been? Twenty years?"

The nickname had nearly got him killed back then, so Mitch wasn't partial to it. "More or less." He shook the reporter's hand, determined to keep it professional and not to mouth off like the bawdy teen Charter had known.

Time had not been kind to the man who was only a few years older than Mitch. He'd hit the beat and started harassing the youngers of the Beale Street Gang fresh out of college. Charter had always seemed to know how the group worked and played that to his advantage. After he caught Mitch "disposing of some borrowed property," he'd exploited the knowledge to gain inside access to the gang's activities. And as a result, Charter Vance always had the scoop. But over twenty years on the trail of the seediest residents of Memphis had sucked the youth out of the man. He looked like a desiccated mummy.

"Still doing PI work?" Charter indicated a chair opposite the desk before he sat back down.

Mitch shifted a pile of newspapers to the floor and sat in the chair, which appeared to be older than either of them. The reporter wasn't working out of The Beetle anymore, but his digs weren't screaming success. "Yeah, nothing better's come up."

Charter laughed, reached for his lit cigar, and leaned back in his chair. "Good to know you stayed on the right side."

Mostly. He partially owed his success as a PI to his illicit youth. It was much easier to track down bad guys if you knew how they operated. His criminal record, plus his fondness for operating outside the box, had kept him from pursuing a career in law enforcement. He'd never been good at doing what he was told, which was why he either needed to become "management" in the gang or get the hell out. Luckily, he'd met Harry and defected before he could get into a hole he couldn't climb out of. Moving to Asheville had permanently severed all ties to the gang. Except when Carla had pulled him back in.

"So, Mitchell Kline, what can I do for you?" Charter puffed on his cigar and the scent mingled with old newsprint, a week's worth of fast-food waste, and the coffee percolating on a 70's console, making the small office smell like the dumpster behind Dyer's Burgers.

"I was hoping you could fill me in on what the gang's been up to. Specifically, Jason Malick."

Charter's left brow hitched up, but he took another puff on the cigar before he answered. "This got anything to do with that good-for-nothing woman of his? Or you planning to mount a rival gang?" He said it with a snicker, but the gleam in his eye betrayed his lust for a story.

"I just need to know what he's up to." Insecure sixteen-year-old Mitch may have been a snitch, but now he was the one who pressed for information.

Charter considered for a beat, then yanked open a drawer in his desk and pulled out a scrapbook. It was old, similar to the one Betsy kept Mitch's lock of baby hair and first ticket stub to Graceland in. He held it to his chest, reluctance on his face. He even went so far as to move the book back toward the drawer, but then apparently changed his mind and opened it on the desk. "I have a theory."

Mitch could sense his hesitancy, so he stayed put in his chair, mouth shut, and waited.

Charter removed the cigar from the corner of his mouth and pushed the book forward. "Jason's been bad news from the beginning. He's a devious motherfucker."

No surprises there.

"Before he took over, the gang was into minor stuff, like the crap you did. Stealing, drugs, a little racketeering." Charter set his cigar down, stood up, and closed the door to the office. Coming back around the desk, he flipped through the pages of the book. "Jason took it to a whole new level, and I think he started as early as while you were still around." He turned the book and pointed at a newspaper clipping.

The paper was yellowed with age. A date printed at the top in Charter's tight scrawl. *April 22, 2003.*

Teen Recovering After Alleged Accident

Memphis – An unidentified minor female is recovering at The Med after a purported accident near the Orpheum Theater late Saturday night. When questioned, the teen reported that she stumbled on the curb in the alley behind the theater. Business owners in the district, including Beale Street, have long complained about the lack of streetlights and the increasing levels of criminal activity in the dark alleyways off the main strip. The injured teen is not believed to be involved in any illicit activities.

Mitch leaned back in his chair. "What does some girl falling down have to do with Jason?"

"I wrote that piece. It was my first." Charter skimmed his hand over the page. "It wasn't even long enough for a byline." He stood, lost in his own thoughts, until Mitch cleared his throat. Charter looked up. "Sorry, I have a point." He dropped into the chair behind him, raked his hand through what little hair remained on his head. "I saw this girl. She couldn't have been more than fifteen, sixteen at the most. And she was lying her ass off. The girl had a black eye, a sprained wrist, and according to a nurse who was sweet on me, a *lot* of bleeding. There's no way falling off a curb explains all of that.

"I was just starting out, hanging on those streets all the time, trying to get an in with the gang." He smirked. "That's how I found you peddling that stereo equipment behind The Beetle. Don't you remember me asking about her? She was tall, blonde, probably real cute before someone beat the crap out of her."

Mitch had spent the last twenty years trying not to think about his involvement with the Beale Street Gang. He had no illusions about the crimes he'd committed, and he had plenty of his own theories about just how nasty Jason was. It was the reason he'd gone to Vegas the first time. To save Carla. Only she hadn't wanted to be saved.

But he'd spent a lot of time, too much time, with Jason in those early days, and he'd never seen him rough a girl up. "Surely the police checked into it."

"Fuck no. You knew the MPD back then. As long as the crime stayed off Beale Street and away from the tourists, they couldn't care less. This girl was probably a runaway. Lied about her age, wouldn't tell anyone her real name. And when she slipped out of the hospital a few nights later, no one even looked for her."

"Well, it's one girl, over twenty years ago." Mitch needed to know what Jason was doing *now*. Then he was getting the hell out of Memphis.

Charter flipped the pages of the scrapbook. "It's forty girls. Spanning two decades. Not long after you took off, he graduated to rape." He pointed to another article. Another girl who wouldn't cooperate with the police.

Cheating was the least of Carla's worries.

"I never thought you fit with those guys. Hell, you wouldn't even carry an *unloaded* gun. If Harry hadn't pulled you out, I would've."

Mitch tried to digest everything Charter had told him. He'd started with the gang for something to do, something to get him out of the house while his mother "worked." Then he'd met Jason—two years older, rode a motorcycle, had a hot, young girlfriend. Carla had never been the brightest bulb in the chandelier, but she'd always been desirable. And she'd always wanted Mitch. He'd known he was playing with fire when he slept with Carla, but his raging hormones and idealism couldn't be stopped. She'd fall in love with him, leave Jason, start a real family with him. But she hadn't done it when they were teens, and didn't do it years later when he risked everything he'd worked for to get her. She'd chosen wrong. She'd chosen pure evil. He would tell her as much, and then he'd leave. And try to make things right with Jennings.

"Thanks for the information, Charter." He rose to leave.

"No problem, Snitch. Drop me a line if you find anything good."

Chapter Twelve

If Jennings had to listen to one more Elvis song, she was going to lose it. Avoiding Mitch wasn't worth this.

She'd been excited about visiting Graceland, but hadn't considered that she would be touring it with Elvis's NUMBER ONE FAN. Betsy Kline knew more about The King than anyone who worked at the tourist destination. She'd detailed *every single time* she'd seen him perform—live, televised, and even the DVD collection she'd ordered from Time Life Books. She'd spoken in reverent tones about his favorite food, song and color. Mitch hadn't been exaggerating when he said Betsy considered Elvis a deity.

God, how Jennings missed Mitch.

When Betsy maneuvered the Cadillac into her circular drive and Jennings saw Mitch's truck, with wire holding the passenger door on, she wanted to jump out the window and embrace the hunk of metal. Hopefully they'd be setting out for Asheville in that truck soon. This was the second time Memphis had taken her to the end of her rope.

She placed her hand on the door handle, ready to push it open as soon as the car rolled to a stop. "Betsy, this was a really special day. Thank you so much for taking time out of your busy schedule to show me around."

Betsy slowed the car but didn't put it into park. "Oh, honey, I don't mind one bit. Graceland never gets old. Besides, these days there isn't much for me to do." Her forehead furrowed, and Jennings softened toward the older woman. She wondered what her mother would look like if she was still alive. Would she dye her hair like Betsy? Likely not. Her mom had been born to privilege and had ditched it to run away with her dad. She'd been a hippie through and through, by anyone's definition.

"You know, I lost my parents when I was young. Spending this time with you has meant a lot to me." She moved her hand to rest on Betsy's knee.

"Oh dear," Betsy grasped Jennings's hand, "you must have been so lost." She turned to face her, and the car inched forward.

"Betsy!" Jennings freed her hand and grabbed the gear shift, slamming the car into park. The bummer came to rest against a flowering azalea bush, but luckily, they were still several yards from the porch.

Mitch's mother flung the door open and rushed to the front of the car. "Son of a bitch. Now my car's all scratched." She kicked the bumper. "The damn thing's only three months old." She looked across the hood at Jennings, who was straining to hold back laughter at the crass woman who had slipped out of her Southern belle shell. "I'll just make Gary get me a new one. He owes me for being such a lousy husband." With that, she left the car where it was and climbed the steps.

Mitch had implied that his mother wasn't what she appeared to be, and Jennings figured a bit of the true Betsy Kline had just poked through her spit and shine veneer. Now *that* was a woman she could get along with.

The front door opened, and Mitch stepped out wearing only a pair of running shorts.

Holy hell, I love his chest.

"Did you ladies have a nice day?" He threw his leg up on the porch railing and stretched. "And are you speaking to me now?"

Betsy swatted his foot. "Just because you weren't the center of attention this morning doesn't mean we weren't speaking to you. Don't be so sensitive." She blew through the door and slammed it behind her.

He switched legs and smiled down at Jennings. "What's her problem? She get thrown out of Graceland again?"

Heat coursed through her midsection, and she struggled to remember why she was mad at him. "They threw her out? She knows more than anyone in the place." She itched to run her fingers over the bulge of his shoulder and upper arm.

"Obnoxious, huh?" He bounded down the steps and stopped in front of her. Close enough to touch. "She got real heated one time about one of the exhibits. Said they got it wrong. Swore she was there, so she should know. Some beady-eyed manager threw her out on her duff."

"I think I saw him watching us. Real pointy nose?" They stood a mere two feet apart, and she could make out every ripple and dip of his toned torso. Her hand reached out before she could stop it.

Mitch swallowed, his Adam's apple bopping. "Yeah. That's him." He put his hand on her waist, pulled her closer.

"Sorry if you thought I was mad this morning." She sensed him staring at her and tilted her head back.

"I'm sorry if you *were* mad." His lips brushed against hers, and she moaned.

His hand slid up her back, pushing her closer, his mouth meeting hers in a crush of passion. She wound her arms around his neck, holding on, never wanting to let go. The kiss was fire, heat starting in her mouth, racing through her body, melting her joints until the only thing holding her up was Mitch's firm embrace. He stepped forward, pressing her against the Cadillac, lifting her feet off the ground, and somehow her limbs worked enough to hook her legs around his waist.

His mouth left hers, moved down her neck, over her shoulder, across her chest.

"If the neighborhood association doesn't want us having sex in your truck, I'm guessing your mother's front lawn would be unacceptable."

"Screw the association."

She snaked her hands through his hair. "That was my suggestion."

He raised his head and smiled. "A suggestion I should have taken." He lifted her and carried her to his truck. Flinging open the driver's door, he laid her on the seat. "Why is my mother's car in the bushes?"

***

If Jennings kept starting Mitch's engine and not driving him anywhere, he was going to blow a gasket. He'd gone out for a run and ended up in the front of his truck with a nearly naked woman when his mother tapped on the window holding his cell phone. It was as if Benny had a sixth sense about when Mitch was getting somewhere with his sister. And there was still the tiny fact that Benny had asked him not to sleep with her.

He guessed Benny's concern was that Mitch would sleep with Jennings and then dump her, and since he was pretty sure he'd fallen in love with her, that wasn't going to happen. So, in reality, Benny should be thrilled that his best friend and his sister were getting together. That was if Mitch could get Jennings on board. She still had a few walls up, and it'd take a wrecking ball to get through them.

By the time he'd talked Benny off the pre-wedding-and-my-sister-isn't-here-yet ledge, Jennings had put her shirt back on and buttoned her pants. Now the three of them (Betsy was hovering like a chaperone at a tenth-grade dance), were eating dinner in the formal dining room. It was Monday, and apparently that was when the Cajun chef worked, so they feasted on

Jambalaya and sweet muffins. He kept trying to catch Jennings's eye and feel out her no-clothes-off-in-his-mother's-house stance. But she had her chatter switch flipped on, talking to Betsy about light topics such as poker, Norma Jean and Elvis. Mitch hadn't realized Jennings *had* a chatter switch.

He needed to get her out of the house, and away from Betsy. Plus, he needed to track Jason down so they could get the hell out of Memphis. "I'm going to head down to The Beetle again and it would help if I had a cover." He waited until Jennings met his eye. "Taking a beautiful woman out for a drink would work well." As much as he didn't want her tangled up in this mess, he did want to get her out of the house, and after hanging out in the bar alone last night, could use the diversion of a female.

"Mitchell, she's had a long day. Don't go dragging her downtown this late." Somehow Betsy had turned into a protective mother hen, fiercely guarding a chick she'd met two days ago.

Jennings reached a hand toward his mother. "It's fine, Betsy. Mitch came all the way out to Vegas to get me, it's the least I can do."

He wondered if she meant that, or if maybe she wanted some alone time as much as he did, but either way, his mother relaxed and shooed them on.

In the truck on the way downtown, he couldn't get the image of a few hours earlier out of his mind. It was still cheap and vulgar to do it in the truck, and she deserved so much more, but the short skirt she'd put on to go to the bar was doing things to his logic. Maybe he should pop for a hotel. If it was a real fancy, then it could be special instead of shameful.

"Why are you so convinced that he'll show up at The Beetle?" Her casual question forced his mind away from the image of her sprawled across a king-size bed and back onto the case.

He cleared his throat and flexed his hands on the wheel. She may as well know the truth about his not-so-stellar past. Maybe it'd even be the first crack at those walls. "The Beetle is sort of his headquarters. Where he does his business."

"He does his business in a bar? What kind of...oh."

"It's not like the mob or anything, just a small-time gang that operates in town." From what he'd learned today, The Beale Street Gang had graduated to bigger and more dangerous criminal acts under Jason's leadership, but he didn't want to scare Jennings.

She turned her body toward him, rested a hand on his leg. "And you were part of this gang?"

He jerked the truck into a deserted parking lot and turned off the engine. "Yeah. I was a stupid punk who wanted the cool kids to like him." He slid his hand up her arm. She was fuzzy in the ambient light from a streetlamp a block away, but his breath still caught in his throat. "Guess I had a warped definition of what was cool back then."

"Most teenagers do." Her hand slid off his leg, and she shifted further into the shadows. "I thought I knew everything at sixteen. And that got me into trouble too."

"Jennings…" He wanted to follow her into that darkness, hold her, tell her that the past didn't matter, but she had retreated, physically and emotionally. They were only a few feet apart in the truck, but she felt miles away. He wondered if the guilt of leaving her brother had kept her shut down for the last twenty-two years. He started the truck, turned up the radio, and pulled back onto the road. "It's not much further."

He swung a left on South Main, and when they reached the intersection at Beale Street, he nodded his head to the east. "That's where all the famous blues clubs are, and that's," he pointed out the windshield, "The Orpheum." The light changed, and he drove past the theater and pulled into a parking deck. By the time he parked, she still hadn't uttered a word and was pressed so tight against the passenger door he feared it would fall off again. He turned the engine off and went over everything they'd said before she'd gone mute.

Was her silence about Benny? *Or is she upset because I was in a gang?* They hadn't talked about anything else. "So, it was because of the gang that I met Harry." No response. "Carla hung around with us, and of course, my raging hormones wanted her." He laughed, but Jennings still sat there like she wasn't hearing a word he said. He slid toward her, cupped her cheek, pressed his forehead to hers. "Jennings? Please let me in."

She quivered, and he wrapped his arms around her, held her as tight as he could, murmured assurances, kissed the top of her head. She clung to him, and he could hear and feel her struggling for breath.

"Please, baby, tell me what you're scared of." She was so tough most of the time that her vulnerability rocked him to his core. He could feel her pain all the way to his heart. He wanted to fix it, take it away, keep her safe forever.

"I can't be here." It came out in a breath, so hushed he almost didn't hear it.

His chest seized up, so tight he couldn't breathe either. He didn't want to let go of her, but he knew getting her out of there was the most important thing. He didn't know why, but suddenly the place he'd felt so comfortable as a kid scared the hell out of him.

He slid back behind the steering wheel, keeping one arm hooked around Jennings, started the truck and peeled out of the parking garage. There was a line of cars parked in front of The Beetle, and as he maneuvered around them, he saw a familiar black leather jacket and brown ponytail. Pressed up against the car in front of Jason was a young blonde who didn't look like she wanted to be there. Mitch thought back to the scrapbook Charter had shown him earlier in the day, and anger rose like bile in his throat. He slowed the truck, but then Jennings whimpered, so he pulled her closer and sped off down the road.

He was tempted to drive straight through the night to Asheville, but Mitch could sense that Jennings was too fragile for a trip like that right now. She hadn't loosened her grip on him, even though he could feel her drifting into sleep before they even got back to his mother's. He pulled in the driveway, threw open the door and kept one hand on her while he stepped out of the truck. Sliding a hand under her legs and the other behind her, he cradled her close, kicking the door shut and climbing the steps. Betsy had left the door unlocked, but he struggled to reach the knob and get them both through the door.

Jennings snuggled close to his neck as he carried her to her bedroom through the dark house. "Please don't leave me."

He gripped her tighter. "Never." Laying her on the bed, he slid off her shoes, then kicked his own toward the closed door.

Her eyelids were heavy as she pulled her shirt over her head and squirmed out of her skirt. A soft light filtered through the sheer curtains, possibly from a security light on the house behind them, but it was enough that Mitch could see the lacy detail in her purple bra and matching panties. His groin tightened, and he admonished his throbbing desire. This was not the time. Jennings wiggled under the covers, jerked around, and then threw her bra in his direction. The last time he'd been this close to a naked Jennings, he'd had to go sleep in his truck.

A battle waged between his head, his heart and his cock. *Sex can be emotionally soothing, right?* He unbuttoned his jeans.

Her hair splayed out on the pillow, the blond roots like a halo around her head. He knew she was a year older than him, but right now she looked like the sixteen-year-old girl who had run away after losing her brother. He redid the button. Their first time couldn't be like this. It shouldn't be a raw moment of passion in the cab of his truck, or comfort sex. He wanted her to know that he cherished her, wanted to take care of her, had fallen completely in love with her.

"Mitch?" She didn't open her eyes, just reached her hand out to him.

He crossed the room and slid into the bed fully clothed. She scooted back toward him and pressed into the curve of his body, sighing deeply. He held her close, kissed her shoulder and mentally recited Ty Cobb's career hitting stats. All twenty-four years.

Chapter Thirteen

Jennings was still sleeping when Mitch slipped out of bed the next morning, but before he reached the door she spoke. "I miss Norma Jean."

"I'll get her." Betsy Kline be damned. The woman needed her dog.

After he returned from the kennel and the ecstatic Norma Jean reunited with her owner, he locked himself in Gary's office to make a few calls and do research on the computer. Apparently, Betsy had kicked her husband out cold, because the office was still full of framed degrees and law books, and a very expensive iMac. Poor bastard.

His first call was to Benny.

"I need to know everything you remember about when your sister left."

"Hello to you too." His usually upbeat friend sounded grumpy and putout.

Mitch took a breath and reminded himself that Benny was justifiably worried. "Sorry, B. What's on the agenda for today?"

"Well, the groomsmen were *supposed* to be golfing."

Damn, he'd forgotten about the pre-wedding activities. Benny had taken the whole week off—as one last hurrah. "Supposed to be?"

"We've only got three, and besides that, it's overcast. They're calling for scattered showers."

"That sucks, man. Maybe we can go Thursday or Friday?" Mitch prayed he'd make it back in time.

Benny groaned. "Aimee's family is coming into town tomorrow night, and there's this whole brunch, shower, country club thing on Thursday. Friday's lunch with her dad and brothers. You have to be back for that, Mitch. I can't face all of them on my own. Her dad was a colonel."

He'd find a way. "Not a problem. Hopefully it'll be sooner. Just need to wrap up some things here." He stuck the phone between his shoulder and ear and booted up the computer. "So, about your sister, did you have any contact with her after she left?"

"Isn't she there with you? Why can't you ask her this? Did you piss her off?"

"We're getting along peachy. Don't worry. She's just a little guarded about the past." He opened a browser window.

"Please don't scare her off. She's my only family, Mitch."

He'd always considered Benny to be family. And he realized he wanted Jennings to be too. "I won't, B. Promise. But is there anything you remember?"

Benny sighed. "Not much. She showed up at my foster home one night and tapped on my window. Told me she loved me and that she needed to go away for a while." He paused, possibly to collect himself. "She gave me a song written on a scrap of notebook paper, told me our mother wrote it when I was born. I asked her where she was going and she told me it was better if I didn't know, but she'd be okay."

"Did she have anything with her?"

"She had a ratty old backpack and our dad's guitar. I heard my foster mom on the phone a few weeks later saying that she probably took the bus out of town."

Mitch typed "Greyhound" into the search window. He wondered how far back their records went.

"Oh, and I got a postcard from her. I still have it. Hold on." He set the phone down.

Clicking through the site, Mitch found a contact number for someone in Administration.

Benny picked the phone back up. "I found it. You won't believe this, Mitch, but the postmark is Memphis."

He believed it. Something bad had happened to Jennings in this town, and he needed to know what it was. "What's the date, B?"

"April 21, 2003."

Mitch almost dropped the phone. He didn't believe in coincidences. But he had to be sure. "I've got to go, B, but you've been really helpful."

"I've missed her so much, Mitch."

"I know, Benny. We'll be there soon." He ended the call and closed the browser window. He didn't need to call Greyhound. Scrolling through his address book, he called Charter Vance instead. "Do you have plans for dinner?"

***

Mitch had been doting on her all day, treating her like she was a proper lady who'd come down with a case of the vapors. He'd certainly been all gentlemanly coming to bed fully clothed the night before. After what happened, she'd wanted to escape for a bit. And sex was always good for escape. She'd been escaping for the last twenty years.

Instead, they'd spent the night spooning, his warm body and quiet strength pressed against her, making her feel safe. She knew it was an illusion, but she was willing to hold on to it for a while. Anything to deal with the horror of seeing that alleyway again.

She'd convinced herself she was over it. After all, she didn't have issues with men or sex. She loved men. She just made sure to never fall in love with them.

That didn't have anything to do with Memphis though. Her heart was already shattered when she got to Memphis. Honestly, she'd been surprised that her heart could hurt even more. But laying in that hospital room almost twenty years ago to the day, her heart had taken its last breath and shut down for good. It'd still pumped the blood necessary for her body to survive, whether she wanted to or not, but its function had become purely biological.

Swinging her feet over the side of the bed, Jennings tried to muster up the strength to shower and get dressed. Norma Jean danced around her, excited to be doing something besides snuggling. At some point during the night, Jennings had gotten cold, and Mitch had given her his shirt. The comfortable tee was worn perfectly, the cotton soft from washing, the lettering faded enough to make it interesting. She hugged it close to her body, brought the hem up to her face to breath in his smell. Her heart kickstarted, skipping a beat or two, making its presence known. Somehow, this man, in this city, had taken hold of a listless heart and brought it back to life.

Norma Jean jumped off the bed and ran to the door. She spun in tight circles, whining—her plea to go out. It was why Jennings had taken the little dog home the day she found her huddled in the back of the alley near her apartment. She needed something in her life to get up for. Something to make her keep getting out of bed each day. It was easy to love a dog. Did she have what it took to love a person again?

She rose off the bed, pulled her skirt on and slid her feet into her black flip flops. She dared a glimpse in the mirror over the dresser. Mitch's shirt fell to her mid-thighs and almost covered the short skirt. She had bedhead and her drugstore dye job was on its last legs. She fingered the blonde at the crown of her head. After leaving Memphis twenty-two years ago, she'd become Jennings Lee, and a brunette. She honestly didn't know if she could go back to being Caroline, but it was time to show her true colors. She'd ditched the brown contacts as soon as Mitch showed up. No point in hiding anymore. She'd been found.

Gathering her hair into a ponytail, she opened the bedroom door and headed toward the kitchen. Norma Jean trotted in front her, likely lured by the smell of bacon. Did Betsy make the fatty temptation *every* morning? For a woman in her fifties, Mitch's mother was lithe and beautiful. She probably dabbled in a little Botox, but she had the body of a dancer. Jennings prayed her body held up as well.

It wasn't bacon she smelled, and it wasn't morning. The clock on the microwave showed it was closer to lunchtime, and there wasn't a frying pan in sight. Betsy stood at the counter going over a menu with a large man in an apron. She jumped when Norma Jean licked her foot. "What the h—?" As soon as she saw Jennings, she swept toward her arms outstretched, nearly kicking Norma Jean out of the way. "Sweetie, Mitchell told me you weren't well. Are you hungry? Is there anything I can get for you?" The entire time she spoke, she shot suspicious glances at the little dog, as if it were stalking her. Which Norma Jean kind of was. She weaved in and out of Betsy's feet, her tongue darting out, slapping her paw at the poof of feathers on Betsy's open-toed kitten heels.

"I'm fine, thank you," Jennings covered a laugh, and scooped Norma Jean up. "But what is that luscious smell?"

The man in the apron beamed and gestured toward the crock pot on the counter. "Those are my famous slow-cooked pork ribs. You'll be having a feast tonight!" He rubbed his belly and chuckled like St. Nick minus the beard.

Betsy scowled in Norma Jean's direction. "Yes, Chef Ghille is preparing our dinner for the evening. He's known throughout Memphis for his excellent barbeque." She turned to the chef and murmured something in low tones, then led Jennings out of the kitchen. "He'll be in there most of the day, but if you need anything you just let us know."

"Okay, thanks. I'm not really hungry." She hadn't been until she smelled the ribs, but she didn't want to impose. "What's the occasion?"

"Mitchell's invited someone for dinner. But Chef Ghille comes every Tuesday."

They stepped out onto the back deck and Jennings set Norma Jean down. The little dog scampered down the steps and sniffed around the bushes.

"Dear," Betsy placed a hand lightly on Jennings's arm, "not to sound paranoid, but have you been hiding that dog in your room for the last three days?"

Jennings laughed and squeezed Betsy's hand. "No, I haven't been hiding her. She was at a kennel, but Mitch picked her up this morning. I hope it's okay, I really missed her."

Betsy appraised Norma Jean as she explored the yard, stopping to tinkle on the spots with just the right smell. "I suppose so. She's a little dog, after all. I only ask that you wipe her feet before she comes inside. We don't want to make extra work for Greta."

"Of course. You won't even know she's here." She made a mental note not to leave Norma Jean unattended for any length of time. One indiscretion and they'd be out on their bums. "Betsy, I was wondering if you could give me a ride somewhere later today." Talk about pressing her luck.

"I have an appointment at two for my nails. You're welcome to drop me there and take my car wherever you need to go." She smoothed the skirt of her dress. "And not to be high maintenance, but maybe Mitchell can watch your dog while we're out of the house?"

Jennings had a feeling Betsy defined high maintenance. "That won't be a problem. Norma Jean and he are thick as thieves." She clapped her hands, and Norma Jean came running across the yard at full speed, leapt up the stairs and hit the deck in a full slide, stopping only when she slammed into Betsy's feet.

"Goodness," Betsy stepped back and appeared to study the beast at her feet, "is something wrong with her?"

She laughed, unsure if Betsy was asking about her behavior or her mangy appearance. "Nope. She just has loads of character." *Like me.* Norma Jean followed her into the house and down the hall, stopping at a closed door. She scratched, and before Jennings could scold her, Mitch appeared.

His eyes lit up, seemingly appreciating the bedraggled pair. Maybe he needed to get his vision checked. "Good morning." He glanced at his watch. "Or rather, afternoon." He stepped forward, placed his hand at her waist. "You look good enough to eat."

"You need glasses." She let him pull her closer and snuggled close to his chest, breathing in the scent of him. His smell was becoming imprinted on her brain. Soon she'd start following him around like a little lost duck.

"I see just fine." He kissed her and then moved back into the office and turned the computer off. "How are you feeling?"

She watched Norma Jean, tracking close to his heels, another female that had fallen under Mitch Kline's spell. "Better. But I'll feel great after a shower. Can you watch the beast for a bit?" She gestured at her dog, who was lying unabashedly on her back, legs spread, waiting for a belly rub.

He laughed and bent down to acquiesce. "No problem. We'll manage."

"Thanks." Jennings started off down the hall but could feel him staring. She swung around.

His mouth was set in a hard line, and the soft spot above his right temple pulsed.

"What is it?" They'd just been canoodling in the hall, surely, he wasn't already mad at her.

Mitch smiled, but it was obviously forced. "Nothing, just watching you walk away. It's a nice view."

It was believable, but one skill that made her a good poker player (well, a passing one at least), was her ability to read people. And Mitch wasn't thinking about her rearview. She let it drop for now, though, and headed for the shower. He may be the investigator, but she wanted to do a little digging of her own, and she was going to use her afternoon outing with Betsy to do just that.

Chapter Fourteen

Jennings took a little extra time putting on her makeup before dinner. She didn't know who Mitch had invited, but she wasn't primping for the mystery guest anyway. Her emerald-green maxi dress was a bit wrinkled from almost a week in a suitcase, but it showed off her shoulders, and Mitch seemed to be awfully fond of kissing them. She left her hair down, and after a good conditioning, it flowed nicely down her back. Capping the ensemble off with a pair of peacock-feather earrings, she was happy with her effort. *I clean up okay.*

Norma Jean perked up from where she was sleeping at the foot of the bed, and then the doorbell rang. She jumped down, ran to the bedroom door and barked.

"I'm coming, Miss Impatient." Jennings took one last look in the mirror, tucked her hair behind her right ear, and went to meet the mystery guest.

When they entered the parlor, Mitch was speaking in hushed tones to a man with his back to the doorway. Norma Jean ran ahead and sniffed the stranger's feet, then jumped against Mitch's leg. He patted her on the head and told her to sit. The normally stubborn dog followed the order, and there wasn't even a treat involved. Well, unless you counted Mitch's attention. It certainly made Jennings sit up and take notice.

When he looked back up, and saw Jennings over the other man's shoulder, his eyes widened. Smiling, he put a hand on the other man's shoulder and gestured toward her. "Charter, this is Jennings Lee."

She stepped forward, extending her hand. The man wasn't as tall as Mitch, and was thin, on the verge of being gaunt. He sported the comb-over look that so many balding men were prone to. *Someone should tell him it's not working.* He appeared to be in his fifties, but the spark in his eye suggested that maybe he wasn't wearing his age well. "It's nice to meet you, Charter. Such an unusual name."

He shook her hand firmly, appraising her openly. "As is yours, Ms. Lee."

"It was my mother's maiden name, although I'm not sure she intended to call me by it."

His eyebrows raised. "You took it on after she passed?"

Jennings stepped closer to Mitch, sliding her arm around his waist. For some reason, she needed to touch him right then. "Something like that."

Mitch pulled her close, squeezed her shoulder.

"My daddy named me Caroline." She wasn't sure why she was telling this stranger her life story. It was almost like she was being interviewed.

Betsy swept into the parlor, all pink chiffon and freshly coifed hair. "Dinner is ready on the deck." Her gaze narrowed.

Jennings followed her line of sight and saw Norma Jean curled up on the plastic-covered settee. "Oh, Betsy, I'm so sorry." She scooped the little dog up and shook her finger at her. "Not on the furniture, Norma Jean." Although it was covered in plastic, so she didn't see what the big deal was.

Mitch made introductions and the four of them proceeded to the deck. A table boasted a large, striped umbrella and four place settings. The buffet along the wall of the house was akin to a Las Vegas all-you-could-eat delight. But the smells emanating from the dishes were 100% southern. Jennings had forgotten about food like this.

Ignoring any manners she might possess, she grabbed a plate and started shoveling food onto it. Fried okra, homemade macaroni and cheese, corn-on-the-cob, biscuits so fluffy they looked like clouds, and the prize hog of the county fair—slow-cooked baby-back ribs smothered in sauce so tangy the scent tickled your nose. She wouldn't be wearing her skinny jeans for a while.

The chef stood off to one side, like a proud papa guarding his brood.

"Everything looks amazing, Chef Ghille." She pulled off a piece of biscuit and popped it in her mouth. As soon as it hit her tongue, it melted, filling her mouth with an ecstasy better than sex. Well, any sex she'd had lately. "My granny used to let me roll out the biscuits. The only thing that'd make these better is some homemade apple butter."

His eyes danced with merriment as he pointed to a bowl at the end of the table.

She groaned with pleasure and scooped a couple spoonfuls right on top of her biscuits. There wasn't a millimeter of space left on her plate.

Mitch sidled up to her and slid his arm around her waist. "I love a woman who can pack it away."

"Hopefully, you'll like a woman who gains twenty pounds from one meal."

He patted her rear and leaned close to her ear. "I can't imagine not liking you."

Her heart fluttered, and for the second time that day, she realized it was coming back to life. It was as if Mitch was slowly massaging it, helping it learn how to beat again. Her biggest fear was that he'd let go, and it wouldn't be able to function without him.

"Jennings? You okay?"

She looked up at the concern in his voice, shook her head, and smiled. "Yeah." The smells from her plate wafted into her brain, triggering a plausible excuse for her silence. "This food just reminds me of my grandmother. Of home." It wasn't a lie, just not what she'd been chewing on at that precise moment.

He squeezed her tighter, kissed her on the cheek. "I promised Benny we'd be there by Friday. Just need to wrap up a few things here." His gaze was intense, and she saw a spark of something—maybe anger, maybe resolve—but his grip on her was possessive, so she supposed the anger wasn't aimed toward her.

They carried their plates to the table where Betsy and Charter were already seated and engaged in a conversation. Charter stopped mid sentence when Jennings sat down across from him.

"Please don't stop on account of me." She gestured that they should proceed and stabbed a piece of okra with her fork.

"I was telling Ms. Kline that I've known Mitch for many years."

"Please, dear, call me Betsy." She used her knife and fork to cut corn off the cob.

Jennings supposed it wasn't ladylike to eat it straight off the cob. She picked hers up and bit into it. Sweet juice ran down her chin and her taste buds nearly exploded.

"I came to Memphis straight after Harvard because I loved jazz and fine Southern cooking." Charter nodded in Chef Ghille's direction. "Finest ribs in Memphis, sir."

"So, you're a New Englander?" Betsy crinkled her nose slightly, then took a delicate bite of biscuit.

Charter laughed. "Yes, ma'am. Memphis has been my home for well over twenty years, but I'm still a Yank to most folk."

Jennings noticed he blended some Southern nuances into his speech. She wondered if he'd adapted over time or if he'd done it intentionally to be more accepted. She'd certainly banished her own Southern twang after she changed her name and hair color. The closer she got to Asheville, the easier her true voice came back to her. Honestly, she'd thought it was gone for good, but apparently, it'd just laid dormant, waiting until she needed it again. "When did you meet Mitch?"

"He'd have still been in his teens." Charter bit into a rib, then licked the ring of sauce off his lips. "He was quite helpful to me in those days."

Mitch had been awfully quiet, and when she looked at him now, she saw him grimace. She leaned closer to him. "Was he in the gang with you?"

Mitch snickered. "No. Wouldn't have made it a day." He raised his voice, addressing the whole table. "Charter's a reporter. We worked together some when I was first learning the PI business."

Charter's eyes flicked to Jennings, then back to Mitch, and he nodded slightly. "Mitch has always been quite adept at investigating."

"You're pretty good at it yourself." Mitch returned the nod, then took a swig of his lemonade. "But let's not dwell on the past. Mother, what have you got slated for tomorrow?"

Jennings looked between the two men, wondering what had just transpired. One of her strengths in poker was picking up on small nuances that other people didn't notice. And she'd bet her bankroll that a hand had just been revealed.

***

Charter was leaving, and Betsy was in the kitchen supervising cleanup, so Mitch jumped at the opportunity to get Jennings alone. She stood under the entrance chandelier saying goodbye to Charter, the light bouncing off the highlights in her hair. The fading, drab brown had been replaced with a rich golden blonde. Her blue eyes were bright and he saw the woman Benny would recognize as his sister. She was shaking off her new identity bit by bit. He wondered if she'd start using her given name again.

The front door closed, and he stepped closer to her, pining her between the foyer table and umbrella stand. "I really like the hair."

She smiled, her hand coming up to tousle the locks. "Yeah?" She twirled a strand around her finger, and he could imagine her at sixteen. "This is pretty close to my natural color. Needed something new."

"It suits you." He hovered close to her lips, savoring her smell, the way her body tensed as if waiting for his kiss. "You want to go for a walk?"

"Sure." Her gaze moved to his mouth.

He cupped the back of her head, and the soft hair flowed over his fingers like a fountain. Unable to hold out any longer, he leaned forward and gently pressed his lips to hers. Her arms went around his neck, her hands twining in his hair, pulling him closer, deepening the kiss. Breathless, he pulled back. As much as he wanted her, right now talking to her was more important. Charter had confirmed his suspicions, and he needed to see what she remembered, make sure she was okay. Well, she obviously wasn't okay if last night was any indication, but she wouldn't be until it was out in the open.

"Do you want to take Norma Jean?"

She licked her lips, and he almost attacked her again. "We better. Can't trust her alone for a second." Grabbing her leash off the hook inside the door, she clapped her hands, and the little dog skittered around the corner. "What mischief were you getting into?" Norma Jean sat and waited for Jennings to hook the leash to her collar, her short tail vibrating.

Mitch opened the door, and Norma Jean led the way down the steps and out to the street. They quickly fell into an easy rhythm, their footfalls the only sound in the quiet neighborhood.

"If I lived here, I'd be out on my porch every night, soaking up the stars." Jennings leaned her head back, gazing at the sky. "It's impossible to see the stars in Vegas."

"But you get to see other kinds of stars all the time, right?"

She waved her hand in dismissal. "I don't care about any of that. Everybody's the same as any other."

They walked in comfortable silence for another block, then she switched the leash to the other hand, and he stepped closer. He took her hand, winding their fingers together, palm against palm. She turned her head and smiled but didn't comment on his high school moves. Circling the block, they reached a small lake with a gazebo in the middle. Norma Jean strained at her leash like she wanted to go for a swim, and Jennings dropped his hand to chase after the dog.

He watched her move in the moonlight, chasing Norma Jean and laughing. His gut wrenched with the knowledge that he'd soon shatter that carefree disposition with talk of a horrendous night twenty-two years ago. Now that he knew she was the girl who'd been attacked, he needed to help her deal with it, and if it was Jason, bring him to justice. Hopefully, it'd bring her closure.

He caught up to them down by the shoreline, where Norma Jean was splashing through the water and chasing a dragonfly. Jennings had taken the leash off and was watching her dog with a look of contentment on her face. *So much for contentment.*

"Jennings?" He stood by a small bench and reached out a hand to her.

She came toward him, took his hand and pulled him down to the bench with her. "Don't forget about the neighborhood association." Teasing twinkled in her eyes, and she drew his hand up to her mouth, pressing her lips against his knuckles.

She was making it really hard to focus. "I'll try to control myself." He shifted on the bench, angling his body toward her. "I need to talk to you about something."

"So serious." She tapped between his eyes, where his brow was indeed furrowed.

"Unfortunately, this is serious."

Something flickered through her eyes—fear, if he had to guess—but then she smiled coyly and moved closer to him. "I *seriously* want you." Her hand trailed down his chest, over his stomach and landed in his crotch. Really, really hard to focus. *Dodger Stadium opened in 1962, making it the third oldest ballpark in Major League Baseball, behind Fenway and Wrigley Field.* "Jennings," he plucked her hand out of his lap, "we should really talk."

She scowled and turned her body forward—away from him. "I don't want to talk, Mitch."

"I think I know what happened twenty-two years ago." He kept his voice soft, careful not to sound confrontational. He slid his hand up her back, rubbing circles.

She jumped off the bench and faced him, her hands dancing wildly through the air. "The only thing that happened twenty-two years ago is that I ran away from a crappy life." Her volume rose with each word, and by the time she finished in a huff, Norma Jean had come close to see what was going on.

"Losing your whole family must have been horrible, and after you left Asheville, things got worse, didn't they?" He could see the pain behind her anger, and he hated to push her, but he knew she'd feel better after everything got out into the open.

Her eyes narrowed; her mouth set in a pinched line. "I'd like to see any sixteen-year-old do better." She leaned in close, pointed her index finger straight in his face. "At least I didn't turn to a life of crime because I was bored." She scooped Norma Jean off the ground, turned on her heel, and stomped off in the direction they'd walked.

Mitch covered his face with his hand. *That went well.* Rubbing his fingers over his cheek, he realized he hadn't shaved in nearly a week, and was now sporting a full-fledged beard. He was so wrapped up in this woman's drama that he was neglecting basic hygiene. He'd wager that he'd gained about twenty more grey hairs, too. Caroline Jennings Lee was going to drive him to an early grave.

Heaving himself off the bench, he trailed slowly behind her, giving her space. He'd let her sleep on it, then confront her tomorrow. Maybe in the light of day it wouldn't be so scary to her.

Chapter Fifteen

"**M**itchell, are you going to sleep the entire day away?" Betsy's voice came at Mitch as if through molasses. The pounding on the door was more distinct.

Maybe he shouldn't have gone to The Beetle last night. He definitely shouldn't have had that last shot. Or four.

He unglued his eyelids and stared at the clock on the nightstand waiting for it to stay still. 10:45.

"Is Jennings in there with you? Mitchell?"

Jennings...maybe she wasn't mad anymore. He reached his arm beside him, but the bed was empty. Rubbing his eyes, he tried to focus. He remembered sitting in the bar, accepting a dung beetle shot from a hot brunette. He remembered his frustration that Jason wasn't there again. Wincing, he remembered ordering several more shots.

"Mitchell!" The door slammed open, and he sat up in bed, now wide awake. Betsy stood in the doorway, breathing deeply, likely from all the yelling. "Why didn't you answer me? And where is Jennings?"

His neurons finally started firing, and he realized that if his mother was asking where Jennings was, it meant she wasn't in the next room. "She's not in her room?"

"No. All her stuff's gone and so is that mangy little dog."

Mitch scrambled out of bed. His head pounded in protest, but he pushed the pain aside as he swept past his mother and down the hall.

The bedroom looked undisturbed, no evidence of the vixen who had stayed there the past four nights. He stepped further into the room, searching for clues as to where she'd gone. A piece of yellow paper, like the legal pads Harry was so fond of, lay on the pillows. "Betsy" was scrawled on the front.

"She left you a note." His head felt near to exploding. *Where is my fucking note?*

Betsy left her spot in the doorway and reached for the note. She read it quickly and then pressed it to her chest, grinning. "Such a polite girl."

Mitch rolled his eyes. *Yeah, a real Southern belle ready for Cotillion.* "What does it say, Mother?" He gritted his teeth to keep from shouting.

She pursed her lips at him, then sighed. "She thanked me for my hospitality. Said I was delightful company." Betsy looked giddy at the compliments.

As usual, his mother was missing the big picture. Jennings had run again.

He pushed past Betsy and, back in his room, pulled a pair of jeans on over his boxer briefs. He was flying down the hall with a shirt in his hand when his mom came out of the guest room.

"Where are you going?"

"To find her."

"She's a grown woman, Mitchell."

He let the front door bang behind him. That was the problem. She wasn't sixteen anymore, and he was betting the streetwise Jennings Lee would be harder to find the second time.

***

Mitch wrenched Harry's door so hard the glass inside vibrated. He needed to calm down. The drive downtown had been almost as reckless as driving home from the bar last night. Jennings had a way of making his sense go right out the window.

"Where's the fire, boy?" Harry looked up from a pile of folders, his pencil in midair.

"She left, Harry."

"Who left?"

"Jennings!" He fell into a chair, and with a "crack," he was on the floor. "Damn chairs." He stood up, brandishing the broken leg. "Piece of shit is older than you."

Harry rose from his desk, stepped in front of it, and crossed his arms over his chest, surveying the broken pieces. "Don't take your lover's spat out on me and my furniture." He gestured toward the chair that remained intact. "These are antiques. Like me."

Mitch dropped the leg, defeated. "It wasn't a lover's spat, Harry." He leaned against the desk. "Jennings was attacked twenty-two years ago. Right here in Memphis." Sucking in a breath, he let it out gradually, trying to slow the speed of his racing heart. "And I think it was Jason who attached her."

"Whoa." Harry dropped into the remaining chair; his face haggard. "I mean, I wouldn't put it past the prick, but what's your evidence?"

"It's actually Charter's theory. He did a piece on a teenage runaway who claimed to trip on a curb over by the Orpheum. She was pretty beat up. But wouldn't tell anyone her name or admit she was attacked." His mind raced with what he needed to do to track her down, but he knew that the more information Harry had, the more he'd be able to help, so he forced himself to finish the story. "Jennings and I parked in a garage behind the theater a couple nights ago and she had a breakdown just being there. She wouldn't tell me what was wrong, but then

I talked to Charter, who showed me the article dated April 22, 2003. Harry, Benny got a postcard from Jennings postmarked April 21, 2003, Memphis, Tennessee.”

“And I taught you to never believe in coincidences.”

Mitch nodded. “I had Charter over for dinner last night, and he’s positive Jennings was the girl he saw in the hospital.”

“So, she ran because she recognized Charter? Maybe he was into *making* news back then.”

Charter Vance was a weasel who pushed around insecure kids to get the information he needed, but Mitch couldn’t picture him assaulting anyone. *Besides, Jennings hadn’t gotten spooked until I started in on her.* “No, I think she ran because she knew I had figured it out. She’s scared of her past, and I think she’s even more scared of falling for me.” He raked his hand through his hair. “I’m in deep, Harry. I think I love her.”

“You don’t say.” His dry tone implied that he’d figured that morsel out long ago.

“I need to find her, Harry.”

He stood up and went back around the desk. As he sat, he opened his laptop. Harry had never been afraid of technology. He’d always had the latest and greatest toys. “Well, unless she hotwired your mom’s Caddy, she probably called an Uber. Man, I miss the days when you could call the cab companies and find out where people went.” He typed on the keyboard for a few minutes, then turned the computer toward Mitch. “Lucky for you, I’ve found a workaround.”

***

Jennings sat down and slapped her chips on the table. She slowed her breathing, visualizing the cards being dealt, raking the pot in. *Focus on the game.*

Poker had been her escape for the last twenty years. Upon arriving in Vegas, she’d taken a dancing gig at a seedy place downtown called Raz’s. Between acts, the girls had taught her Hold 'em. By the time she was old enough to play legally, she'd graduated up The Strip to a slightly nicer nightclub. She played poker in casinos during the day and danced at night.

It wasn't a glamorous lifestyle, by any means, but Vegas, with its constant stream of tourists, was the perfect place to live a mostly anonymous life. That's what she'd wanted—a life with only herself to worry about, and no one who could hurt her by leaving. The first chink in her isolated armor had been Norma Jean, who, on this trip, she'd had to sneak into the hotel in one of her suitcases. Hopefully she was upstairs sleeping quietly—and not tearing the room to shreds.

She should have realized that cracking open the door to her heart to let Norma Jean in would have dire circumstances. It made her think of the possibilities—if she could love a dog that much, maybe loving a person wouldn't be so bad. And look how that had turned out—Mitch started caring about her and then poked around where he wasn't welcome. Jennings hadn't even allowed herself to love him yet, just like him a little bit, and she still ended up getting hurt. Even seeing Benny again wasn't worth the pain of remembering that night in Memphis.

The dealer tapped the table in front of her indicating it was her turn. *Stop reliving a past that can't be repaired and focus on the game.* She peeked down at her hole cards and called the bet. The pair of eights taunted her. It was the hand she'd held against Mitch the last time she'd played poker. She remembered the way his eyes had dug into her during that hand, as if he was pulling her inside out and discovering all her secrets. She should've run then.

"You fixin' to play?" A hick with a cowboy hat and bolo tie glared at her from across the table.

She shook her head, hoping to jar Mitch from her mind. "Sorry." Looking at the felt, the three cards of the flop swam in from her. If she kept playing this distracted, she'd lose what little money remained in her bankroll after getting out of Memphis. Folding her cards, she stood up, stacked her chips and pushed away from the table. "I'm not feeling well. Good luck everyone."

Jennings didn't even cash out her chips. She hopped on the elevator, rode to the fifth floor, and the moment she was in the door of her hotel room, collapsed on the bed.

***

Harry was a freaking genius. Or at least the kid who developed the program to hack into Uber was. They couldn't see people's private information, but they could track routes and see drop offs and pickups.

Tracking someone down was his specialty, and once he started making headway, Mitch's nerves settled, and he was able to focus on the job. *It's only a job.* He repeated the mantra over in his head on his way to the airport, where the car had likely dropped Jennings.

He knew full well it wasn't only a job, but what was a little denial if it could get him through?

He parked in the short-term lot and headed into the terminal. Airport security had gotten extreme since 9-11, and smooth-talking a cute airline representative out of passenger information was about as likely as Elvis himself manning the controls of a jetliner. Too bad Harry's hacker couldn't get into the FAA.

Nevertheless, he approached the ticket counter and scoped out a young attendant with butterfly barrettes in her hair and a cross around her neck. Pasting on his most charming grin, he stepped forward. "Hi," he glanced at her nametag, "Stephanie. I'm hoping you can help me."

"I can most certainly try." Her smile was shy, but her voice confident. She knew how to do her job, and that's what Mitch needed right now.

"Well, you see, there's this girl." Mitch looked down at the counter and fidgeted with the pen attached to a chain. He lifted his head, and tried to appear forlorn. Which really wasn't a struggle. "I think she ran off to Vegas this morning to marry another guy."

Stephanie's hand flew to cover her mouth. "Oh, my."

"Yeah, pretty bad, huh? Anyway, I can't give her up without a fight, you know?"

"Oh, that's so romantic." She practically had stars in her eyes. "So, you need a ticket to Vegas then?"

Mitch's gut clinched. His last flight from Memphis to Vegas—last flight, period—had ended badly. He'd survived the near crash landing only to be humiliated and almost lose his PI license. Maybe Jennings hadn't gone to Vegas. Maybe she was still in the airport. Maybe he wouldn't have to get on a plane.

"Sir?" Stephanie was looking less enamored with his story and more irritated. "When would you like to fly out?"

How about when Elvis rises from the dead? "Do you know when the flight left this morning?"

"Sir," there was now a definite edge to her voice, "we have twenty or more flights to Las Vegas daily. Obviously, I can't share privileged flight information with you."

Mitch pressed against his forehead. He wasn't thinking straight, and his charm had worn off about five minutes ago. "Of course, I understand. I," he stepped back from the counter, "I'll get back with you on that ticket."

He scanned the terminal, his eyes stopping on the stick figure indicating the men's room. Once inside, he splashed water on his face and studied his image in the mirror. The beard had taken on a life of its own and with his eyes darting around nervously, an over-eager TSA agent could easily mark him as a up to no good. He needed to get his shit together. Now.

Pulling his phone out of his pocket, he dialed Harry's number.

"You find your Lola?"

Who is the hell is Lola? He didn't have time for Harry's obscure references. "I'm buying a ticket to Vegas."

"There's a big difference between buying a ticket and getting on an airplane."

Mitch leaned against the wall of the bathroom, banging his head. "Fuck."

"Do you know for sure she went back to Vegas? I thought she gave up her place."

"She did. But where else would she go?"

Harry grunted. "Boy, this broad is screwing with your head. Didn't I teach you anything?"

He tried to quiet the roaring in his head and focus on his PI training. He'd been doing the work for almost twenty years, and only once before had he gotten off track this badly. That'd been a woman too. Obviously, he wasn't built for relationships. "I got nothing, Harry."

"Fine, I'll hold your GD hand." Harry cleared his throat. "Wasn't there some friend, Maria, or Rosa, or something?"

"Elena! Harry, you're a genius." Mitch ended the call and quickly scrolled through his address book to find Elena's number.

"Mitch Kline." Her smooth Latina voice caressed his shattered nerves. "I was wondering when you were going to update me. I can't get *caca* out of Jennings."

He let out a deep breath. "Thank God, she's with you."

"What do you mean? She isn't with you?"

"Shit." He clenched his fist, then released it, focusing on breathing, or he was going to pass out. "I really thought she'd go back to Vegas."

Elena muttered something in Spanish. "What the hell did you do to my friend, you *hijo de puta*?

"When did you talk to her last?"

"Yesterday. She sounded happy. So help me—"

"She took off this morning, and if she hasn't called you, she must not have flown to Vegas." Mitch sorted through the options. Maybe she'd flown to Asheville.

"Where's Norma Jean?"

He stopped pacing the small bathroom. Norma Jean. She wouldn't have been able to get on a plane with the mutt. Unless she had an airline crate and mess of paperwork stowed away in one of her suitcases. "Thanks, Elena, you've been a huge help."

She strung together a few choice Spanish phrases, but Mitch ended the call before she could ask any more questions.

Leaving the rest room, he walked into the main part of the terminal and spun in a slow circle. Why did she come to the airport if she wasn't going to fly? His gaze landed on an advertisement for Avis Car Rentals. He strode across the lobby floor and took the escalator down to the lower level. A car made more sense than a plane. And it didn't involve him leaving the ground.

At the first rental counter, he sidled up to a middle-aged woman who wore a bored expression. "Busy day?" The woman looked immune to charm, so he decided to try empathy.

She grunted. "Want a car?"

He slid a twenty onto the counter. "Just information."

The woman laid an application over the money, her eyes darting toward the ceiling.

Mitch kept his head still, but slid his gaze up. A dark bubble over their heads signaled surveillance, but it didn't appear to be wired for sound. He leaned on the counter. "Say a woman with a dog wanted to rent a car."

"Hertz does it. Seems there might have been a dog there earlier today." She pointed and slid the application and money back off the counter. "Have a nice day."

"You too." As he crossed to the Hertz counter, he studied his mark, trying to determine the best approach. The attendant was an average guy in his late twenties, no ring, a bit of a beer gut, and untrimmed hair. He'd bet he was straight.

"You need a car, man?" Definitely straight.

Mitch shook his head, raked his fingers through his hair. *I've got to get a haircut.* "You married, dude?" Sometimes he felt more like an actor than an investigator.

Brandon, according to his nametag, scoffed. "Hell, no."

"Well, avoid it at all costs. I woke up this morning and my crazy ex had swiped my dog."

"That's low, man, taking a dude's dog."

Mitch nodded. "Lowest of the lows. Anyway, I think she might have rented a car." He put his hand up to his mouth as if imparting a secret. "At least I got *something* in the big D."

Brandon bobbed his head. "I hear ya, man. Was it a real ugly mutt?"

"Yeah, sad case, lost a bunch of her hair in a fire. Good dog, though, real loyal."

"She was here. And damn, man, your ex is hot."

"Watch out. Hot usually equals crazy." He twirled his finger near his ear in the international symbol for *loco*.

"That sucks, bro, but I can't really tell you anything. You know, private information and all that shit."

Mitch sighed and dropped his shoulders. "Yeah, I understand, dude. You're just doing your job." He looked around and leaned further over the counter. "But maybe in the course of your job you had to give directions to someone."

Brandon pointed his finger like a gun. "I gotcha. You need a map of The South. Like if you wanted to find Tunica." He slid a map over the counter.

Of course. There were lots of casinos in Tunica, and it was less than an hour away. "Thanks, dude. You've been extremely helpful. And watch out for the next hot one."

"Will do. Good luck, man."

Chapter Sixteen

God bless Norma Jean. The stinky little mutt was keeping Jennings within driving distance. And she was making her owner easier to track. No one forgot a balding mixed breed with personality to spare.

Back at his mother's, Mitch jumped in the shower, lathered his face up, and got rid of his mountain man getup. He stepped out, dripping, onto the stupid Elvis bathmat and checked his reflection. His face was recognizable again. He still needed a haircut, but the clean-shaven effect should help in the charm department. The damn beard covered up his dimple, and women seemed to go for that sort of thing. When he got to Tunica, he'd need all the help he could get. First, to gather the information necessary to find Jennings, then to charm the woman herself into coming back with him. There was still a wedding to get to. He'd have to put his vigilante justice on hold.

He wrapped a towel around his waist and padded into the office. As soon as Gary's iMac booted up, he opened a Safari window and searched for Tunica casinos. There were ten major ones, and after a few clicks, he determined that only five of them had poker rooms. He printed the list, threw some clothes on, then stuffed everything back into his duffel. He was almost to the truck when his mother's Caddy pulled in the driveway, blocking the old Ford.

"Are you going off after that poor girl?" Betsy stepped out of the car and gestured at him across the roof. "Can't you just leave her be?"

"I thought you liked Jennings." He tossed his bag in the bed of the truck, tucking the tarp around it.

She walked toward him, her heels clicking on the flagstone. "Of course, I like her. That's why I think you should give her some room to breathe."

It would have been good advice a day ago. Before he'd raced after his theory, with no regard for how it would affect the woman he cared about—hell, loved. "I don't have the benefit of time, Mother. Benny's getting married in three days and I have to get his sister to Asheville or risk being demoted from best man to uninvited."

Betsy rolled her eyes. "Yeah, I sure you're real worried about your hippie friend's wedding." She planted her hands on her hips and stared him down like a mother who just caught her little boy with his hand the cookie jar. "You're in love with the girl, Mitchell. And somehow you've managed to muck it up."

He wondered briefly what his mother knew about love. All of her relationships had been about financial gain, not about matters of the heart. "Maybe, but I can at least finish what I set out to do."

She tossed him her keys and headed toward the house. "Love is always a pain in the ass."

Mitch stared after his mother as she swept into the house and closed the door behind her. *Which one of her discarded husbands had she loved?* He didn't have time to analyze his mother's love life. He wasn't even sure he had time to deal with his own. His first priority was to get Jennings to Asheville. Even if he had to drag her kicking and screaming.

He pulled his mother's car forward, then vaulted the steps and set the keys on the small table inside the front door. "Bye, Mom. Thanks for letting us stay."

No response echoed through the big house and he briefly considered tracking her down and making sure she heard, but he didn't want to waste any more time. He'd wasted enough time fixated on a woman who was completely wrong for him.

***

The two-hour nap gave her scattered mind a break, and Jennings felt ready to tackle the tables again, but first, she needed to get Norma Jean outside for a potty break. She grabbed her phone, snapped on the leash, and peeked into the hallway to check for witnesses. All clear, she dashed out of the room, dragging the little dog behind her. Norma Jean didn't understand the urgency.

A stairwell at the end of the hallway looked promising, and Jennings prayed that it would open to the outside. Five flights down, and the door opened on the side of the building, well hidden from the activity out front. She held the door open with her leg while she stretched to grab a piece of wood to ensure their re-entry into the building. *I'm not just some dumb waitress from Vegas.* She'd bet she'd outsmarted Mitch, too.

Norma Jean strained toward a dumpster, which likely reminded her of home. Jennings scanned the marshland behind the casino while the dog sniffed out the appropriate spot.

Her phone chirped. Mitch had called multiple times, but this call was from Elena.

"Hey, *Chica*, what's up?" She mimicked her friend's Latin flavor.

"What's up? I'll tell you what's up! I'm worried sick about you, Mitch is worried sick about you, and so help me if you've gone off and done something *loco*..."

Jennings didn't understand the rest. "I'm fine, Elena. I just needed to get away from him—everything—it was too much. I'm sorry he called and got you worried."

"*Carina*, why are you running away? Did he hurt you?" The concern in her friend's voice clenched her heart.

How could she explain something she didn't completely understand? "No. But he got really close to a nerve."

"Where are you?"

"I'm safe, don't worry. If you know, Mitch will try to get it out of you." Norma Jean tugged at the leash. Jennings tugged back. Norma Jean barked. She was blowing their cover. Jennings turned and headed back for the stairwell door, then saw what her dog had seen. "Shit."

"What's wrong?"

"Elena, I've got to call you back." Jennings lowered the phone, her gut rolling in disgust. *How the hell'd he find me?*

"You people had better stop hanging up on me," Elena screamed through the phone.

Jennings ended the call. She'd make it up to her friend later. Right now, she had to pray that Mitch hadn't seen her or heard Norma Jean.

The old truck pulled into a parking space at the outer edge of the lot. *Is he worried someone will scratch it?* She didn't wait around to see if he'd made her. Kicking the piece of wood out of the door, she scooped up Norma Jean and raced up the five flights. If she barricaded herself in her room, she'd be safe. It was a big hotel. He couldn't knock on every door.

She'd traveled on the sly enough to know how to stay under the radar. It'd been a long time since she'd worried about her identity, but she wasn't completely rusty. Of course, he'd made it to Tunica, so he must have schmoozed that rental car clerk for information. Was nothing private these days?

Luckily, she'd had the presence of mind to spin a tale for the hotel clerk who checked her in that morning. Getting a room that early in the day had been an accomplishment in and of itself. Mitch wasn't the only smooth talker.

Unwilling to risk Mitch hearing her leave Betsy's that morning, she hadn't showered, so when she arrived at the Goldstrike, she mussed her hair a bit and went with the whole bedraggled look. She'd stuffed Norma Jean in one of her suitcases, and prayed she wouldn't cause a ruckus during check-in. The whole time she was talking to the man at reception, a small brown muzzle kept poking out the hole Jennings had left in the zipper.

She'd explained that she had broken up with a man who'd cheated on her and he wasn't taking it well, and might try to track her down. So, while she knew she needed to show her license to check in, could he please list her reservation under another name? She'd thrown in a desperate "save-me" smile for good measure. The staff member, aptly appalled, had agreed, and registered the room under CJ Diamond.

Now, locked safety in her room, Jennings wished she had a secret camera on the front desk so she could watch Mitch strike out and leave with his tail tucked between his legs. At least she could watch him get back in his truck and drive to the next casino.

***

Mitch stepped into the lobby of the Goldstrike. Harrah's and the Horseshoe had been busts, but there were only three more casinos with poker rooms, so he was optimistic.

The marble floors gleamed in the expansive entrance, and set in front of the reception desk was a sculpture, which, to his eye, resembled a lit-up sea anemone. He watched the staff for a moment, and noticed one guy who kept checking his watch. If Mitch had to guess, he was getting off shift soon, which meant he may have been around when Jennings checked in.

"Hey," he leaned casually on the counter. "I'm meeting my girlfriend. I believe she's already checked in. The reservation should be under Lee." Who knew which first name she was using at this point?

The other man's brow dipped and his eyes narrowed. "I'm quite sure we don't have a reservation under that name, sir."

Based on the daggers the man was shooting at Mitch, he'd bet they did. Jennings had likely told him some story about her big bad boyfriend. "Well, that's weird. I could've sworn she said the Goldstrike. Tell me," he glanced around the pristine lobby, "what's your pet policy?"

"We allow small dogs in specific suites for a non-refundable deposit. Are you traveling with an animal, sir?" The clerk looked confused by the question, but maintained his professional demeanor.

Jennings had either left Norma Jean in the car, which Mitch seriously doubted, or had snuck her in. "Nope, but I'm curious. What would happen if someone snuck a dog in and it, say, destroyed hotel property?"

The clerk's eyes widened and he typed something into the computer. "I'm sure our clientele would never be that underhanded."

Mitch shrugged his shoulders. "I suppose." He pointed to the end of the counter. "I'll just step over here and try her on the phone again." He slid down the counter and dialed Harry's number, keeping one eye on the clerk.

The other man jotted a number down on a pad, tore the sheet off and slipped it to another staff member, whispering something in her ear.

"Did you find her?" Harry's gruff voice sounded like sandpaper. Maybe he'd taken to a mid-day nap.

"Darling, I'm here at the Goldstrike. Haven't you checked in yet?" Mitch watched the employee with the note slip into a room behind the counter. He stepped away from the desk and headed toward the elevators.

"Darling, huh? Can't say anyone's ever called me that. The Goldstrike, huh? So, she went to Tunica?"

The woman emerged from a door and pressed the up button on the elevator.

Mitch stepped closer, trying to glimpse the number on the paper. "I know how you love poker, dear. Maybe after you finish, you can join me in the room." The elevator door slid open and he stepped in behind the Goldstrike employee, who pressed the number five.

"Boy, you get weirder every day. Call me when you can talk straight." Harry hung up.

"Four," Mitch answered in response to the woman's silent question.

When the doors opened at the fourth floor, Mitch smiled and stepped out, barely waiting for the doors to close before he took off for the stairs. He flew up the additional flight, and cracked open the stairwell door in time to see the woman knock on a door down the hall. Closing the door, he caught his breath. *Victory.*

Chapter Seventeen

The knock at the door startled Jennings from her post at the window. Mitch hadn't come out of the hotel yet. If he was standing on the other side of the door, she didn't know what she'd do. She crossed the floor and peered through the peephole. A hotel staff member stood in the hallway.

Shit. Jennings grabbed Norma Jean off the pillow she was sleeping on and searched for an appropriate hiding place. The bathroom seemed too obvious, so she threw open the closet door and set the little dog inside before quietly closing the door. Throwing the security lock open, she cracked the door to the room, praying that Norma Jean would stay quiet. "Yes?"

"Sorry to bother you, ma'am," the woman attempted to peer past Jennings into the room, "I was just making sure you have everything you need."

I'm so sure. She held her body firmly in the crack of the door. "Everything's peachy. Thanks." Norma Jean whimpered, and Jennings coughed. "I was just laying down for a nap, so if you'll excuse me." She started to close the door, but the staff member whipped her hand into the open space like a frog darting its tongue out to capture prey.

"Let me turn your bed down for you."

"Really," Jennings gritted her teeth, "that's not necessary." She went to close the door again and the woman had to move her arm or risk it being smashed. Leaning against the closed door, she sighed. *How did I get here?* She felt like a fugitive on the run from a crime she didn't remember committing.

She jumped at the second knock on the door. *The nerve of this woman!* Jennings wrenched the door open. "Is a little peace too much to ask..." The question died on her lips when her brain assimilated that it was Mitch standing in the hall. Before she could react, he pushed past her into the room.

"We need to talk. You can have your peace later." The deep, masculine voice slid up her back and embraced her entire being like the warm honey baths her mama had given her when she'd been unable to sleep as a child.

Jennings remained in the doorway, unable to turn around, to move at all. She didn't know how to face this man that terrified, infuriated, and aroused her in ways she'd never experienced. Norma Jean barked and clawed at the closet door. The pup had fallen head over tail for the gruff stranger and now she wanted out of her hiding place. The dog's ruckus snapped Jennings out of her fugue, and she let the door to the room close.

"Is Norma Jean in time out, or can I let her out of the closet?"

It was the dog who'd done her in. She wasn't sure what irritated her more: that she hadn't been able to disappear like she'd done over twenty years ago, or that Mitch was so good at his job. Jennings opened the closet door and Norma Jean rolled end over end to get to Mitch.

"I missed you, too." He picked up the scraggly dog and let her indulge in a frenzy of kisses. "Mean old Jennings ran away with you."

"She's MY dog!"

He cocked a half-smile at her, and she realized he'd shaved off the beard she'd become so fond of. And now that damn dimple puckered up front and center. "I think she likes me more."

Jennings clenched her fists and closed her eyes. *One, two, three...*before she could make it to ten, Mitch's arms were around her and his lips were working their magic on her neck.

"I'm sorry I pushed." The kisses moved along the line of her jaw, and she melted a little with each one.

In this hotel room, away from Memphis and the painful memories, she was having a hard time remembering why she was mad at him. When his lips reached hers, she wound her arms around his neck and leaned into the kiss. She'd certainly experienced desire that burned in her gut before, but with Mitch, the heat filled her entire being, and it was deeper than just lust. It filled her heart, her core, and she wanted to drown in it—even though she knew drowning led to death.

His hands slid down her back and he crushed her to him. Backing further into the room he turned, and they were falling, the weight of him pressing her against the bed.

Mitch pulled back, and she missed his lips. He tucked her hair behind one ear, his eyes full of lust, but so much more. "I don't want to be the thing you're scared of."

His weight wasn't on her anymore, so why couldn't she breathe?

***

His plan had been to talk her into going to Asheville. To get her to Benny's wedding. But the moment he'd seen her, all he'd wanted was to hold her.

Now, she lay beneath him, her chest rising and falling in short, frenzied breaths. A tear slid out of her eye, and his gut clenched. Why couldn't she let him love her? He used his thumb to wipe away the tear. "I'm not going to hurt you, Jennings."

She sucked in her top lip, her brow furrowed, and another tear rolled down her cheek. "How can you know that for sure?" The question came out in a strangled whisper.

He wanted to erase the pain he saw in her eyes, take the tremor out of her voice, expel the fear she'd been living with for so long. Mitch couldn't imagine what it'd be like to lose your entire family, and he didn't blame her for guarding her heart. But he'd fallen hard for this mysterious woman, and he'd spend as much time as it took to convince her that he wasn't leaving. "I'm not going anywhere." He kissed her cheek where the tear had been. "Unless it's to chase you."

Her gaze bounced over his face, as if she were trying to gauge a tell at the poker table. Finally, it settled on his eyes, and her breathing slowed. She put her hands on each side of his face and rose up to meet his lips. Her arms snaked back around his neck and she buried her face in his shoulder. "Make love to me, Mitch."

He was in too deep to turn back now. Desire and love were sliding past each other and the line between them had blurred to nothing. His body and heart joined forces to defeat any logic his brain might have tried to throw at the situation. Thoughts of his promise to Benny briefly flickered through his mind, but as Jennings's hold on him tightened, nothing else mattered. He needed to prove to her that he wanted all of her. Her body, her heart, her untrusting soul, the pain of her past.

He slid his hands up her sides, hooking the fabric of her shirt with his thumbs and pulled it over her head. The juncture of her neck and shoulder begged to be kissed. He lowered his head, breathing in her scent, memorizing it, like a bloodhound who might need to track her at a later time. He tasted the soft flesh, and her body quivered in response. Moving along the line of her shoulder, he explored every inch with his eyes, his mouth, his hands. He intended to savor every kiss, every touch, every moment with this woman who had existed only in casual conversation two weeks ago. Now his every thought included her, enmeshed her into his consciousness, his very soul.

As much as he yearned to explore every freckle, every supple bite of her flesh, he missed her lips. He diverged from his trek down her arm, twined his fingers in her hair and raised his mouth to hers. She moaned into his mouth, maybe saying his name, but he stole the words with his kiss. His body urged him to hurry up, but his soul wanted to slow it down, spend the next fifty years learning how to touch Jennings all the way down to her heart.

She tugged at his shirt, and he leaned back to allow her to pull it over his head. Then he sank back down, their flesh meeting, sending shivers across his chest, along his stomach and straight to his groin. Her hands slid down to the button of his jeans, and she seemed to be in as much of a hurry as his thick, throbbing cock.

Slipping his hands beneath her, he fumbled to unhook the clasp on her green, lacy bra. She arched her back, and the bra released. He slid the straps off her arms, and cupped her left breast in his palm. The flesh was smooth and pale, and he dipped his head, sliding his tongue around the pink, hard tip of her nipple. She jerked and moaned. He released the breast from his hand and sucked it into his mouth, causing a sharp intake of breath from Jennings.

"Please, Mitch."

He slid his hand up to cover her other breast, squeezing it while he worshipped its partner with his tongue. She squirmed beneath him, her hands clenching at him, pulling at his jeans.

"Oh, God, Mitch."

Every time she uttered his name, he slowed down, indulging in the pleasure of her husky inflection. Relishing the thought that maybe he was getting a little closer to her guarded heart.

***

Jennings wasn't usually much of a talker during sex. Hell, she usually didn't know the guy's name well enough to use it confidently. She didn't typically spend two weeks getting worked up before the guy closed the deal. And she never used the words "make love."

Everything was different with Mitch. He had wormed his way past her solid defenses, had squirmed into the soft, exposed, vulnerable flesh of her heart. And if she wasn't so turned on, maybe she would have been able to fight it. Focusing on the physical helped her ignore the messy emotional aspects of this long-anticipated encounter. And the physical was so damned good.

He was trailing kisses down her stomach, flicking his tongue against her skin, sparking goose bumps, as if he had all the time in the world. The fire between her legs raged, and his lackadaisical journey down her body was driving her crazy. The man took foreplay to an entirely different level. Come to think of it, they'd been engaging in foreplay for two weeks now. Her engine was past primed.

When his mouth slid past her navel, she got hopeful. But he started back up her body, sliding first his mouth, then his hard chest up and over her stomach, her breasts, and returned to her mouth.

It wasn't that she minded the kissing. Mitch kissed like he was standing on the dock, minutes from being shipped out, and this was his last chance to hold his girl. He kissed her like he cherished her, and Jennings had never felt cherished before. So, while pinpricks of energy lit the heels of her feet, her nipples hardened, and she got wet with anticipation, the strangest effect of Mitch's kisses was how her heart swelled and warmed her from the inside out. She didn't have time to dwell on the feeling though, because desire throbbed from deep in her gut and the only way it would be sated was if she could get him out of those damn pants.

She tugged at the button on his jeans again, but he grabbed her arms, raised them over her head, and pinned them at the wrists.

"I'm not going anywhere. We have lots of time." His eyes were hungry, yet tender, and she almost believed him.

"You're torturing me." She licked her lips and added a little whine. "Please."

He laughed, and pleasure rocked through her.

He's not even touching me! She was in deep and she didn't know how to get out—or if she wanted to.

"Baby," he affected the voice he'd used in their "pretend" relationship scene at the restaurant with Harry and Carla, "you'll never have to beg me." He leaned back down and kissed the sensitive spot behind her earlobe, his breath dancing across her ear and her neck, and any resistance she'd been hanging on to evaporated.

She craned up, and snatched his earlobe in her mouth, sucking and nibbling it. He moaned, and loosened the grip on her hands, so she wiggled free, and propelled both of them over. Straddling his hips, she sat up, smiled, and undid his pants. He may have been taking his time, but he was as ready as she was. She stroked the long, hard rod and watched in satisfaction as his breathing got shallow.

"Honey," she pressed his erection between her legs, "you're gonna be the one who's begging."

He sat up fast, knocking her backward, but his strong arms caught her as he assaulted her with his mouth. He went from carefree meandering to frenzied attack in ten seconds flat. Before Jennings could react, she was on her back again, her pants across the room and Mitch was naked, rolling a condom down his thick, hard cock. Then he was over her again, his knee between hers, his eyes locked on hers as he lowered down.

Just before he entered her, he cupped his hand behind her head and kissed her with such tenderness the door to her heart swung open and Mitch Kline walked right in.

Chapter Eighteen

ennings awoke before Mitch. They were tangled together in a mass of arms, legs, and sheets. She slid out from under his arm and sat up in the bed, watching him. His hair was damp and stuck to his forehead, and his jawline boasted a fine brown stubble. His chest rose and fell rhythmically, and she couldn't help but rest her ear against it to hear his heartbeat there. He hooked his arm around her again and pulled her close. His eyes were still closed, but his fingers traced lazy patterns on her hip.

She settled into his embrace and sighed. The safe, calm feeling was foreign, and she wanted to soak it in, test it out, figure out where it'd go wrong. She closed her eyes, imagining what it be like to wake up next to Mitch every day. His big, strong presence, his fresh, manly scent, his hands, gently soothing her and turning her on at the same time. Sex with Mitch had been unlike anything in her life. As much as she'd tried to focus on the intense physical pleasure, the emotional connection had overwhelmed everything else. The way he touched her, the way his kisses sliced straight to her heart, it was like something Jennings had never dared to dream about. She'd felt adored, treasured, loved…and she knew that when he left her, her heart would never recover.

He kissed her shoulder. "We should get going."

Going? "I'm not ready to go back to Memphis, Mitch." *How could he even suggest that?*

His laughter tickled her neck. "Not Memphis, although some of my stuff's still at Betsy's." He kissed her again and sat up. "To Asheville. I assume you were running from me, not Benny."

Benny. He was why she'd gotten a rental car instead of hoping on a plane. Well, that and Norma Jean. She'd planned to get her head on straight, maybe make some money playing poker, and then drive to Asheville in time for the wedding. She may be unwilling to revisit parts of her past, but Benny was the part too long ignored. "I never ran from Benny." She'd run from the pain of him being taken from her. From the loneliness she felt every day she couldn't see him. And the secret DSS couldn't know about.

Mitch laid his hand against her cheek. "I know." He leaned forward and kissed her lightly. "You don't have to be nervous about going back. He loves you. He's not holding any grudges."

"I don't want him to be disappointed." She sucked her bottom lip in, chewing on it.

"Jennings," he gripped her shoulders, "no one could be disappointed by you. What you went through, it would have made most people crumble. But you kept going. Took care of him and yourself. You were just a kid." He pushed her hair behind one ear. "He's proud of you. I'm proud of you."

She'd turned off her emotions twenty-two years ago, and the last two weeks had been like irrigation to a dusty and parched field. Tears sprang to her eyes again. Digging out her memories and remembering how much she loved her brother was hard enough, but dumping the torrent of her feelings for Mitch on top of it was like soaking a houseplant with enough water for a swimming pool. She was drowning. Her heart had only served biological purposes for so long, containing all this new emotion was kicking it into overdrive. She raised her hand to her chest and pressed, trying to slow it down. She looked up at Mitch, and the tears spilled over.

He pulled her into his arms, and she clung to him with the realization she couldn't handle this on her own. Needing someone was a foreign concept to her, and it scared her more than remembering that night in the alley behind the Orpheum.

***

He'd held her until she stopped crying, and now she was in the shower and Mitch was smuggling Norma Jean out of the building. Benny accused him of having a superhero complex when it came to women, always seeking out the ones that needed to be saved. He'd learned too late that Carla's cries for help were simply manipulations and that she didn't want him to save her at all, just to know that he would. Jennings was different. She'd been saving herself for so long she didn't even know how to let someone else do it. But he'd felt a wall crack last night. A chunk of her defenses had fallen, and she'd let him in. He'd never experienced such a fusion of passion and emotion. Her vulnerability had allowed them to connect on a level he'd never experienced before, and he felt bound to her in a way he'd never felt with Carla. Even as he'd stood at that altar in Vegas.

Mitch unlocked Jennings's rental car and pulled Norma Jean out of his jacket. He'd likely resembled the Hunchback of Notre Dame as he strolled through the lobby of the Goldstrike. He started the car and rolled the windows down a third of the way, then patted the little dog on her head. "You stay put. We'll be down really soon."

It was already nearing eighty, and he wanted to be sure not to leave Norma Jean in the car for too long. Which meant he couldn't go up to the room and get in the shower with Jennings.

They'd made love three times during the night, the first time frenzied and hot, the second slow and sweet and the third half asleep but not sated. Mitch had never been one to use the phrase "make love," but with Jennings, the term "sex" didn't begin to encompass it. Even with Carla, who he'd pledged his love to on a hundred occasions, sex and emotion had remained separated. Now he wondered if it was because the emotion had been one-sided. He wondered if Carla even possessed the ability to love. Look who she'd chosen to be with—a man who controlled a group of hoodlums and likely raped girls for fun.

He was done with Carla. Never again would he come to her rescue; never again would he fall for her ploys. She had chosen Jason, and now she had to live with him. Mitch had spent too long believing she was the one for him, and it had blinded him to what love truly is. *Love is being so real it hurts. Love is letting someone else in. Love is fighting for justice.* And so, while he was done with Carla, he wasn't done with Jason. Jennings wasn't ready yet, and he wouldn't force her, but some day, she'd tell him about that night in the alley, and if he thought for a second that it was Jason—he'd make sure he paid.

When he got back in the room, Jennings stood in the window, wrapped in a towel, her blond hair wet and dripping down her back. Mitch had always considered himself an ass man, but this woman's shoulders gave him a hard-on. He came up behind her, wrapped his arms around her waist, and kissed a water droplet off the crook of her neck. "You okay?"

She nodded, and covered his arms with hers. "Just thinking about Benny."

He squeezed her tighter, unsure of what to say.

"Norma Jean's in the car?"

"Yup, windows down. But it's already getting hot."

She sighed. "Then I should get ready."

He loosened his grip, and she turned in his arms.

Her eyes rose to his, and she rested her hand against his face. "Last night..."

She chewed the inside of her cheek and her eyes misted.

"I know." He kissed her gently and released her from his embrace. Patting her towel-covered ass, he grinned. "Now get some clothes on."

She headed toward the bathroom. Standing in the doorway, she faced him and dropped the towel. "And here I thought you preferred me with my clothes off."

He almost leapt across the bed to get to her, but just shook his head, knowing they didn't have time, or they'd have a roasted mutt in the car. "I'll take you any way I can get you."

A shy smile spread across her face, and she bent her head before closing the bathroom door.

***

Mitch had ridden her ass all the way to the airport to drop off the rental car, likely worried she'd try to give him the slip. She should probably tell him she'd decided to stop running. Maybe she was under the spell of that silly female hormone that was supposed to bond women to men when they had an orgasm. Lord knew she'd had plenty of those last night. But she'd had orgasms before, and she'd never wanted to stick around to see what developed. She'd never wanted her heart to get involved. Regardless of what was at work, she'd made a decision to stay in Asheville after the wedding and see if there was something to this thing with her and Mitch. He'd have to stop digging around in her head for memories that she wasn't going to relive, but if he could do that, she could maybe see them together.

Jennings hadn't dreamed about a future with a man since she was sixteen and Jack had told her he loved her. Of course, now she knew he'd only said that to get her under the bleachers—and out of her pants. Then her whole world had fallen apart, and daydreams were replaced with cold, hard reality. Even after she'd been settled in Vegas, and didn't have to look over her shoulder every other minute, she'd only had the energy to dream about paying her rent and buying a few groceries. Sure, she'd tried to become a professional poker player, but that was more of a practical goal than a dream—a way to make a living that wasn't dependent on grubby men ogling her body.

They'd dropped off her rental car, stopped at Betsy's for a proper goodbye and to retrieve Mitch's stuff, and now they were cruising down I-40. The driver's side window was down, and the wind stirred the ends of Mitch's hair. She wanted to reach up and stroke her fingers through it. His hand rested protectively on her thigh, and she had bumped Norma Jean to the passenger side to steal the spot beside him. When he caught her staring, he smiled, and her insides heated up. What was stopping her? This man wanted her. All of her. Even her sloppy, painful, secretive past. Even her jobless, no plan for tomorrow, sorry ass. There must be something seriously wrong with him. She'd have to ask Benny when they got to Asheville. *Hey, Bro. Been a long time. Give me the dirt on your hot friend.*

Mitch drummed his fingers on the steering wheel to the beat of Earth, Wind and Fire. Her parents would approve. She could picture them sitting outside the van, swaying to the music on the CD player, lost in a world full of love and rhythm. Her parents had been kindred spirits, drawn together by a common passion, overthrowing barriers of society and etiquette. They'd fought for their love, her mama turning her back on a wealthy family and their expectations. Jennings couldn't imagine loving someone that much. It was hard enough to imagine love, let alone a love worth fighting for.

"You okay?" He lifted her hand and kissed her palm.

He kept asking her that. She wondered if she'd ever be able to honestly answer yes. She laid her head on his shoulder. "My parents loved this song."

"Tell me about them. What was it like growing up on the road?"

She smiled. "It was a never-ending adventure. We'd pull over to the side of the road and build a fire and roast hot dogs. Dad would sneak into orchards and pick apples for us. Mama had a little tomato plant on the dash of the van."

He rubbed his thumb across her leg, and it reminded her of how her mama used to rub her back at night to help her sleep.

"My daddy sang to me every night. The Beatles, Bob Dylan, Elton John."

"And Neil Diamond?"

Jennings pressed her hand to her mouth. She could remember laying her on her blanket, made of pieced together patches of old clothes, staring up at the designs Mama had painted on the roof of the van, listening to Daddy singing "Sweet Caroline." She nodded, knowing if she spoke the sob would break through.

He must have sensed her sadness, because he moved his hand from her thigh and stretched his arm around her, moving her closer into the crook of his arm. "I never knew my father."

It was a simple statement. Not meant to elicit pity or to compete in some way with the loss of her parents. But as if he wanted to let her in.

"That must have been hard." As much as it had hurt to lose her parents, it was better to have ten happy years with them than to never have known them at all.

He shrugged. "Betsy provided for me. I know it was hard for her sometimes, but I never wanted. And then I met Harry."

She understood why it'd been so important for Mitch to come to Memphis and help his mentor. And she'd screwed it up. "I'm sorry you didn't finish your case."

"It's not important." His hand slid up her arm and he kissed her on the head. "You're more important than any case."

Craning her neck to look at him, she reached up, wound her fingers through his hair and kissed him on the cheek. "You're a good man, Mitchell Kline."

"You're an amazing woman, Caroline Jennings Lee."

***

She must have fallen asleep after lunch, because when she woke up, they were in the thick of the Appalachians, racing around winding curves alongside signs that warned of falling rocks. They passed through a tunnel and as they rolled back into daylight, Norma Jean rose up on her hind legs and whined at the window.

"We've been driving a long time. She probably needs to pee." Mitch flipped on his blinker and pulled into a scenic overlook.

Jennings stretched her arms and noticed a small wet spot on the sleeve of his shirt. She swiped at it, embarrassed. "I'm sorry."

He gave her a slow, sultry smile. "You can drool on me anytime, baby."

She swatted at him and laughed, and when he opened the door, Norma Jean launched her compact body over both of them. "She definitely has to go."

Norma Jean bolted to a grassy area overlooking a deep, rich valley and sniffed twice before she squatted. Jennings slid out of the truck after Mitch, keeping her eye on the little dog to make sure she didn't venture toward the road. She wandered over to a split rail fence and took in the view. She hadn't returned to these mountains in two decades, but the familiar scent of lilac and mountain laurel tickled her nose, and she was transported back in time. Mitch came to stand beside her, his hand resting casually on her waist, and she leaned into his embrace, closed her eyes, and let herself remember.

Benny used to hide in the overgrown azalea bushes in front of Grandma's place, and when she'd "find" him, he'd run out laughing, red and pink petals in his hair. One year, when he'd been three or four, she remembered it was fairly soon after the fire, he'd gotten the bright idea to climb a dogwood. The tree hadn't been much older than him, and its juvenile branches couldn't support his chunky little body. He'd come tumbling down, and Jennings had caught him before he'd hit the ground, but he'd cried like the Earth was going to stop spinning on its axis. Grandma had promised he could sample the cookie dough and his world had righted itself. Even then, as a preteen, Jennings had known it would take a lot more than cookie dough to make her life right again.

Mitch rubbed her side and kissed her cheek.

Was it possible this man could mend thirty years of pain?

"I haven't been back, you know. To these mountains." She followed the line of the mountains, feeling the dips and rises more than seeing them. The trees were full and green, like a soft velvet blanket covering the entire valley. It almost made you want to dive in, certain that you'd bounce back off the cushy carpet of green.

"Stark contrast to the desert, huh?"

A cool breeze ruffled her hair. It was luxurious, like a sinful escape from the inferno of Las Vegas. "I didn't realize I missed it." She had buried the memories, pushed them deep where they couldn't hurt, where she wouldn't have to think about Benny. Pushed them down to fill the gaping hole of grief that churned in her gut every day until she'd gotten numb and only remembered once or twice a week.

"I went to Asheville for a case, but within a day I knew I had to stay. There's a comfort to it that I haven't felt anywhere else."

Jennings hadn't felt comfortable anywhere since that DSS woman had dragged her out of her grandmother's house kicking and screaming. Certainly not in the group home where she shared a ten-by-ten bedroom with three other girls. Certainly not in Memphis, where the Greyhound bus had dumped her off when her money ran out. And while she'd made a life in Vegas, because she'd been too tired to run anymore, she'd never felt truly comfortable there. *What would it take to feel that again?*

Mitch whistled and Norma Jean trotted over. He squeezed Jennings, then scooped up the dog. "Well, are you ready to go see your brother?"

"Yes?" She hadn't intended it to come out as a question, but truthfully it still scared the snot out of her. No doubt she wanted to see him, be part of his life again, but there was still the nagging assertion that he'd be disappointed.

"Jennings," he faced her and cupped one hand on the side of her face, "you have nothing to worry about. You're incredible. He's going to be completely stoked."

She stared up at him, unconvinced. Mitch was biased. They'd had significant naked time together.

He laughed. "Well, you have a little more than an hour to get over it." He kissed her on the nose and walked back to the truck.

Chapter Nineteen

Mitch set Norma Jean in the truck, and when it looked like Jennings wasn't coming back from the overlook right away, he pulled out his phone.

Benny didn't even give him a chance to say hello. "If you're calling to tell me you aren't going to be here for lunch tomorrow, I'm revoking your best man privileges."

There are privileges? "Actually, I was calling to say we'll be there in about an hour, and I thought you might like to have dinner with your sister."

"Seriously?"

Mitch squeezed his eyes shut and held the phone away from his ear. "Dude, you're going to have to calm down. Your sister spooks easy."

"You better not be messing with me."

He laughed. "I'm not screwing with you. We're almost to North Carolina and she's standing about thirty feet from me."

"Caroline." Benny sighed. "I can't believe I finally get to see her."

Mitch wasn't sure where she stood on the name thing, so he'd let her deal with that. "We're going to stop at my place and get ready, but we'll meet you at Wasabi at seven, ok?"

"Your place? Mitch. I asked nicely."

"Let's just focus on your reunion and wedding." He'd try to explain in person. He knew he'd have some convincing to do. As far as Benny had seen, Carla was the only woman he'd even attempted a commitment with, and they both knew how well that had turned out. Jennings turned toward the truck. "Gotta go, B. See you at seven." He ended the call before Benny could argue the point further.

"I'm ready." She smiled, and it wasn't the pinched fake one. She looked at peace, and when she got close enough, he wrapped her in his arms and tried to borrow some of it.

He didn't have any doubts about his feelings for her, but his friendship with Benny was one of the most important relationships in his life and he hated that he had jeopardized it. He'd just have to make sure B saw what a great thing this was. Who knew? Maybe they'd be brothers-in-law someday. Or better yet, Jennings could explain it to Benny. He'd never get mad at her.

They drove in comfortable silence, the only sounds besides the radio Norma Jean's bodily functions. Man, that dog could let one rip. With the windows down, the smell dissipated eventually, but Mitch would be happy to get the mutt out of his truck. Jennings didn't seem to notice, maybe she'd become accustomed over the years, or she was in a trance. She hadn't said a word since they'd left the overlook, not even when he changed the radio to a country station.

She'd seemed okay after he talked to Benny, but ever since they passed the sign welcoming them to North Carolina, her shoulders had tensed under his arm and she'd stared straight ahead at the traffic in front of them. If she was playing the license plate game, she was in bad shape, because they'd been following a truck from Tennessee for about forty miles. He almost made the joke out loud, but sensed that this homecoming was a far bigger deal than he'd originally thought.

He was starting to get a read on Jennings, and her quiet, contemplative side was strong, likely from years on the run and no one else to talk to, let alone lean on. Most of the women he dated suffered from verbal diarrhea, a constant stream of everything in their heads, so he never really had to wonder what they were thinking. There was so much Jennings didn't say. And he found himself wanting to know everything.

Merging onto I-240, Mitch moved his arm from around her shoulders to navigate the denser traffic. She turned to him with a doe-eyed expression, so he patted her leg to reassure her. "We'll be at my place in a few minutes. Then we have some time before we meet up with Benny."

She slid closer, and his heart clenched to think maybe his presence brought her comfort. Maybe this could work. Maybe she could release her defenses and really let him in.

He took the exit for downtown and as they rolled down Patton Avenue, she peered out the window at the gathering dusk. Mitch had only lived in Asheville for the last ten years or so, and the city had morphed and grown significantly in that time, so he imagined it was a stark contrast to the Asheville of her youth.

In a matter of minutes, he pulled into the garage of his building and parked the truck near the elevator. He remembered the last time they'd sat in a parking garage, just a few days ago, and braced for Jennings's reaction.

"You live downtown?" Her hand balanced on his knee, and while she sounded normal, he could feel its clamminess through his jeans.

He covered her hand with his and opened the driver's side door. "Yup. Urban living at its finest." Climbing out, he tugged on her hand and she followed, then he pulled her into his arms. "Let's head upstairs, have a glass of wine, and relax for a bit. We've got over an hour before dinner."

She stepped back, looked up at him and smiled. "An hour, huh?" Her seductive grin and raised eyebrows confused him. Surely, she didn't want to have sex right now. "You know what's more relaxing than a glass of wine?"

Hot damn, she wants to have sex right now. "We'll have wine with dinner anyway."

Rising up on her toes, Jennings kissed him hard and deep. He backed her against the truck and slid his hands down her body. She was nearing forty, and she was ten times hotter than most of the twenty-somethings that gave Mitch the eye on the infrequent occasions he hit the bars. And given that they were getting ready to have sex for the fourth time in twenty-four hours, her sex drive shot those young girls out of the water as well.

"Oh, Mitch," she moaned into his mouth, her hand hovering over his crotch.

They needed to get upstairs NOW. Or they'd be having hot parking garage sex and the building's co-op board would probably kick him out. Considering he'd dumped every dime he had into this condo, that wasn't an option. He stepped back, his heart racing, his breath coming in short huffs. "Upstairs." He flung the tarp back, grabbed her suitcases, and headed for the elevator.

***

Jennings scooped up Norma Jean, grabbed his duffel and stood beside him waiting for the elevator to arrive. His breathing appeared to be as shallow as hers, and she was wondering if he lived on a high enough floor to accomplish things on the elevator ride. She couldn't imagine there was a building tall enough in Asheville. The doors slid open and an older woman with a black Pomeranian stepped out.

"Mr. Kline." She nodded her head crisply, a frozen smile on her face, but the little dog squirmed in her arms, obviously excited to see Mitch. Apparently, Norma Jean wasn't his only canine admirer.

"Mrs. Blitz, good evening." He set down a suitcase and patted the little dog on its head. "Hey, Queenie."

Norma Jean growled, which Jennings didn't get, because she loved other dogs. They stepped into the elevator and her dog jumped out of her arms and sat at Mitch's feet, her front paws in the air.

"Someone's jealous." He squatted down to her level and ruffled the patch of fur on her head. "Don't worry, Norma Jean. I only have eyes for you." His gaze slid up Jennings's body. "And your mama, of course."

Jennings dropped the duffel and stepped toward him, ready to press him against the wall and slap the emergency stop button. The elevator dinged, and the doors slid open. She'd have to make it the few steps to Mitch's apartment.

"I'm still trying to figure out the difference between your 'you-want-to-hit-me' face and your 'you-want-to-rip-my-clothes-off' face." He laughed, picked up her suitcases and headed down the hall.

She huffed, picked up his bag and trailed him and Norma Jean out of the elevator. Her plan had been a little seduction to take the edge off before they met Benny, but when he looked at her like that—like he wanted to possess every inch of her—it set off a blaze in her gut that threatened to consume her if he didn't put it out. She wasn't used to a man wielding that sort of power over her. Sex had always been a fun activity, but not something she needed. But here she was, an hour away from meeting the brother she hadn't seen in two decades, and all she could think about was getting Mitch naked and inside of her. She liked to think it was just a craving for distraction from her nervous energy, but deep down, she knew it was far more. Her soul had bonded to his and when he left, it wouldn't be like ripping off a bandage, it would be like removing the top two layers of skin when you accidentally superglued your fingers together.

"Jennings?"

She snapped her head up, and he was standing in a doorway a few feet away, that familiar concerned expression on his face. She was so used to living inside her head—she had to learn how to stay focused now that another person was in the room, so to speak. "I'm coming." She caught up to him, and he took the duffel bag from her and kissed her.

"Welcome to my home." His voice was muffled as he kissed the crook of her neck and dropped the bag to slide his hands up under her shirt. "If there's anything I can do to make you more comfortable…" He yanked, pulled it over her head, and tossed it onto a granite island in the middle of the kitchen.

The apartment was nothing like she expected. It was a modern, open loft with contemporary furniture and floor-to-ceiling windows with a view of Pack Square and the iconic pink city building. In the fading light, she could see a new park stretched all the way to the courthouse. She'd expected Asheville to have changed in the twenty years she'd been absent, but she hadn't expected Mitch to have stainless steel appliances and an espresso machine.

His hands reached behind her and unhooked her bra, and when his mouth located her nipple, she sucked a breath in and steadied herself against his shoulders. "This place is amazing."

"You sound surprised." His tone held a hint of laughter, but he moved to her other breast.

"Well, your truck is older than you and held together by wire." She reached across his back and pulled at the hem of his shirt.

"The truck is sentimental, and don't be too impressed, I have a mortgage the size of Peru's national debt." He stood up straight and helped her get his shirt off, then grabbed her hand and pulled her across the room.

"I assume you're exaggerating." The most expensive thing she'd ever bought was a television, and she'd had to make payments. Who was this guy? All responsible and settled with a mortgage. Why wasn't he married?

He shrugged. "Doesn't matter." Jerking her hand, he hooked his arm under her knees and swept her off her feet—literally. He carried her to a big, cozy bed covered in a red and white quilt and dropped her.

A man who makes his bed before he leaves town? She was having trouble reconciling this with the guy who had fast food wrappers in his truck of places that had gone out of business ten years ago. "You have a cleaning lady, too?"

"Hell, no." He laughed. "What makes you say that?" He loomed over her, his eyes roaming her half-naked form.

She sat up on her elbows and peered around the room. Books littered the nightstand and through the cracked closet door, she could see a jumble of shoes. Okay, so it wasn't OCD neat. "Just surprised your bed is made, that's all."

"That would be Benny."

She furrowed her brow. "My brother is your cleaning lady?"

He burst into laughter. "That's an image I didn't need." Shaking his head, he sat beside her on the bed, and some of the heat left his eyes. "Benny's a neat freak. I asked him to feed Cash while I was gone, and he always straightens up."

Jennings fell back onto the bed, smoothing her hand over the quilt. Her brother had been here, had touched this bed, had seen this view. Suddenly, she felt exposed. She crossed her arms over her chest and turned onto her side. "Who's Cash?"

Mitch laid beside her, facing her, and traced the line of her jaw with his index finger. "He's my cat, although he thinks he's a Rottweiler. Norma Jean and he had it out while you were fantasizing about me in the hallway."

She pushed against his chest, knocking him back and almost off the bed.

"Hey, you gonna deny it?" He righted himself and slid his hand down her shoulder, her arm, across her hip.

"You were going to maul me in the parking garage." She inched closer to him. Warmth radiated off his bare torso like a kerosene heater. She spread her fingers across his chest, soaking up the heat.

His hand slipped behind her, cupping her ass, and in one motion, he pulled her against him. "And now I'm going to maul you in my neatly made bed." He leaned toward her, taking his time, his eyes starting the kiss before his lips reached hers. It was slow and deep, and she considered telling him to hurry up because they had to meet Benny, but it felt so good that she couldn't stand to stop it. His hands roamed from the top of her body to the bottom, and somewhere in between their pants were off, and he was inside her and they were still in that first hot, deep, long kiss that felt like it would never end.

They moved in a gentle rhythm, rocking their bodies together like the cogs of a machine, producing heat and passion. He kissed down her neck, sending stabs of fire into her gut, and when she turned her head to give him better assess, she stared out at darkness falling over a city skyline that was etched in the recesses of her mind. She gripped his shoulders, digging her fingers into his flesh, drawing him closer, wanting him deeper inside her. And when the tingles lit the soles of her feet, she gasped. He murmured her name, kissed her again, and held her tight as she climaxed in rolling waves of ecstasy. With one final thrust, he collapsed on top of her breathing heavily.

"Damn."

"You can say that again." Jennings raked the wet hair off his forehead, letting the soft strands fall between her fingers.

"Damn." He was still panting, but he turned his head slightly and kissed her just above her right breast.

She kissed his head, and scraped her nails over his back, stroking the taut muscles between his shoulders. If sex with Mitch was going to get better every time, she was going to have to hit the gym. She needed endurance training.

"Shit." Mitch wrenched up, and their sweaty bodies made a noise like a suction cup popping off the window. "We're supposed to meet Benny in ten minutes."

She couldn't meet her brother with eau de Mitch all over her. "I've got to shower."

"It's just around the corner, but I'll text him and tell him to give us fifteen." He dug around on the floor for his pants and pulled out his phone. "Start the shower, I'll be in in a minute."

"Maybe you should tell him 7:30." She slapped his bare ass and headed into the bathroom.

Chapter Twenty

They walked to the restaurant, past buildings that were familiar and businesses that weren't. Mitch had his arm around her, his hand lightly settled on her hip, and it eased some of her trepidation. The passionate interlude that started in the parking garage and ended in the shower had taken the edge off her nervous energy, and she felt balanced and ready to see Benny. She tried to remember the last time she'd seen him. It'd been past midnight, and she'd snuck over to his foster home and rapped on the window to rouse him from his sleep. His hair had always been thick, with enough curl to make it interesting, and that night it had stuck out from the sides of his head like an unkempt porcupine. He'd rubbed his eyes and when he focused them on the window, his whole face had lit up.

His expression had gone the opposite direction when she told him she was leaving. She couldn't expect an eight-year-old to understand, besides, he seemed content with his new family, even though he missed her. So, she'd put on a brave face and told him the biggest lie of her life. "Everything will be okay, and I'll be back before you can sing all the words to *Rocket Man*."

She'd considered pulling him out that window and taking him with her, but she knew life on the run wasn't an option for a little boy. He deserved stability and fun and a life free of worry. All the things he'd had for his first eight years, before a bureaucracy decided Jennings couldn't take care of him. And as much as she grieved leaving him, there was someone else to consider now, and damned if DSS would get their hands on someone else she loved.

Mitch stopped walking and dropped his hand from her hip. She turned to face him, firmly back in the present. "What is it?"

He took her left hand, his thumb flicking across her knuckles. "Before we go inside, I…" He licked his lips, looked down at the sidewalk, then slowly raised his eyes to meet her. "Jennings," he stepped closer, his voice shaking slightly, "I care about you a lot."

She nodded. "I know." Despite the acrobatics in the shower, she knew there was more between them than really hot sex.

"Benny's my best friend. He's stood by me through a lot, and I'd do anything for him." He smiled. "That's why I tracked you down." He dropped her hand and raised his arm to cup her cheek.

"I know." What was he trying to say?

His eyes shifted down again, and she could tell he was nervous. She prayed he wasn't going to make his declaration of love on this sidewalk moments before she saw her brother for the first time in twenty-two years. It was more than a girl could take.

"Mitch—"

"No, I need to finish." He dropped his arm and took a half step back. "Your brother isn't going to be happy with me."

She didn't have much experience with declarations of love, but this didn't seem like one.

"I haven't really had *relationships* much since Carla. If you can even call that a relationship, but the point is, B had some concerns that I might, well, try to sleep with you."

So, my little brother's pretty intuitive. "And?"

"And I think when he finds out he's going to want to kick my ass. Or at the very least demote me to usher or something."

The snicker came out before she could stop it. She could tell Mitch was serious about this, but the idea of Benny kicking anyone's ass was ridiculous. Forcing a straight face, she put her hand on his arm. "We're both adults and nobody took advantage of anybody. I'm not exactly a prude."

A smile cracked through his stoic expression. "No, you aren't, thank God."

An image of Mitch pressed up against the wall of the steamy shower heated her gut. "Anyway, Benny will understand. It'll be fine."

"Oh, there's no way he'd be mad at *you*. He put you on a pedestal thirty years ago."

Her stomach dropped and the early heat morphed into a cold lump of anxiety. That's exactly why she hadn't tried to find the brother she'd missed all these years. Why she hadn't come home before now. She wasn't proud of some of the choices she'd made since she left and the thought of disappointing Benny scared her more than the ache of missing him.

"So, I was thinking maybe you should tell him."

She shook her head, trying to figure out what Mitch had said after she stopped listening. "Huh?"

"If you tell B that we're, um, together, I think he'll take it better, and maybe I won't lose my best friend."

He wants the first conversation I have with my brother in two decades to be about the fact that I'm sleeping with the PI he sent to find me? This was supposed to be a happy reunion. And Benny was getting married in two days. "Or maybe we don't tell him."

Mitch's eyes widened and he shook his head. "Oh, no, I couldn't keep—"

"I just mean right now. He's getting married the day after tomorrow. This," she waved her hand between them, "is drama he's better off without for right now. Besides, I don't want my first words to my brother to be that I'm boinking his best friend."

He seemed to be considering it.

"We can keep our hands off each other for a few days. After Benny gets back from his honeymoon, we'll tell him." Maybe by then they'd have a better idea of what *it* was.

"Okay, I guess that makes sense." He hooked his hand on her waist and pulled her close again. "Although keeping my hands off of you is going to be an extreme challenge." He kissed her, melting a little of the worry in her stomach.

"Well maybe we just keep our hands to ourselves when Benny's around."

"Speaking of Benny, we're late." He let go of her. "You ready?"

Hell no. "Sure."

***

Nearly every table in the restaurant was full, but Jennings picked her brother out of the crowd with just a glance. His hair was a shade darker, and he wore it cut close to his head, but she would know him anywhere—even without having seen the Facebook pictures. She wondered if he kept it short to keep the curls at bay. He'd always hated them as a kid, but their parents loved it on the longer side, so she'd kept it that way after they were gone. She'd been considering cutting it as she chopped the cucumbers from Grandma's garden. Then the DSS worker had pulled in the driveway.

Mitch touched her elbow and jolted her back to the present. Her brother's gaze locked with hers and he rose from his chair. Her heart raced in her chest and when Mitch moved forward, her feet wouldn't cooperate to follow him. Benny was tall, almost six feet, taller than anyone she knew from their family. Of course, she hadn't been to any family reunions lately. Save this one.

A hostess asked if they needed a table, and Mitch explained they were meeting someone, because Jennings's mouth wasn't working either. She was proud to still be standing up.

Benny crossed the restaurant in four strides, and she wished it was a bigger place. The trip across the country, even the detour in Memphis, hadn't been enough time to prepare for this meeting. *Another twenty-two years should do.* He stood before her, a lifetime from the little boy she'd hugged goodbye, and cried over leaving for the next three years. Eventually, she'd run out of tears, and folded her grief into a secret compartment in her heart. Hidden in the dark, with no one to police it, she feared the pain may have morphed into a creature of such ugliness, of such enormity, that it couldn't be conquered.

His breathing matched hers, and he raised a hand to tug his earlobe. Uncertainty lined his eyes and he licked his lips before he spoke. "Caroline."

It was a whisper, barely a breath, and over the din of the restaurant, she felt it more than heard it. Like a voice-activated lock, the door to that secret place in her heart flew open, and musty, decayed grief tumbled out. Her legs turned to gelatin and Benny's image blurred.

Before she could fall, Mitch's strong arm slid around her waist, pressing her to his side. He bent close to her ear. "I'm right here."

Jennings blinked, took a deep breath, and assessed the damage. Her heart still beat, oxygen still filled her lungs, and it was like her mama had shone a flashlight under her bed to prove that no monster lived there. Her grief hadn't grown out of control, instead the balm of time had soothed some of the pain. And now her little brother, less than two feet away, offered further healing.

She stepped away from Mitch, stood straight, and stuck out her hand. "Hi, Benny."

He smiled, transforming into the little boy she'd known, and pulled her into an embrace. "Hey, Sis. I've missed you so much."

She waited for the questions, for the accusations, but he just held her, so she relaxed into the hug. It was familiar and foreign all at once, and she found herself wanting to feel all of it—the good and the scary—to etch this memory in her brain.

Who knows how long they would have stood there, blocking the entrance to the restaurant, but a crowd of young patrons broke through the door and forced sister and brother to disengage and move to a table.

A pretty brunette sat in the fourth seat, waiting patiently. Jennings hadn't noticed her, she'd been so focused on Benny, but she was the type of woman who exuded confidence and calm energy. Her hair fell in ringlets around her round face and she wore her extra weight well, complimenting her curves with a simple black wrap dress.

"Caroline, this is my fiancé, Aimee." He gazed adoringly at his future wife. Then he turned to Jennings, a similar gleam in his eyes. "Aimee, this is my sister."

"It's great to finally meet you." Aimee extended her hand across the table, a smile lighting her face. "Benny hasn't been able to talk about anything else since he found out you were coming." She jabbed him playfully with her elbow. "Luckily, I haven't needed him to focus on wedding plans."

"Luckily, I'm marrying the most organized woman on the planet. I'd just screw it up." He put his arm around her and kissed her cheek.

Jennings envied their easy and obvious affection. But she was excited that her brother had found love—and had the capacity to embrace it. *I wonder if I'll ever be able to enjoy Mitch like that.* She shook her head. *Where did that come from?* Surely, she didn't believe a relationship with Mitch could actually work. Besides, this night was about reuniting with her brother, not being distracted by the man whose hand rested on her knee. Hadn't they agreed to keep their hands to themselves? "Aimee, it's great to meet you, too. So, tell me, where are you having the wedding?"

Benny grinned, like he'd just crawled up the kitchen cabinets to sneak a cookie. "Didn't Mitch tell you? I've been fixing up Granny and Pap's house. We're having the wedding in the backyard."

For the second time that evening, Jennings couldn't speak. She hadn't just returned to Asheville, and her little brother. She was returning to the house she'd grown up in—the last place she'd ever called home.

***

Jennings excused herself, and as soon as she was out of earshot, Benny leaned across the table.

"Why is she so quiet? Did I say something wrong?"

Mitch sighed. He could only imagine what Jennings was feeling, but he had an active imagination. "It's a lot to take in, B. I hadn't told her you're renovating your grandparents' house. That was probably a bit of a shock to her. Give her time."

Aimee leaned close to her fiancé, whispered something. Benny nodded. He let out a rush of air, and then picked up his menu.

They'd been eating here since the place opened and Benny was a creature of habit. Mitch wished he could say something to reassure his friend, but even more, he wished he could go after Jennings and make sure she was okay. Following her to the bathroom would likely raise suspicions and so far, Benny hadn't brought the subject of their relationship up. Mitch wanted to postpone that conversation as long as possible.

"What time's the lunch tomorrow?" He stole a glance at the back of the restaurant. Still no Jennings.

"Twelve-thirty at Deerpark." Aimee answered for the sullen Benny.

Deerpark. That meant a suit and tie. Good thing he loved Benny like a brother. "I'll be there. You want me to pick you up, B?"

"Will they let that atrocity you call a truck onto the grounds of the Biltmore?" Aimee's eyes twinkled despite her straight face.

"We can take my car, Mitch."

Benny drove a practical and boring Pirus. Mitch had never thought the car suited him.

"Sorry, about that." Jennings took her seat and buried her nose in the menu. Her eyes were rimmed in red and her right leg jiggled up and down.

He reached his hand under the tablecloth and squeezed her thigh. When she glanced at him, he sent her a look meant to reassure. Instead, she looked like she might burst into tears. He quickly marked the sushi menu, tossed it at Benny and pushed back his chair. "Order for us, we'll be right back." Grabbing Jennings's arm, he tugged her from her chair. Her menu fell to the floor and her eyes widened in surprise.

"Um, excuse us."

He threw his shoulder against the door of the restaurant and led them into the cool night air. She didn't protest, and when they rounded the corner, he pulled her into a recessed storefront and took her in his arms. As if she'd been granted permission to let go, she pressed into him and the tears came in a torrent. He stroked her hair, held her tight, and let her cry. With every sob, his heart ached for her. His childhood hadn't been sunshine and lollipops by any stretch of the imagination, but he'd never had the weight of responsibility Jennings must have felt. Twenty years of emotion assaulted her and she clung to him as if she couldn't bear it.

After a few minutes, he could sense the deluge wasn't lessening, so he fumbled to get his phone out of his pocket without letting her go. With his hands behind her back, he punched out a text to Benny saying that Jennings wasn't feeling well and he was taking her back to his place to rest. If she felt better, he'd call him later.

He pocketed the phone, then slid one arm down under her knees and cradled her in his arms. She gripped him around the neck and buried her face in his shoulder. Kissing the top of her head, he stepped back onto the sidewalk and headed for his condo. He may have shown his hand to Benny, but right now the only thing he cared about was making Jennings feel safe and comforted.

Chapter Twenty-One

Mitch carefully slid his arm out from under Jennings and checked to make sure she was still sleeping. She'd held on to him most of the night, alternating between crying and dozing. Around five she'd fallen into a deeper sleep, relaxed her grip and rolled onto her side. His phone rang again, and he hurried out of the room.

"Is she with you?"

He checked the clock on the microwave. 7:10. Early even for Benny. "Yes, she's here." Mitch didn't have enough strength to have this conversation. He'd hoped to sleep until just before his lunch commitment.

"All I asked you to do was find her and invite her to the wedding."

"I know, B. I'm—"

"Hold on, I have something to say." Benny cleared his throat, took a swig of something. "I didn't really think about how this would be for her. I just wanted my sister to be at my wedding. It was selfish and immature to expect her to come back here and bam! everything would be same again."

"B, don't be so hard—"

"Let me finish, Mitch."

He leaned against the counter and stared out the window where the sun was coming up between the buildings, driving the wisps of fog away.

"I should have asked you to look for her a long time ago. But I was scared. Scared that she didn't care about the brother she left behind."

"She cares, B." He could see her through the open door to his room, her blonde hair spread across the pillow, her body tucked into the fetal position, the rise and fall of her chest. It took courage to come back here, to face the past she'd run from, but everything Caroline Jennings Lee had done in her life showed more guts than any woman he'd ever met.

"Are you in love with her?"

Mitch dropped the phone. Fumbling to get it back to his ear, he wondered when he'd become so transparent. Jennings stretched on the bed and her eyelids fluttered open. Her eyes locked with his and a sleepy smile filled her face. "Yeah." If he disowned him, at least he wouldn't have to go to the stuffy luncheon with Aimee's family.

"Good. She's lucky."

"This isn't a casual fling, I really—wait, what did you say?"

"I said, 'good.' I went into last night with no consideration for her feelings. And when she got upset, you didn't hide your concern for her, you took care of her. You put her first."

Jennings slid out of the bed and walked slowly toward him. He'd helped her out of her clothes last night, and she now wore only a camisole and matching panties. It was hard to have a serious conversation with a hard-on. He held her gaze. "She's a remarkable woman."

She stopped, blinked, took a step backward.

"Benny, I've got to go. Pick me up at noon."

"Mitch, this conversation—"

He ended the call, laid the phone on the counter, and held out his hand like he was approaching a startled deer. "Jennings..."

She took another step back.

"This is nothing to freak out about. It's good news." He took a cautious step forward. "Benny isn't mad. He knows I'm not just in it for the sex."

"What are you in it for?" She stopped, rested her hand on the door to his bedroom.

It was one of those trick questions women asked that had no right answer. He raked his hand through his hair. He was ready to go to that stuffy luncheon now.

"Well?"

"Have I told you how beautiful you are when you first wake up?"

With a flick of her wrist, she slammed the door.

***

Mitch had pleaded with her for nearly half an hour, telling her that he lusted after her body and had no feelings for her whatsoever. Finally, he'd given up and said he was taking Norma Jean for a walk. She heard the front door close, and poked her head into the living room. Unless he was crouched down behind the kitchen island, he was really gone.

They'd left before dinner last night, so Jennings hadn't eaten anything since lunch the day before. Forging through Mitch's refrigerator confirmed that he was a bachelor and produced some shriveled grapes, Chinese leftovers of an unknown vintage, and beer. His cupboards yielded slightly more, but she wasn't interested in nuking Minute rice for breakfast. She'd jump in the shower and then venture into the city. Asheville was no Vegas, but surely, they had at least one Starbucks. She rushed to get ready, hoping to get out of the apartment before Mitch could return. Her eyes were puffy and swollen from the marathon crying session the night before, but she didn't have time to mess with makeup. Who'd she need to impress anyway? She'd already disappointed the only person in town who she gave a rat's ass about.

She grabbed her purse, considered and dismissed leaving a note, and wrenched the front door open. Norma Jean barked and ran past her into the apartment. Mitch scrambled to his feet, which wasn't an easy task, considering he was balancing two steaming cups and a brown paper bag. "I don't have much to eat in there." He nodded toward the kitchen, but didn't advance. "Been out of town."

"Thank you, Captain Obvious." She crossed her arms over her chest. It took all of her willpower not to grab the coffee and bag out of his hand.

"You don't have to break out the sarcasm." He extended one cup toward her. "A peace offering."

She looked from his face, to the cup, and back again. Sighing, she took the cup out of his hand and stepped back into the apartment. "This does not mean I forgive you."

He followed her into the kitchen and shut the door behind him. "I can't say I've ever had a woman mad at me for caring about her." Pulling two muffins from the bag, he offered one to her. "Maybe a muffin will tip the scales in my favor?"

It *was* a ridiculous reason to be mad. And if she was honest with herself, she wasn't mad at Mitch. She was mad at herself for relying on him so heavily. He'd become a lifeline for her, and she was terrified she wouldn't be able to pick up the pieces when he left. She took the muffin. "Sorry," she mumbled as she took a bite.

"Jennings," he rounded the counter and put his hands on her shoulders, "I get it. Neither of us was looking for this. You're dealing with a lot of shit right now, and thinking about a relationship—or whatever the hell this is—only makes things more complicated."

Amazingly, he did get it. Part of it, at least. She set the muffin down and stepped closer to him. He'd touched on a solution. She just wouldn't think about it. She'd live in the moment and not read into every word, every little action. *I'll get through Benny's wedding, and deal with being back in Asheville. Then I'll worry about Mitch.* But for right now, she needed him to lean on. As he pulled her into his arms, she knew he was offering just that.

***

Jennings leaned her weight into him, and as her body molded against his, carnal thoughts invaded his mind. His earlier erection had deflated when she slammed the door in his face, but his sexual fortitude was rebounding with the eagerness of a teenager on prom night. Hooking his arm under her knees, he lifted her into his arms. "And to prove that my intentions are purely lecherous..." He stepped toward the bedroom.

"Mitch! Wait." She leaned back, stretched her arm, and grabbed her muffin off the counter. "Proceed."

How can I not love this woman? He carried her, muffin and all, into the bedroom and dumped her on the bed. "You better eat that muffin, because you're going to need your strength." Grabbing the back of his shirt, he pulled it over his head and flung it across the room. Cash hissed and darted out from under a chair, and Norma Jean raced in from the living room, barking her fool head off. The cat leapt over the bed and Norma Jean gave chase.

Jennings shook with laughter. "Wow, breakfast and a show."

A clatter rose from the kitchen and Mitch ducked his head out the door in time to see Cash leap onto the counter and then to the top of the refrigerator. Norma Jean took up post below, growling in frustration. "They've got things under control out there." He closed the door. "As far as in here, *you* are getting crumbs all over your shirt." Reaching the bed, he crawled toward her, his heart rate accelerating when she licked her lips.

She scooted backward, until she hit the pillows, then held the muffin out. "Don't come any closer, or I'll crumble." A smile played at the corners of her mouth, but she kept a straight face.

He slid a hand up her leg, over her knee, to the inside of her thigh. "I can reach everything I need from here." With his other hand, he grabbed her ankle and tugged, catching her off guard and forcing her into a prone position. The muffin vaulted from her hand and landed on the bed beside her. He picked it up, set it on the nightstand, and leaned over Jennings. "I'm much more satisfying than a pastry."

"Technically, it's a baked—"

He captured her mouth with his, devouring her like a breakfast buffet. Her hands slid up his back, leaving scalding impressions where they moved. This woman was heat and passion and vulnerability and resolve, all rolled into one. He didn't think he'd ever tire of touching her, of kissing her, of that luscious moment when he entered her and she sucked in her breath like she was savoring the air around them.

She arched her back, and the camisole grazed against his flesh. He slid against it, enjoying the sensation of her pert nipples, covered in smooth silk, bumping along his torso. Moving down her body, he teased one of those nipples with his tongue, evoking a gasp and a moan from Jennings. She clutched at his hips, pulling him against her, squirming underneath him. Her hands moved to the front of his pants, and she tugged at the button. He loved her eagerness, but he wanted to stretch it out, savor the feel of her, the taste of her, the way every nerve ending in his body prickled when she moaned his name.

Capturing her wrists, he pulled them above her head, leaned down, trailed his tongue along her ear, sucked in her earlobe.

"You get some sick, morbid rise out of torturing me, don't you?" She sucked in a breath and squeezed her eyes shut as he moved down her neck, exploring every inch of her soft flesh.

"Oh, you definitely give me a rise." He thrust his hips against hers to prove his point.

She squirmed again, trying to free her hands.

"I think I'll keep you right here. Chain you to the bed so you can't disappear on me." Leaning down, he kissed her, gently at first, but harder as she bumped her lower body against his.

"Mitch." Her voice was muffled against his mouth, but he could tell it was more conversational and less erotic moaning.

He broke the kiss, waiting for her next smartass retort. *God, she's beautiful.*

"Let me go."

He kissed her on the tip of her nose. "Nah."

She writhed underneath him.

He wasn't going to be able to hold out much longer. Every bump of her pelvis hardened his cock a little more and soon he'd be forced to rip those silky panties off.

"Please. Let. Me. Go." Her bottom lip quivered and her eyes were full of fear.

Releasing her wrists, he sat back, held his hands up. "I'm so sorry, Jennings."

She struggled underneath him, trying to sit up. He slid off her, cursing himself for his insensitivity. If Charter's theory was correct, Jennings had been raped twenty-two years ago in the alley behind The Orpheum. And he'd just held her down and refused to let go.

Her back was to him, her feet hanging off the side of the bed, her arms hugging her torso. He reached out, touched her back, and she jumped to standing.

Had he ruined it for good? Would she ever welcome his touch again? "Jennings, please. Look at me."

She turned slowly, her hand swiping at her eyes. Then she straightened, shook her head. "It's fine. No big deal."

He slid off the bed, stood in front her. "It is a big deal. I'm so sorry for holding you down." He reached out tentatively, scared to touch her, but more scared not to.

Sighing, she took his hand. "I overreacted, really. I'm fine."

He stepped closer, raised his other hand to cup her cheek. "We need to talk about what happened in Memphis."

She dropped his hand, stepped back. "Nothing happened in Memphis."

"I know you were attacked twenty-two years ago."

"I don't know what you're talking about." She crossed her arms over her chest, set her jaw.

"Jennings," he stepped forward, "it's okay. You can tell me. We can make it right." If he found out that Jason was, in fact, the man who attacked her, he'd move heaven and earth to make it right.

She backed away like a snarling tiger was advancing. "You need to drop it, Mitch. If you want this," she gestured at the space between them, "whatever the hell *this* is, to work, you need to stop poking around in my past, making up fairy tales."

What he was talking about hardly constituted a fairy tale, but the brave front she was putting on thinly veiled the terrified girl behind it. He needed to back off, or she'd run again, and he was in too deep to lose her now. "My mistake." He took a step back. "I won't bring it up again." *For a while, at least.*

"Thank you." She let out a shuttering sigh, and leaned against the wall. "Don't you have a lunch to get to?"

She looked so fragile, so vulnerable, like the wall was the only thing holding her up. He wanted to rush to her, wrap her in his arms, shake her until she let it out. All the fears, all the hurt, all the worry. Make her understand that he'd never leave, that he'd keep her safe. But she was stacking the bricks. Rebuilding the damn wall. And if he wanted back in, he'd have to find another way. "Yeah, I should get ready."

***

Jennings sat curled up in an armchair with a front-row view of the city. Occasionally, she glanced down at the book in her lap, but mostly she stared out at the skyline—familiar, yet vastly different from the city of her youth. Norma Jean had dragged a throw pillow off the couch and claimed it as her own. She whimpered in her sleep, her little legs pumping the air, chasing down a dream squirrel or rabbit.

Mitch had left shortly after their confrontation, even though his luncheon wasn't for two hours. Apparently, he'd figured out she needed space. He seemed fairly intuitive most of the time. It was a wonder he wasn't attached. Intuitive, gorgeous, funny men didn't grow on trees. And Lord knew a girl could get used to his sensitive, yet deeply passionate, lovemaking. If said girl was looking for a relationship.

For an available woman, he seemed ideal. But Jennings Lee hadn't been available since she was sixteen. Losing her parents had been hard enough, but then her grandparents died, and Benny had become her whole world. She hadn't considered dating even then. But Jack had been so charming, and he seemed jealous of her lifestyle. He loved the freedom it afforded them— always told her his parents were overbearing, too concerned with his every little move. She never had the guts to tell him she would have given up all the freedom to have her parents back.

When he'd come over, he'd play with Benny, chase him around the yard, wear him out. She realized now that he probably just wanted her little brother to go to bed so he could get her into one. But at the time, she pretended they were a family. Imagined what it'd be like for Jack to be there all the time, to help her shoulder some of the responsibility of raising an eight-year-old. And when she'd realized she was pregnant, it seemed like the final piece to bring that dream together.

She hadn't had time to tell him the good news before DSS found out about the two Lee kids living alone in the house on Bear Mountain Road. One day she was dreaming about what color to paint the nursery, and the next the social worker was dragging a screaming Benny to the car. After she was dumped off at the group home, Jennings knew they'd take her baby away. So, she'd snuck out and over to Jack's house. They'd run away together. Start their family. Then fight for Benny.

Only Jack didn't see it that way. He told her they'd had fun, but he was going to college next year, and he didn't want to settle down. He'd handed her a fist full of money and told her to take care of it.

That was the day she learned not to count on anyone else. She altered the dream. She'd run away. Start her family. Then get Benny back.

She got as far as Memphis before that dream was shattered, along with any fight she had left. She'd switched courses yet again—keep a low profile and survive. Blend in, become someone else, leave all the pain in the past. And never get attached to someone again.

As great as Mitch seemed, he was a PI. He dug into people's pasts for a living. And he was already digging too deep for her liking. She wasn't sure how he knew about what happened in Memphis, or if it was just guesswork, but either way, she wasn't revisiting that night twenty-two years ago. She'd leave again before that happened.

She was startled out of her reverie by a knock at the door. Had Mitch forgotten his key? Was he coming back to apologize? She crossed the living room, threw open the door, ready to get one more orgasm out of him before she broke things off.

But it wasn't Mitch standing in the hall. It was Benny's fiancée. "Aimee. What a surprise." She didn't want to imagine what this woman must think of her after her behavior the night before. Probably that Jennings was mentally unstable and shouldn't be associating with her new husband.

"Are you okay?" Aimee leaned forward, as if ready to grab Jennings if she felt the need to collapse.

Yeah, she definitely thinks I'm unstable. "I'm fine. I was just really tired last night."

"Oh," she took a step back, "I wasn't talking about last night. I, uh, well, you're crying."

"What?" Jennings put a hand to her cheek, and sure enough, there was moisture there. She swiped away the tear. "Oh, no, my eyes are watering. Allergies." She stepped aside to let the other woman in. "I've been living in the desert, you know. Cacti don't make pollen." She hated that she was chattering, but she needed the distraction to compose herself. Further proof that nothing good came from revisiting the past.

"I'm sorry to show up like this, but after last night, I realized how hard this must be for you." Aimee set her purse on the kitchen island and took a seat on one of the stools.

Jennings had little experience as a hostess, unless the two-month stint seating people at the Lucky Strike café counted. She grasped the handle on the refrigerator door. "I'd offer you something, but all Mitch has is beer."

Aimee laughed and waved off the apology. "Please, I don't expect any-thing. That man is a bachelor through and through. The last time I was over here, he couldn't even produce a clean glass for tap water."

"I was surprised at how neat the place was, but he told me it's because Benny tidied up." She leaned on the counter, more at ease.

"Yeah, he's very neat for a guy. Someone raised him well." She smiled.

Jennings's heart clinched. She couldn't take credit for how Benny turned out. She stared at the pattern in the granite, counting the light specks.

"Anyway," Aimee cleared her throat, "I do have a reason for intruding on you."

She looked up so quickly the blood rushed into her forehead, and she had to blink the ache away. "No, it's not an intrusion."

"I could see that you were pretty surprised we're having the wedding at your grandparents' house. I imagine it'll be a bit of a shock to go back there after all these years. So, I wondered if you'd like to go with me now, before all the hubbaloo starts."

Jennings rubbed at her temple. *A week out of Vegas and I've already lost my poker face.* "What is it you do for a living, Aimee? If you don't mind me asking."

She smiled, her eyes twinkling, and it was apparent why Benny fell for her. "I'm a psychologist. I work mostly with foster children—which is how Benny and I met."

The headache morphed into a freight train roaring through her cerebellum. "I'm sorry," Jennings rounded the island and headed for the couch, "I need to sit down." She collapsed on the leather sofa, leaning back and slowing her breathing. Norma Jean jumped onto the couch beside her and licked her hand. She patted the little dog on the head and the train slowed down.

Aimee sat on the other side of her and placed a hand on her arm. "Can I get you something?"

Raising her head off the back of the couch, Jennings attempted a smile. The pain didn't get worse, so it was a start. "I'd say some water, but I doubt Benny did the dishes while he was here."

"I can always pour out a beer." She crossed to the kitchen, rummaged through the cupboards and produced a glass. "This one looks reasonably safe." She ran the tap, filled the glass, and returned to the couch.

Jennings took it from her and sipped the water. She had to find a way to bow out of this impromptu chat. Aimee seemed nice enough, but she was bound to start psychoanalyzing at any moment. It was probably second nature.

"I'm the youngest in my family. I never even babysat." Aimee stared out the window. "I can't imagine taking care of a little kid when I was a kid myself."

Am I supposed to lay down on the couch now? "It wasn't a big deal."

She turned to face her. "I couldn't keep a hamster alive. You *raised* Benny. It's a huge deal."

Jennings jumped up from the couch, startling Norma Jean, who barked in protest. "I don't think I'm up to seeing the house." She strode to the door. "Thank you for coming by."

Instead of following her to the front door, Aimee took a seat in the armchair Jennings had previously occupied. "If it's cool with you, I think I'll just hang out 'til the boys get back."

No, it's not *cool with me.* "I guess Mitch won't mind. But I've got to be somewhere." *Anywhere but here.*

"Okay," she waved from the chair, "just leave the door unlocked. I'll guard the beer." She picked up an ESPN magazine and started flipping through it.

This is who my brother is choosing to marry? Apparently his young, impressionable mind was damaged by being forced into foster care, because he'd been normal the last time she saw him. Jennings grabbed her purse and Norma Jean's leash. She clapped, but the dog barely looked at her from her spot curled up in the corner of the couch. "Norma Jean, let's go." She clapped again. No response.

"I'll watch your dog, too, if you like." Aimee didn't look up from the magazine.

Walking Norma Jean had been the extent of her plan. Standing in the doorway, the leash hanging limply in her hand, Jennings realized how pathetic it was to run away. If she intended to have a relationship with her brother, she wouldn't be able to avoid his new wife. She might as well get the dirty laundry out of the way and attempt a truce. "I loved my brother and I did the best I could. I was sixteen," *and knocked up,* "when they took him from me. We didn't have any family left. There was nothing I could do. But I love my brother." She braced her arms against the walls of the small entrance.

"Oh, Caroline, no." Aimee jumped out of the chair and flew across the apartment. "I never meant to imply that you did anything wrong. Nobody blames you for leaving, least of all Benny."

"I blame me."

"No." She gripped Jennings's arms and held her gaze. "You did absolutely nothing wrong."

She seemed so certain, but she didn't know the whole story. And suddenly, Jennings couldn't think of a reason to keep it secret any longer. No one cared about a runaway from over twenty years ago. She wasn't hiding anymore. "I did a lot wrong." She straightened, took a deep breath, and decided she was done running. "Would you like to hear about it?"

Aimee's eyes watered as she nodded. "I'm up for anything you'd like to share."

Chapter Twenty-Two

The Colonel's toast sounded more like a West Point commencement address than an encouraging sentiment for his future son-in-law. Honestly, Mitch had tuned out after Aimee's father compared marriage to a militia unit. His phone vibrated, and he slid it out of his pocket and tried to read the text while keeping the phone hidden under the white linen tablecloth. He didn't want to incur a demerit for misconduct.

Charter Vance

> Leaned on a low-level, Jason bragging about first "conquest." A match for Jennings. Any luck on your end?

Apparently, Charter Vance was back on the story he'd started over two decades ago. Good, because Mitch wasn't getting anywhere with Jennings.

He knew in his gut she was the girl that was attacked in the alley behind The Orpheum, and as much as he wished it wasn't true, he was certain she was raped. Pinning her down this morning had been a stupid mistake—one he'd give anything to do over.

She'd lied back then and had likely been lying to herself all these years. Why would she suddenly want to tell him the truth? Maybe Charter could find definitive proof on his end, and Mitch wouldn't have to involve Jennings at all. He would take care of Jason, and if she was ever ready to deal with the trauma of the attack, he'd be able to tell her that the bastard had paid. But he had to be careful. If he pushed her, she'd likely run again. And he wasn't sure he could live without her at this point.

Benny elbowed him.

Everyone held their glasses high except Mitch. He thrust the flute in the air. "Cheers!"

The Colonel looked like he was ready to throw him in the brig. But everyone clinked glasses and took a drink.

A server set a cake in the middle of the table. The other two groomsmen snickered. The design in icing showed a blond-headed man standing in front of a firing squad. Five men holding guns on the groom clearly resembled Aimee's father and brothers. One of her brothers, Mitch couldn't tell them apart, laughed. "That's what'll happen if you hurt our little sister."

Benny smiled. "The only way I'd hurt Aimee is if five guys held guns to my head."

Mitch didn't envy his friend's position. Taking on a clan this size was overwhelming for anyone, especially a foster kid who'd grown up without a family of his own. Thank God he'd gotten Jennings back to Asheville, despite the rocky journey. Benny deserved to have his own blood at his wedding. Even his foster parents had died, although he was long out of the house before they passed. Mitch had met them a couple times. A nice older couple who'd never had kids of their own and doted on Benny like he was still eight.

"Was that Caroline?" Benny leaned close to whisper in his ear. "That texted you?"

"No. Something for work." Mitch took a plate offered by the waiter who had cut the cake. His piece featured a long rifle.

"Aimee just texted me. She's at your place with Caroline."

He hoped to hell Aimee didn't push the wrong buttons. Her casual conversation could make a person question their entire moral identity. "Maybe we should get back."

"I'm kind of the guest of honor here, Mitch." Benny stabbed the blond man's head with his fork. "She said they're having a nice talk."

Exactly what he was afraid of.

"So, young man," the Colonel loomed over his future son-in-law, "when are we going to meet this sister of yours?"

"She should be at the rehearsal dinner tonight, sir." Benny slid his gaze over to Mitch.

He nodded. He'd get her there. Even if he had to throw her over his shoulder and carry her. Hell, that sounded like a fun fantasy even if it wasn't necessary.

Mitch shoveled the last bite of cake into his mouth. *Once the cake was gone, they could leave, right?* "There's a ton to be done before then, we should probably..." He jerked his head toward the door. Aimee had drawn up a whole list of best man duties for him, but Mitch figured he'd accomplished the most important thing. And he intended to make sure she stuck around through the wedding. Hopefully Aimee hadn't spooked her.

"Yeah, I suppose Mitch is right. It's his job to keep me on track today. Best man and all." Benny pushed back his chair. "Thanks for the lunch, everyone. And the cake was great." He shook hands with Aimee's dad and brothers and clapped his other two groomsmen on the back. "See everyone tonight."

Saluting the Colonel, Mitch followed Benny out to the parking lot. "Let's hope Aimee hasn't broken out the therapy dolls."

He punched Mitch in the shoulder and laughed. "She can have a normal conversation."

"Man, she digs around people's psyches in her sleep."

Benny backed out of the parking space. "You watch for cops."

***

Jennings collected the last bits of rice and pork and raised the chopsticks to her mouth. It was good to know Asheville had decent Chinese delivery. "Thanks for lunch, Aimee. I was starting to get lightheaded from lack of sustenance." The muffin Mitch brought her for breakfast had gotten caught in the crossfire.

Cracking open a fortune cookie, Aimee smiled. "Everything's easier with food." She read the fortune to herself and chuckled. "'You will be going on a great journey.' Do you think they mean the marriage or the honeymoon?"

"Where are you going?" Jennings leaned back against the cushions. She couldn't remember the last time she felt this content. *Who knew divulging all of your deepest secrets to a practical stranger could be so freeing?*

"Aruba." Aimee rubbed her hands together. "Benny wanted to go to Big Sky Country. I won."

She had so much she wanted to share with Benny. Now he was getting married, taking off for at least a week, and then would be a newlywed. Would there be any time for her to reconnect with her brother?

"Benny's so excited you're here, I'm surprised he didn't ask to postpone the trip." Aimee bounced on her seat like a kid anxious to get to Disney World. "But as soon as we get back, I know he can't wait to catch up with you."

The woman could read minds. Jennings made a mental note to avoid gambling with Aimee. "There's no hurry. I don't plan on going anywhere." Asheville didn't seem scary anymore. And now that her darkest secret was out in the open, revealing the truth to Mitch wasn't as scary either. "Benny's really lucky to have found you, Aimee." She squeezed her soon-to-be-sister-in-law's hand. "I'm lucky he found you, too."

"Are you kidding? I have four brothers! I can't wait to call you my sister." She threw her arms around Jennings.

I could get used to all this hugging. She squeezed Aimee tight.

"We're back." Mitch rushed through the door; Benny close on his heels. "Everything okay in here?"

Aimee pulled back, laughing. "Where's the fire, boys? You think I was going to shrink my new sister-in-law's head?"

From the looks on their faces, hers wasn't the only mind Aimee had read. Jennings wondered if she knew how to play poker. She'd be a natural.

Mitch recovered first. "No, of course not. We just missed our ladies." He plopped down on the couch next to Jennings and leaned in close. "Seriously, are you okay?"

Jennings smiled. She didn't want to clue him in that he was right. And she never would have guessed how valuable a little free therapy would be. "I'm great. Sorry about this morning."

"No, I'm sorry. I screwed up." He leaned his forehead against hers. "Won't happen again."

She noticed movement out of the corner of her eye. Benny and Aimee moved quietly toward the door. "No, wait." She leapt off the couch, knocking a surprised Mitch back. "Sorry, hon." She patted his leg and then moved toward her brother. "Benny, wait. I need to tell you something."

Aimee smiled then gestured toward the couch. "Come on, Mitch, I'll buy you a coffee. Or a beer."

He stood, but Jennings shook her head. "No, it's okay. You guys can stay. I'm not keeping secrets anymore."

They settled in the living room, and Jennings pulled the coffee table closer to the couch to use as a seat. Her knees bumped against her brother's, and she braced her hands on his legs and stared into his eyes. "Benny, I missed you *every* day."

He opened his mouth, but she held up a hand.

"Please, let me finish." Doubt crept in, but she focused on her brother's eyes, the eyes that used to stare up at her while she read *Charlotte's Web* and *Stuart Little*. "It killed me to leave you. But it wasn't just about you and me." She sucked in a breath and felt Aimee's strong hand on her back. "When I left Asheville, I was three months pregnant."

She dared a glance at Mitch, who gripped the arm of the chair so hard his knuckles turned white. Then she focused back on Benny. She'd have to face Mitch later—this moment was about making things right with her brother. "I knew if I had the baby while I was in the system, they'd take it from me. I intended to get established somewhere, have the baby, and come back to fight for you."

Benny covered her hand with his, his brow knit with concern so much like their father's when he was worried about Grandpap.

"It was a grand plan for a teenager with $47 and an old guitar. I see that now." Jennings stared down at her brother's hands, locating the scar from the time he'd touched the hot tailpipe of their parents' van. How had she lived twenty-two years without him? Her eyes teared up, but she pressed forward, determined for him to know the whole story. "So, I took the bus as far as Memphis, saving my last twenty dollars for a few meals. It was a cool city, Mama and Daddy would have loved it. I thought it'd be as good a place as any." She bit her lip and snuck a glance at Mitch, whose mouth was set in a hard line. Aimee rubbed her back, encouraging her to continue. "I was sleeping in an alley one night when I was attacked. The guy took my money and Daddy's guitar, and I," Jennings bit the inside of her lip, "I lost the baby." The agony was as raw in this moment as it had been all those years ago when the doctor with the gentle eyes told her she'd had a miscarriage.

Benny's hand flew to his mouth, and her pain was reflected in his eyes. "Oh, Caroline, I had no idea. I..." He pushed forward, wrapping his arms tightly around her. "I never blamed you for leaving. Never. I just hoped you were happy."

Jennings clung to her brother, letting the tears flow, knowing there was so much more to say but this was enough for now.

***

Benny and Aimee had left to prepare for the rehearsal dinner and Jennings lay curled up on the couch, drifting in and out of sleep. Mitch had been watching her for over an hour, his rage growing each time she bit her lip or shuddered in her sleep. After her revelation, all the pieces fell together. And while she still hadn't admitted to the rape, or the perpetrator, Mitch knew. And he finally knew how to prove it.

As soon as she'd mentioned the guitar, it'd come back to him in a flash. Jason, propped up on one of the booths in the back of The Beetle, strumming a battered old guitar with Woodstock stickers on it, singing an off-key rendition of Bad to the Bone. He'd been extra cocky that night, pumped up from some unknown triumph, sitting high upon his "throne," waving his conquest around like a kid with a shiny new penny. He'd been tightlipped about where the guitar had come from, and after that night, Mitch had never seen Jason in public with it again. But he had seen it tucked under Jason's bed, so he knew it held some importance for him. And he'd bet the bastard still had it, a trophy from the first victim of his depravity.

As soon as the newlyweds were on a plane to Aruba, he'd go back to Memphis. And he wouldn't dance around the matter this time. Jason would pay.

"Are you angry with me?"

He'd been staring out the window, fantasizing about finally giving Jason his due, and hadn't noticed Jennings awaken. Shifting onto the couch, he brushed the hair back from her face. "No, of course not."

She appraised him, her blue eyes clear and unblinking. "You're definitely angry."

"Yes. But not at you." He slid his hand down her arm, entwined his fingers in hers. "The guy who attacked you stole your innocence, and a life, and he needs to answer for it."

Her gaze shifted to the floor. "I was hardly innocent."

He gently grabbed her chin and forced her to look at him. "Caroline, you were sixteen years old. And no one ever deserves to be raped."

The word hung in the air between them, but she didn't deny it. "Why do you call me Caroline whenever we talk about the past?" She sucked her bottom lip in and stared up at him through her eyelashes.

"Honestly, I hadn't noticed." He took her hand again. "You are Caroline to me. And Jennings. Caroline is my best friend's sister, and Jennings is the woman I've fallen in love with." His impulse was to block her way, not allow her the chance to escape, but he forced himself to remain seated.

Silence sat between them, like a courtroom waiting for a verdict. Her eyes darted from his face, to the window, to their hands entwined together.

He watched the erratic rise and fall of her chest and continued to stroke his thumb across her hand. Carla was the only woman he'd ever said those words to, and she'd thrown them back in his face like counterfeit money, not once, but twice. Lesson learned; he hadn't allowed himself to get emotionally attached to the women he dated after that. He treated them with respect, and never led them on, but the moment he started to feel something, he'd move on.

Jennings was different. The stories Benny told about his older sister had always intrigued Mitch. Being an only child—especially one who'd received little in the way of nurturing—it was hard to imagine a connection so strong that it endured twenty-two years of no contact and what some would describe as abandonment. Caroline had raised Benny for his first eight years, until he'd been taken away from her. She'd been a child, then a teenager, but from what he knew, she'd given her whole world to the little boy. Then that world had been ripped away. And things only got worse. The fact that she was here at all was amazing. The fact that she was a strong, sensual woman moved Mitch to his core. What he knew about Caroline Jennings Lee, he could fit on the head of a pin, but he wanted to spend the next fifty years discovering the rest.

"I don't know who I am." Her quiet words brought him back to the moment, to find her with a single tear on her cheek.

He kissed the tear away, licked the saltiness off his lips, and smiled to reassure her, although he couldn't claim to know any more answers than she did. "You can be whoever you want. And I'm here, no matter what."

She let out a breath, and a smile peeked out of her worry. "Thanks for finding me, whoever I am."

With her blonde hair splayed across the cushions of his couch, and her blue eyes glimmering under unshed tears, she was like a vision conjured up by a lovesick teenage boy. Mitch couldn't remember ever feeling so deeply about another person. With Carla, it'd been about infatuation, and maybe about winning. His ego had been more wounded than his heart.

With Jennings, or Caroline, or whoever she decided to be, his heart felt whole. He hadn't even realized it wasn't before.

He brushed a soft kiss across her lips. "Anytime, babe."

Chapter Twenty-Three

Jennings needed more time to deal with the emotion of the day. Five or six years, tops. She'd turned off her heart so long ago that it was having trouble keeping up with all the new activity. Sharing the story of her attack and losing the baby, being reunited with Benny, and then having Mitch profess his love—she felt like a mouse on a treadmill that would never reach the cheese at the end. Now, as Mitch turned onto Bear Mountain Rd, she had to deal with one more thing. She was going home.

A new subdivision had taken over Jesse Wallingburg's farm. Around the next curve, Mae Oberaton's Victorian had been converted into a Bed and Breakfast.

Her name wasn't the only thing that had changed in twenty-two years. No junked cars littered the yards of the well-maintained homes lining the winding road and there wasn't a couch in sight. *You really can't go home again.*

But as Mitch crossed Bear Creek and rounded the final curve, Jennings caught a glimpse of the green gabled roofline, and she was transported back in time.

"I don't understand why we have to stay at Granny's. I can help take care of the baby."

Mama turned in her seat, a feat, considering her huge belly. "Caroline, you're eight years old. All you have to do is be a kid. And the best big sister ever."

"This van's not big enough for four, kiddo." Daddy turned the radio down. "We want you to have a yard, and your own bedroom. I grew up in this house, you know."

"I know and you walked four miles to school—barefoot." She stuck out her lip. "Hey! I'm not gonna have to go to school, am I?"

"Your mama's going to be busy with the baby. She won't have time to home-school you anymore. But school will be fun. You'll make lots of friends."

This is getting more rotten by the minute. "Well, it seems to me if Granny's gonna help with the baby, then Mama can still teach me stuff."

Mama laughed and patted Daddy on the arm. "Can't argue with that logic, can we?"

"I suppose not. I guess we'll give it a try." He put his hand back on the radio dial. "But you're missing out. The school has a groovy playground." He spun the dial, and the sound of the Bee Gees filled the van as they rounded the corner and Granny & Pap's house came into view.

Benny had done a lot of work to the house. It gleamed with fresh white paint and appeared to have new windows. The driveway that wound around back had fresh gravel and he'd trimmed back the oak tree in the front yard, so it no longer scraped the roof of the house. He had freshened everything up but hadn't changed the overall look. The azalea bushes surrounding the porch exploded with brilliant blossoms and the tire swing swayed in the breeze like he had just jumped off. As they pulled in the driveway, she could see the butterfly wind chimes hanging outside her bedroom window. She wondered if the matching quilt was still on the twin bed.

How had this place survived so many years of neglect?

"You ready?"

She hadn't noticed Mitch stop the truck alongside a row of other cars, because she'd been staring at the spot where the van had been parked when it caught on fire. In its place stood a metal arbor, entwined with bougainvillea and clematis, surrounded by forget-me-nots. At the peak of the arch, two copper crosses shone in the sunlight.

"Jennings?" He'd climbed out of the truck and held the door open. "Norma Jean is on her third lap around the house."

"Oh." She glanced from him to the crosses and back again. "Sorry." She took the hand he extended and slid across the seat. "I guess I'm a little distracted."

"Take all the time you need, babe. The ceremony isn't until three tomorrow." He quirked his lips into a grin and winked at her.

She wrapped her arms around his waist and leaned against his chest. "I'm so glad you're here."

"I got nowhere else to be." He kissed the top of her head.

"Caroline!" Benny's voice traveled over the backyard.

She spun around and saw him coming across their granny's garden, carefully stepping to avoid the tomato plants, squash and peppers. *Just how long has he been working on this place?* He stopped as he reached the edge of the patch and plucked a flower off a vine. Beaming, he crossed the backyard and held the blossom out to her.

"Benny, I can't believe everything you've done here. It's exactly the same, except better."

He tucked the flower behind her ear. "When I started working at DSS, I looked up our file and found out that the house was in both our names. Ever since, I've been spending weekends out here trying to fix it up. I remembered the garden and the front, but I'm fuzzy on the inside, so I just cleaned it up and got rid of the stuff that was decaying. Maybe you can help me." He looked hopeful, like a little boy asking his mother to stay up half an hour later.

"I would really like that." She hooked her arm in his. "But Granny had awful taste, so I'd say it's safe to change things up."

***

Mitch watched brother and sister walk toward the back door and felt a sense of satisfaction. *I actually did something right for once.* His phone vibrated, and he pulled it out of his pocket.

"You got a minute to talk?" Charter sounded out of breath.

The rehearsal dinner didn't start for over an hour, and Mitch knew if he ran into Aimee, she'd give him a job to do. He walked around the front of the house. "Sure."

"There's some serious shit going down here. I just had a meet with Paulie Austin, Jason's second. Apparently, Carla's gone off her rocker and is threatening to expose Jason's extra-marital affairs. Including the ones that were one-sided. Says she has proof."

Finally. Maybe the woman had some sense after all.

Charter continued. "Jason's gone underground and Carla's scared out of her wits, understandably. Says she'll only talk to you."

Mitch swore. Would he never be free of her? "Tell her to go fuck herself. I've got a wedding tomorrow."

"You're getting married?"

"Not hardly." Although the idea didn't completely terrify him anymore. "I'm the best man. Gotta be here." Not that he'd rush back to save Carla's ass anyway.

"I guess I misunderstood. I thought you wanted justice for Jennings."

Mitch kicked a small boulder near the mailbox. "I do, dammit. And I already figured out how to do that. But it will have to be *after* the wedding." And not on Carla's terms.

"Did Jennings remember Jason?"

"Not exactly."

Aimee called his name from the front porch.

"Listen, Charter, I've got to go, but thanks for the info." He ended the call and headed up the front walk. "Aimee, I need to make one more phone call, then I'm at your beck and call." He lifted his eyebrows and grinned.

She put her hands on her hips but laughed. "Okay, you've got five minutes. Then I need you up on a ladder."

"Yes, ma'am." He saluted her, then turned back toward the road, dialing Harry's number. He didn't want for the old man to speak. "You need to go talk your crazy-ass niece off the ledge until I can get there." But he wasn't going to Memphis to save Carla. Hell, if he could figure out a way to throw her under the bus with Jason, he'd be more than happy to oblige.

***

Benny and Mitch had strung white lights from the side of the house to the surrounding trees and back again, marking a patio of sorts. Aimee's brothers arrived with a truck full of tables and chairs. Soon, everyone was seated around the tables with heaping plates of Carolina barbeque, corn on the cob and collard greens. Jennings had met each of Aimee's brothers and their wives and now sat at a table with their friends from work. If you had told her she'd be laughing and comfortable with a table full of DSS employees, she would have told you your head wasn't screwed on right. She'd spent the last 20 years blaming that grey-haired social worker for everything that had gone wrong in her world. The people around her were young, positive, and obviously cared a great deal for the children they were responsible for. Perspective was hard for a sixteen-year-old who had lost everyone in her life. For a woman nearing 40 and finding out that her heart wasn't completely shriveled and dried up, a new light was shining on everything she thought she knew.

After they ate, the wedding party assembled near the arch to run through the big day. When she realized that Benny and Aimee were getting married on the spot where her parents had died twenty-eight years ago, Jennings excused herself and slipped through the back door of the house. She leaned on the wall and fought against tears. Benny was honoring the parents he hardly remembered by sealing his love in the place they drew their last breaths.

The door creaked open beside her. "You okay?" Mitch gently took her hands.

Jennings nodded but kept her eyes squeezed shut.

He pulled her over to the couch and sat her down, never releasing her hands. "You know, Benny welded that arch himself. He took a class during college. The crosses took him like a 100 tries to get right. I swear he wasted more copper than he used." Mitch chuckled. "But he stuck at it until they were perfect. You can't see it from the ground, but he engraved their names on them."

Tears slid out of her lids. Jennings had cried more in the last two weeks than in the last two decades. Surely, she'd dry up soon.

"For a kid that lost his parents, grandparents and even his sister, he sure is well adjusted. I think he owes that to you." He stroked the tears off her cheeks then placed a kiss on either side of her nose. "I'd come out here with him some weekends to help paint or what not, and he'd talk about you the entire time. How you'd build forts to sleep in and create maps to find a treasure. I hardly remember my childhood and Benny knows what flavor of ice cream you hand-churned for the 4th of July. Caroline, he holds zero resentment for you leaving. He just wants you back in his life."

She slowly opened her eyes and bit her bottom lip, trying to stem the flow. "Me too."

He cupped his hand around her head and pulled her into his chest, his strong arms settling around her.

She felt safe in his arms. Safe in this house that had once been her home. Safe as Benny's sister again. She sat back and swiped at her face. "I feel like Caroline here."

The left side of Mitch's mouth twitched up.

The back door opened and Benny and Aimee came in. "Here you are, we've been looking for you!" He moved in front of the couch with his hands behind his back and a Cheshire grin on his face. It was like Benny was seven again and had snuck a salamander into the house. Aimee had her arm hooked in his and her eyes were twinkling like the lights strung up outside.

"Is the rehearsal over?"

The couple nodded their heads in unison. "We have a surprise for you." Benny looked like he might burst.

"Is it an amphibian?"

He dissolved into laughter and brought both his hands up to his face. That's when she saw the glint of metal. So, it wasn't a slimy creature.

Aimee looked a little confused, but she was still as excited as a bride on her wedding day. Which really didn't explain anything.

Mitch cleared his throat and punched Benny on the shoulder. "Dude, get to it."

Jennings had zero clue what was going on here, but obviously Mitch was in on whatever it was.

Benny composed himself and held out his hand, a key dangling from his pointer finger. "It's yours."

She must have looked as confused as she felt, because Mitch nudged her and whispered, "The house."

The house? Gran's house? This house? "What do you mean its mine? You said it's in both our names. And you did all this work."

He crouched down in front of her and held the key out. "Aimee and I have a place in town. We have to be on call for work, and this is too far out. Besides, it still needs some more attention. Especially the inside."

Jennings looked around and saw peeling wallpaper and threadbare furniture. She saw her grandmother standing at the kitchen sink scrubbing it with steel wool. She saw a young Benny driving his race cars across the worn wood floor. She blinked and saw what it could be. Her home. Again.

She nearly knocked Benny off his feet with her embrace. "I don't know how to thank you." He regained his balance and squeezed her tight.

"Thank me by staying."

"For you, anything." Caroline wouldn't leave her brother again.

Chapter Twenty-Four

It was the perfect day for a wedding. Not that Jennings had a lot of experience with weddings. The last one she attended had been Elena and Martin's in a tiny chapel on the Vegas Strip. She was pretty sure she wouldn't see Elvis at this event.

The ceremony was lovely. Now Jennings sat next to Mitch, his arm draped around her shoulders, while they watched the new couple wind their way around the dance floor. Jennings closed her eyes and remembered Daddy spinning her around the backyard while Mama looked on nursing Benny. The nights had always been so magical. After Granny and Grandpap had gone to bed, the four of them would sit outside and look up at the stars and reminisce about their adventures. They had been planning a road trip to a festival a few hours away shortly before the fire. It would have been Benny's first adventure. Jennings wished more than anything that he could have known their parents.

"Where you at?" Mitch's breath tickled her neck as he leaned in close and whispered.

"Right here," Jennings assured him. *If not right now.* She squeezed his knee. "Just wishing my parents could be here. Could see how good he's turned out."

"Both of you."

She had very little to be proud of. She'd gotten knocked up, abandoned her brother, lost the baby, held nowhere jobs and basically failed at the only career she attempted. But looking around the backyard of the home she grew up in, and seeing her brother, whole and in love, gave her hope for a new beginning.

Mitch stood and held out his hand. "May I have this dance?"

Accepting his hand, Jennings allowed him to pull her onto the makeshift dance floor. He wrapped his strong arms around her, and she settled into his embrace, just soaking in the moment. *Feels Like Home* came over the speakers and she gripped Mitch even tighter as the words sank into her soul, soothing her lonely heart and making her realize that she had a chance at a future—a future that included her brother, a new sister-in-law and a good man who loved her. After being alone for so long, could she learn how to let others in? Could she learn how to love again?

She laid her head on Mitch's shoulder as they swayed to the music. Maybe she didn't have to figure everything out right now. Maybe she could just be happy in this moment and push down the worry that everything would eventually fall apart.

***

Mitch leaned close to Jennings' ear and brushed her hair back. "We should have stayed in bed."

"I think that might be what's keeping the happy couple." Jennings turned in her chair to face him. She slid her hand up his thigh and his body immediately responded to her touch. "We'll give them 10 more minutes, and if they don't show, we can go back to bed." She licked her lips and gazed at him with hungry eyes.

He willed his body to relax. The Grove Park Inn was not an appropriate setting to be sporting a woody. "I don't know why they insisted on brunch anyway. Newlyweds should want to stay in bed too."

"Morning!" Benny slid out the chair across from Mitch and Aimee took a seat. She was beaming, her cheeks rosy and her eyes sparkling. Benny rounded the table, gave his sister a quick hug and then took the seat across from her. "It's a beautiful day, wouldn't you say?"

Yup, the sun was shining straight up Benny's ass, and Mitch was so happy to have woken up beside a gorgeous blonde with a heart of gold, that he didn't even hold any ill will toward his friend. And now said blonde's hand was creeping closer and closer to dangerous territory beneath the white linen tablecloth. He squeezed her fingers, and removed her hand from his crotch, while shifting in his chair. "Yes, Benny. It's a beautiful day." He glanced at Jennings, who had a devilish gleam in her eyes. All he wanted was to move this brunch along and take her back to his loft.

Jennings gestured over the veranda and to the view beyond. "Can't beat the view. Could you see it from your room?"

"All I saw last night was my beautiful wife." Benny kissed the back of Aimee's hand and looked lovingly at his bride.

Mitch was getting ready to reply when Jennings' hand crept back up his leg. *Montgomery, AL. Juneau, AK. Pheonix, AR.* He picked up his menu and tried to ignore what was happening under the table. "What's everyone having?"

A waiter approached the table and took their drink order. His eyebrows arched slightly when he noticed Jennings' arm snaked under the tablecloth. Cheeks flushed, she withdrew her hand and sat back in her chair.

"What time does your flight leave?"

"Not until 4, but we have to go by the house on the way to the airport and get the rest of our luggage." Benny took a swig of the beer the waiter set in front of him. "Actually, if you guys want to follow us there, you can grab my car to use while we're gone, Caroline."

"Oh, no, I don't want to put you out, I'll be fine without a car."

He shook his head firmly. "When I get back, I'll help you get something permanent, but you can't be that far out without transportation."

Mitch hadn't even considered the fact that Jennings would be so far from town without a way to get around. And based on the text messages he'd been getting all morning, he had to get to Memphis sooner rather than later. "That's a great idea, Benny. Not like you'll need it."

Jennings looked unsure but finally nodded her head. "Ok, just until you get back. But I don't need much. I'm going to clean up the house and settle in a bit. And find a job." She sucked her bottom lip in, and Mitch recognized fear creeping into her features.

He lightly squeezed her thigh. "Aimee, I bet you can't wait to get to Aruba."

"Those palm trees are calling my name. Benny's gonna have to pry the book out of my hands and my ass off the sand."

Jennings choked on her water. *Distraction successful.*

Benny scooted Aimee's chair closer to him. "Don't let her fool you. I'm better than any book boyfriend she may have."

The waiter reappeared and took their orders, then silence fell over the table as everyone stared over the golf course at the skyline of Asheville and the mountains surrounding them.

"I haven't been to the beach since I was little. Gotta admit, I'm a little jealous about Aruba." Jennings turned toward him. "What about you, Mitch? Ever been?"

"Ha!" Benny slapped the table. "Mitch going to Aruba? Not unless they built the world's longest bridge to get there."

"Huh?" Jennings looked between Mitch and Benny. And before Mitch could cut him off, his friend continued.

"Mitch doesn't fly. Not since the incident." He even had the nerve to use damn air quotes.

Both women at the table leaned forward, their eyes bright. Jennings was the first to speak. "The incident?"

"Oh yeah, this sounds juicy. Tell us, Benny." Aimee bounced in her seat.

Mitch raked his hand over his face. This was not the kind of distraction he was looking for. "It's nothing, just had a bad experience the last time I flew."

"Oh, it's not nothing. The plane had to crash land." Benny paused for dramatic effect. If Mitch could have, he would have kicked him under the table. "In Vegas, no less. Why else do you think he'd drive that hunk of metal across the country?"

People were always slandering his classic truck.

Mitch knew he had to rein this in, and quickly. "But luckily, no one was injured. End of story."

"Nope, that's the beginning of the story." The waiter brought their meals, and Benny only paused long enough to take a bite of his omelet. "He went out there to stop Carla's wedding. See, Carla had told Mitch that she was pregnant with his baby but that she was going to Vegas to marry some other dude, Jackson, or something." He paused again and took a bite of bacon.

Mitch willed his friend to shut the fuck up and attempted to plead with him through telepathy but Benny was too focused on buttering his toast.

Jennings and Aimee were completely enthralled by the story and hadn't even touched their food. Mitch felt like he could puke.

"Really, we should eat before the food gets cold." Mitch tried to take a bite of his eggs, but he really didn't think he could stomach it at this point.

"No, I want to hear more about Carla." Jennings pushed her plate to the side and shot Mitch a look that he wasn't able to read. One day he'd figure out all her looks, if this story didn't send her screaming for the hills.

"Yes, yes!" Aimee's enthusiasm was not helping.

Benny shoveled in another bite and then wiped his mouth. "So, Mitch survives a plane crash, finds Carla, professes his love to her, and she tells him she's marrying Jackson anyway."

This is not how Mitch planned to tell Jennings about what happened with Carla. Okay, he hadn't actually thought about telling her at all, because he knew now that he never loved Carla, but maybe it would be better coming from him instead of Benny's sensationalized version.

"Benny, eat your eggs." Mitch reached for Jennings' hand, and focused his attention on her, even though he knew Aimee was listening with rapt attention. "Carla is a manipulator. You know that. You met her."

"You met Carla? What's she like? Is she a slut? She sounds like a slut." Aimee rattled the questions off like a firing squad. Which seemed appropriate to Mitch.

"Anyway, she called me and said that her and Jason were in Vegas to get married."

"Jason! That's it!" Benny held up his fork triumphantly.

Mitch glared at him, then refocused on Jennings. "I was young and stupid and thought I was in love with her."

Benny opened his mouth, but Mitch pointed at him before he could get his next inaccurate thought out. "Let me tell it." Benny clamped his mouth shut and busied himself putting ketchup on his hashbrowns.

"I got there and Carla wouldn't even tell me where they were. I went to about a dozen wedding chapels before I finally found them, and Carla had on really heavy makeup, and I'm almost positive there were bruises on her face. When I asked her about the baby, she acted like she didn't know what I was talking about and assured Jason that she wanted to marry him. And she did."

Aimee downed her mimosa in one gulp. "Did she have the baby?"

Mitch shook his head and turned back to Jennings. "I'm guessing there never was a baby, she just told me that to see if I'd chase after her and make a fool out of myself. Which I did."

Jennings reached out and cupped his cheek. "That's on her, not you. She was just toying with you."

"That's not the whole story."

Everyone at the table looked at Benny, who was grinning like a Chesire cat. Aimee and Jennings looked shocked, and Mitch was tempted to throw his fork straight at Benny's chest.

Aime clapped her hands. "This is the best brunch ever!" She hadn't even touched her French toast.

All these years, and up to this point only five people knew about "the incident." Down the drain because his friend had two beers before lunchtime.

His phone buzzed in his pocket, and he took the opportunity to get out of there. Benny might tell it wrong, but Mitch didn't think he could handle seeing the disappointment on Jennings' face when she heard about the biggest regret of his life.

Chapter Twenty-Five

Mitch held up his phone and stepped away from the table. Jennings watched his retreating back and worried that he was embarrassed. She had done many things in her life she regretted, so she would never judge another person, especially in a moment of great turmoil.

"Benny, maybe you shouldn't tell the rest. Let's just drop it."

Aimee shook her head. "How are you not dying to know?"

Part of her definitely wanted to know, mostly because she wanted to understand Mitch fully, but it seemed wrong for them to discuss it without him here.

She pushed her chair out from the table and rose. "I'll be right back."

Crossing the stone veranda, she stepped inside the massive lobby of the hotel. Mitch was near one of the large fireplaces, leaning against the stonework, looking at his phone. His posture was rigid, his brow creased. He was likely pissed about Benny spilling his secrets.

He looked up, his eyes locking with hers. As she walked toward him, she focused on those eyes, the ones that seemed at times to bore into her soul.

He met her halfway, his hand going immediately to her waist and drawing her closer.

"I'm sorry we put you on the spot like that. Benny shouldn't have—"

"No, it's fine, really. I don't want to keep anything from you. It's just not my proudest moment." He leaned his forehead against hers, his fingers gripping at the waistband of her skirt. "I'm not that man anymore. I got mixed up in a world I had no business being in and made a lot of mistakes."

She cupped her hands around his face and pulled back enough to stare into his eyes. "We've all made mistakes. Trust me, I would win if this were a contest."

He cracked a smile and her heart swelled. Her feelings for this man were so intense, so unlike anything she'd felt before. She swept a light kiss against his lips.

"Will you come back to the table? No need for embarrassment. I made Benny stop with the story."

He shook his head slightly. "I didn't leave because of embarrassment." He held his phone up. "Carla's in the hospital. Jason beat her within an inch of her life."

***

After he broke the news to the table, everyone sobered up and they rushed through their meal. Jennings had said very little since their moment in the lobby and Mitch wished he could climb inside her head and figure out what she was thinking. He was torn between staying in Asheville and making sure that she knew how important she was to him and getting to Nashville to be there for Harry, who sounded sincerely worried about Carla. She was a royal pain in the ass, but no one deserved to be beaten half to death.

He also needed to get Charter on the phone and see if he had any leads on where Jason was hiding out. Mitch might not be able to convince the police about Jason's past crimes, but he was certain they'd be more than interested in dragging the thug in now. He'd never been so brazen in his debauchery before. That fact worried Mitch. He wondered if Jason was spiraling out and this was just the beginning. He wouldn't go after Harry, would he?

The valet brought Mitch's truck around to the front of the hotel and tossed the keys at him. "Sweet ride, man."

The kid seemed sincere, and Mitch was impressed that someone so young could appreciate fine American workmanship. He slipped him a larger-than-normal tip.

Jennings scooted across the front seat, and Mitch glimpsed a patch of skin when her skirt rode high up her thigh. Yeah, Memphis could wait one more day. He wasn't ready to leave her for the shitstorm that would likely greet him when he reentered the messed-up world of the Beale Street gang.

Settling in the truck, Mitch reached over and pulled her toward him.

Her eyes rounded and she let out a little gasp.

He patted her leg, then left his hand there as he started up the truck. "Just need you a little closer."

She leaned into him and laced her fingers into his.

They rode like that all the way to Benny's place where Jennings picked up his Prius. As Mitch drove back to his loft, he kept his eyes on her in the rearview mirror and tried to convince himself that everything was going to be okay. He would go to Memphis, track down Jason, turn him into the cops, tell them all his many sins (starting with that night in the alley) and then get back here as fast as possible. Jennings would be waiting for him, and they could start their lives together without the past weighing them down.

***

"I'll get my stuff together and head to the house so you can get on the road." Jennings swept into Mitch's loft and headed for his bedroom.

"Hold on there, spitfire." He grabbed her by the waist and pulled her back into his arms. "There were some promises made at brunch and I'm not leaving until they are fulfilled."

Her back was pressed against him, and she could feel the hard planes of his chest, abs and erection. His hand slid up her outer thigh and dipped underneath her skirt.

"This skirt has been driving me crazy all day."

"It's just a regular black skirt." She rocked her ass against him, and he groaned.

His thumb hooked under the thin strap of her thong. "It's so short, it's almost indecent. But I'm not complaining." His other hand followed the same path up her right leg.

She shimmied her hips as he pulled the scrap of red lace down. "My Vegas wardrobe probably isn't appropriate for normal life in the mountains of Western North Carolina." She dipped her chin to her chest. She had a decision to make. Blow her bankroll setting up a new life here in Asheville, or get a job immediately, which wouldn't leave her much time to work on the house. And there was the whole matter of not having a car and living 20 miles outside of civilization.

Mitch held the lingerie up before he pitched it toward the couch. "Well, let's not be hasty. This is hot as fuck." He spun her in his arms and lowered his mouth to hers, delivering a kiss full of passion and heat. He gripped the back of her head, his fingers tangled in her hair, and he walked her backwards toward the bedroom.

She got lost in the kiss, in the feel of his lips covering hers, his tongue probing her mouth, sending pulses of heat straight to her core. Her hands roamed down his back, over his ass, and around to the front where she started unbuttoning his shirt.

"What the fuck?" Mitch pulled his lips off her neck, and his hands stilled on her back.

Jennings froze, unsure of what was happening and so turned on and flustered that she couldn't quite process why he had stopped. "What?"

His eyes closed and a sigh escaped his lips. Then the corners of his mouth turned up, and a rumble started deep in his chest and crept up until it erupted fully from his lips—lips that were marked with her lipstick. "Norma Fucking Jean. What the hell?"

She turned, dreading what her terror might have accomplished in the hours they'd been gone. Norma Jean had destroyed nearly everything Jennings owned, but since she furnished her place in dumpster décor with a hint of Goodwill chic, she'd never much minded. And usually only if she was left alone for more than 9 or 10 hours. Her feet planted, and her back to Mitch once again, she peeked her eyes open to see what the mutt had done.

Mitch was still laughing, and Jennings let out a sigh of relief. Not everyone would take this situation so well. Most people don't expect to walk into their bedroom to find their bed covered in goose down with a tarred and feathered hairless mutt laid out in the middle of it, on her back, legs spread like a Playboy centerfold.

Jennings dropped her head into her hands. "Norma Jean." She surveyed the mess and realized there was also a roll of toilet paper spread from the bathroom doorway, up onto the bed and amassed into a makeshift nest of sorts for the prima donna. "Mitch, I'm so sorry, I'll clean this up." She started toward the bed, but he hooked his arm around her waist once more.

"It can wait." His breath tickled her ear, and he peppered kisses along her neck. He was no longer laughing, and from what she could feel pressed against her ass, he was ready to continue what they started. Spinning them both, he now directed her toward the couch, apparently happy to utilize whatever surface was available.

They fell to the couch together, their lips locked and their hands exploring. He situated her on his lap, his hands on her bare ass, squeezing just enough to make her whole body light up. She pulled her shirt over her head and tossed it on the coffee table, revealing a red lace bra that matched the long-gone thong.

His eyes roamed over her body, hands following closely behind, and she never felt more beautiful than in that moment. Mitch made her feel like she was enough, even when she had her own doubts about her usefulness in this world. She wanted to stay in this bubble with him as long as possible, where passion and pleasure were in focus and the rest of the shit was blurry and unimportant. She cupped his face, and bent down, brushing her lips against his. "I could stay here forever."

"I hope you will." He pulled her close, deepened the kiss and promised a delightful afternoon without saying a word.

Chapter Twenty-Six

Mitch awoke to an awful noise and the semi-darkness of early evening. He was alone on the couch, his skin sticking to the leather, and a serious crick in his neck. As he sat up and tried to gain his bearings, he realized the high-pitched whirling noise was coming from his bedroom. A sliver of light shone under the double doors, so he rose to investigate.

Not bothering to find his clothes, he flung open the doors to find Jennings on her hands and knees in only his Braves t-shirt, which was currently riding up and over her very fine, very naked ass. She was stretching the hose of his vacuum cleaner under his bed as Norma Jean looked on from her spot curled up amongst the feathers.

He bent down and turned off the vacuum to stop the annoying sound.

Jennings startled, and her head hit the bottom of the mattress. "Omph."

"Sorry, didn't mean to scare you." Mitch braced himself in the doorway and kept his eyes on the show unfolding before him. She crawled out from under the bed, dragging the hose of the vacuum cleaner behind her. The shirt rose even higher and Mitch's body came alive.

"I hope I didn't wake you. I was just trying to clean up..." Her apology died on her lips as her gaze lit on a very turned-on, naked Mitch. Her tongue peeked out from between her lips, and she sat back on her heels.

His white t-shirt did nothing to disguise her pert breasts and hard nipples, and he believed he'd forever get turned on when the Braves played from here on out.

They had spent the afternoon enjoying each other on the couch, but his little nap was giving him a second wind and seeing Jennings in his loft, half-naked, cleaning, was doing things to his libido. He stalked toward her, a tiger pushing through the vegetation, if feathers could be vegetation. She held his gaze, shifting slightly, but not looking away. "I think you broke my vacuum cleaner."

She pulled her bottom lip into her mouth and broke their staring contest. "It didn't sound right after it sucked up that muffin from the other day. I honestly had forgotten that it fell under the bed while we were..." She looked up at him through her eyelashes, her gaze a mixture of contrition and hunger.

Mitch took one more step and dropped to his knees in front of her. He reached his hand up and tangled his fingers in her long blonde hair. "I'll get a new one." He crashed his mouth to hers and knew he'd never get enough of this unpredictable, unassailable woman.

She pulled back long enough to tug his shirt over her head and then pushed him backward and climbed on top of him.

He could feel the heat between her legs and as she slid her dampness over him, his cock grew with each stroke. He reached up and cupped her breasts, massaging them, causing Jennings to arch her back and moan. He'd been ready to go seeing her fine ass sticking out from under his bed, but now he felt like he could explode on the spot. "Babe, reach over to the nightstand and grab a condom. I need inside you now." He slid his hands down her body and gripped her hips.

She stopped moving and a pensive look took over her face.

Mitch was starting to figure out some of her tells and this was definitely Jennings' contemplative face. *What the hell is she contemplating right now?*

A smile crept over her face and she lowered down, her tits pressing against his chest and kicking his heartrate up. She kissed him lightly and then pulled back and stared into his eyes. "I haven't," she slid her velvet soft pussy up his cock and tilted her hips before pushing back the other direction, "been bare since I was a teenager."

"Fuck." Mitch couldn't believe how amazing it felt to be inside Jennings with nothing between them. He'd never slept with anyone without a condom, and now that he knew how good it felt, it would be hard to go back. "Are you sure?" *Please be sure. Because damn.*

She kissed him again and nodded. "I'm clean and I'm on birth control."

Thank God. He gripped her hips and pushed up to fully insert himself. She rocked against him, and he worried he'd blow right then and there. He sat up, gripped her ass, and lowered his mouth to her neck. "Jennings, you feel so damn good. I'm not going to make it long."

She shifted again and they got closer than he thought possible. "Me neither. Oh, Mitch, yes!"

Their sweat-soaked bodies slid against each other, as their hands gripped and their lips sucked flesh. Mitch slid a hand between them and pressed his thumb against her clit. Almost immediately, he could feel her walls clench, shuddering around his cock. He drilled into her two more times and exploded with the most powerful orgasm he had ever experienced.

Words escaped him. Feelings overwhelmed him. All he could do was hold this woman he loved to the depth of his being.

***

Jennings couldn't believe she'd gone bare with Mitch. It felt so right in the moment, but now she was over-analyzing the decision. They were laid out on the rug in Mitch's bedroom, fluffy white goose down sticking to their sweaty skin. She'd tried to clean it all up, but the vacuum cleaner wasn't cooperating.

Mitch traced lazy circles up and down her arm and she felt safe and happy. Which was terrifying. It was hard to sit back and take stock of her feelings when they attacked each other every chance they had. She'd never wanted anyone the way she craved Mitch. The last time she'd been this wrapped up in a guy was as a teenager with Jack. And look what had happened then. What the hell was she thinking? She hadn't been on birth control as a foolish teen, but you could never be too safe. The need to keep her heart, and her body, safe, had been at the forefront of her mind for the last 22 years. She still wasn't sure how Mitch had blasted through those shields.

She needed a little distance to get her feelings in check.

"Isn't Harry expecting you in Memphis?"

"You trying to get rid of me?" His fingers continued their wandering, and his tone was light.

"Of course not." She tucked her body in closer to his. "I just know you always honor your commitments."

He tipped her chin up so he could see her face. "I do. And one of those commitments is to you."

She tried to hold his gaze, but her heart kicked up, and was that numbness shooting down her arm? She ended up studying the way his hair curled at his neckline.

"Jennings." He gripped her chin. "Look at me. Please."

Closing her eyes briefly, she counted to three. Slowed her breathing. Garnered the will to meet his gaze. Forcing her eyes open, she met his gaze. And saw so much love there. Tears filled her vision.

Mitch slid his thumb up her cheek and wiped away the tear that had spilled over. "You have quickly become my first priority. I didn't plan it, and I know it scares you, but it's the truth. So, yes. I have to go to Memphis because I owe it to

Harry. But I want to make sure you have everything you need here before I leave. Because I'm not sure how long I'll be gone."

Several more tears leaked down her cheeks and a lump in her throat blocked any response.

"I want to be with you, Jennings. I need to know that you'll be here when I get back." His voice broke, and his strong gaze slipped into one of worry.

She swallowed, bit her lip and worked to find her voice. "I'll be here."

He squeezed his eyes shut, then leaned forward and brushed his lips against hers. "Just know, I will chase you if necessary. I'm a detective, after all."

***

Mitch had slept several hours that afternoon, so he decided to head to Memphis as soon as Jennings was settled at the old house on Bear Mountain Rd. They cleaned up most of the goose down, which resulted in more than one feather fight and a little more naked time. Then Jennings left to run to the store and Mitch threw a week's worth of clothes into his duffle. He hadn't had time to do laundry since he returned from Vegas, so if he needed more clothes, he'd have to buy them.

After checking the loft one more time, he grabbed Norma Jean's leash and let out a short whistle. She peeked her head out of the bathroom, where she'd been hiding out since the feathers started flying. Apparently, she was the only one allowed to make a mess. "Come on, girl. Time to go destroy a different place."

As he hooked the leash to her collar and patted her on the head, he realized he was going to miss the little dog. Just like her owner, she had wormed her way into his heart despite the fact that he wasn't looking for love.

In the hall, Mitch knocked on his neighbor's door. Shawn, a rail-thin, 6'4" star basketball player answered. "Hey man." They bumped knuckles and he caught the teen staring at Norma Jean.

"Dude, did you get another pet? That thing is ugly."

Mitch laughed and realized how light he felt despite what he would be facing the next day in Memphis. "She grows on you." He slid his wallet out of this pocket and grabbed a couple twenties. "I'm heading out for an indetermined amount of time. Can you look after Cash for me?"

"Sure thing. But didn't you just get back?"

"Yeah, Benny got hitched on Saturday and I've got to head out to finish up a case."

"I don't have to watch that do I?" He gestured at Norma Jean, who had rolled on her back and was busy licking herself in a private way in the very public corridor.

The dog truly had a mind of her own, just like Jennings. "Nah, she's my girl—" he caught himself and backpedaled, not having time to get into a drawn-out conversation with the teen. They were buds, but it seemed like a big deal to tell him about Jennings. "My friend's dog. I'm taking her home on my way out of town."

Shawn arched one eyebrow, but he let the slip slide. "I got Cash for you. Stay real." He offered his fist again and the two bumped. It was like Ahola, a greeting that could mean both hello and goodbye.

"Tell your mom I'm going to need some of those peanut butter cookies when I get back. The last batch didn't make it to the state line."

The teen laughed. "Word."

As the door closed, Mitch thought for the hundredth time that he hit the jackpot when it came to neighbors. The single mom worked hard, had raised two respectful kids and baked when she was anxious. With two teenagers, she was anxious on a regular basis, which kept Mitch in a constant stream of cookies, brownies and the occasional pie.

He also enjoyed attending Shawn's basketball games and had even written a letter of recommendation for a basketball clinic he was attending this summer at the local college. Mitch's lifestyle didn't really lend itself to complicated relationships, but the friendship he had formed with his neighbors helped make him feel a little less alone in the world.

Now, with Jennings and Norma Jean, his life and heart suddenly seemed very full, and he was surprised to find that it didn't scare him. Instead, he was excited to see where it led. He could picture a future with Jennings, despite the way he felt after things with Carla blew up. Despite "the incident."

Eventually, he'd need to tell her the rest of that story. But he had some unfinished business to attend to first.

***

Jennings put away the groceries and made a list of the most immediate projects that needed to be tackled. The fridge hadn't likely been cleaned in several decades, and honestly if she had the money to burn, she'd probably just replace it. But she'd already made a large dent in her bankroll after buying new towels, toiletries and food for the next week or so. As soon as she scrubbed her way through the house, she needed to find a job. But it would be hard to commit to something until she had her own vehicle, so she had at least until Benny got home to get the house in shape.

Pulling out a fresh roll of paper towels and a spray bottle of cleaner, she scrubbed away the layers of grime that had built up on her grandmother's kitchen table. The Formica had once been a deep yellow with daisies circling the edge. Now, the color was closer to brown and Jennings could barely make out a single flower. The paper towels and eco-friendly cleaner weren't cutting it.

She dug through her bags and found some steel wool. She filled the porcelain farmhouse sink with hot, soapy water and then went to the hallway. The linen closet held sheets, threadbare towels, lightbulbs, the world's oldest box of Kotex. She grabbed a stack of towels and stirred up a storm of dust. Sneezing, she mentally added the linen closet to her list of things to clean.

After her vision cleared, she spotted something at the back of the shelf. She stretched her arm over the deep shelves and snagged an orange and green photo album. A thick layer of grime covered the plastic-coated book. She carried it with the towels over to the sink.

Dipping one of the towels into the sudsy water, she soaked it through and then wrang out the excess water. The kitchen table forgotten; she rubbed the towel across the photo album. The word "Memories" appeared from under the grime and Jennings felt that word hit her hard in the chest.

She used a dry towel to finish cleaning off the book, then took it to the couch where she curled up in the corner. She took a few calming breaths before cracking the cover open.

The first picture showed her mama and daddy, young, happy and barely dressed. They were standing in the middle of a crowd, flowers in their hair and their fingers forming a "V." Written underneath the picture in her mother's distinctive scrawl were simply the words "The Beginning."

Jennings stroked her fingers over the picture, summoning up all the memories she had kept locked in her heart for so many years. Her childhood had been full of music, adventure and most of all, love. It hadn't been traditional by anyone's definition of the word, but she had been happy. Until that fateful night. The night when her childhood was ripped away from her. The night a raging fire lit the sky behind this house. The night when her parents had been taken from her and Benny. When everything started to crumble.

***

As soon as Mitch pushed open the screen door, Norma Jean raced through and launched her compact body at Jennings who was curled up on one end of the couch. He wasn't thrilled that she was out in the middle of the country with her front door wide open, but when he went to open his mouth, he saw her wiping her cheeks between Norma's kisses.

Her eyes were rimmed in red and a book laid open in her lap.

"Everything okay?" He slid onto the couch beside her, the springs of the old sofa creaking.

She nodded, while still trying to settle the dog down. "A combination of decades of dust and too many memories to count."

Norma Jean was stepping all over what Mitch realized was a photo album. Based on the cracked corners and yellowing of the pages, he figured it was old and grabbed the mutt before she could destroy it. He set her gently on the floor and then moved closer to Jennings, hoping to catch a glimpse of a tow-headed little girl. "Your parents?"

The album was open to a spread of pictures featuring a beat-up old van and two smiling, long-haired, bell-bottom wearing young adults. He guessed them to be in their late 20s.

She nodded and turned the page.

The couple stood on a cliff overlooking the ocean, the woman's hand resting on a pronounced baby bump and the man holding her tight. The wind had whipped long blonde locks across her face as the camera flashed, and both were squinting at the sun. The woman looked so much like Jennings that it nearly stole his breath.

The opposite page showed a bigger belly and even bigger smiles on the pair's faces. The backdrop a vast desert with distant plateaus and a lone cactus.

She flipped the page again, and there was her mother, sitting in a field of wildflowers, her long hair in a braid flipped over one shoulder, and a tiny, naked Caroline in her arms. The joy on her face was unmistakable.

"You look so much like her. Beautiful." His fingers traced the picture, wanting to soak in the joy of that moment.

"I was born in that field."

He turned to look at her, his mouth gaping open. "No."

She nodded, a smile lighting up her face. "Yup. My parents didn't really believe in hospitals, so when it was time, they stopped in a small town in Nebraska and found a midwife. They had driven by this massive wildflower field on their way into town and they knew that's where it should happen. My mom circled that field for almost two days until I decided to make my entrance. They washed me in a nearby creek and camped there for a week before they took off again."

"That's gotta be the best birth story I've ever heard." He was fairly certain his mother asked to be knocked out and woken up when her baby could fend for itself.

Jennings turned another page and Mitch sucked in a breath.

"Can I see that?" He reached for the album and slid it into his lap. It was a small, square picture, likely from a Polaroid. Her parents sat in camping chairs in front of the van, her dad strumming a guitar and her mother clapping her hands. A blonde-headed toddler danced between them. "Did you own any clothes as a child?" As cute as Caroline's little baby bottom was, he was more interested in the guitar. The guitar that he was 100% positive Jason had been playing that night in the bar.

She chuckled and pulled the album back into her lap. "My folks practiced what you'd call 'free-range parenting.' I rarely wore clothes, and I didn't attend a formal school until I was eight."

"Well, I can get on board with the no clothes thing." He pulled on the collar of the shirt she was wearing to expose her shoulder. "And you seem plenty intelligent to me." He nibbled on the curve between her neck and her shoulder and snuck another look at the photograph.

Jennings squirmed away from him. "Not that I don't enjoy that, but shouldn't you get on the road? It's late and I'm all settled here."

He looked around the room, his gaze lighting on the kitchen table with rags piled on top, the bags piled on the floor with towels spilling out of them, and counters loaded with cereal boxes and bags of chips. She had supplies. She had

Benny's car to use. She even had cell reception out here in the boondocks. So why was he so worried to leave her?

"I'll go. But you have to promise to lock all the doors and windows. No more leaving the door open."

"There's no one out here to bother me. Besides, I've got Norma Jean."

Mitch turned to find Norma sprawled out on the rug, her feet in the air, twitching to the rhythm of her dreams. "Lock the door, Jennings."

Chapter Twenty-Seven

After forty-eight hours of deep cleaning, the place looked about a million times better, and Jennings never wanted to see another rag. In Vegas, her housecleaning was mostly in response to one of Norma's tirades. She was no Martha Stewart. Which is why she was eating cereal for dinner.

She wasn't sure if she could survive this far from civilization—Uber Eats did not deliver to Bear Mountain Road. She checked.

In Vegas, there was a Starbucks on every corner and a literal smorgasbord of food options on the Strip. You could get pork lo mien or filet mignon at 3 am. Not that she could afford filet mignon, but she liked knowing it was an option.

Now that most everything was free of the two decades of dust that had accumulated in her absence, she was struggling to find a way to occupy her time and her mind. No cable, no smart TV to stream on—or Internet for that matter. No twenty-four-hour casino steps from her door. No job. No plans. No Mitch.

There was so much grass and loads of trees and fresh air out here in the country. So why did it feel like she was suffocating?

She scooped up the last bite of her Special K and set her bowl in the sink. The window was open, and the chirp of crickets filtered into the house. Closing her eyes, she flipped through her memories trying to capture one from the days before things got complicated. When it was just her parents and her, living on the road, parking the van wherever they were for the night.

Exploring nature, appreciating the great wide open, crickets and frogs and howling wolves the soundtrack of her nighttime. When had she stopped appreciating the simple things?

The answer was obvious, but she didn't want to dwell in the grief. She wanted to figure out how to be part of a family once again. To learn about everything she'd missed with Benny. To make new memories with him. But he was in Aruba. And she was here. Alone. In this house, where grief hid in the shadowy corners.

"Argh!"

The release only served to startle Norma Jean out of her sleep. She ran to the door, barking, ready to fight the non-existent intruder.

Since the couch was now available, Jennings flopped in the middle and rotated to prop her feet up. Her foot scraped against something hard. Reaching between the cushions, she pulled out the photo album she'd been looking through the other night. After Mitch left, she crashed and had forgotten all about it. Settling against the arm of the couch, she tucked her feet under her and flipped the book open.

The first few pages held pictures of the place where it all started. Her father barely had his license before he drove to New York to attend Woodstock. Her mom wasn't even old enough to drive but hitched a ride with a cousin and her boyfriend—against her parents' wishes.

Their shared love of music brought them both to the place where they met, and over the next week, fell in love.

But reality soon splashed cold water on their budding romance, and her mother had to return home and finish high school. Over the next decade, they wrote letters, sent postcards, even occasionally talked on the phone. They never wavered from their intention to be together, and once her father had saved up enough money for the two to survive, he drove back up to New York and picked up the woman he loved.

When she got into that van with a single suitcase, she knew she was choosing love over her family, over privilege. She knew there was no going back. Her parents would have nothing to do with two hippies living in a van.

The album jumped from the teens at Woodstock, to pictures from every corner of the country. The two of them at Mt. Rushmore, in Yellowstone National Park, overlooking the Pacific Ocean. Between the old van and their fondness for the style of the 60s, most people wouldn't realize these pictures were from the early 80s.

Then that tell-tale bump appeared, and soon a baby took the focus. Caroline's birth did not stall the adventures. The young parents were more than happy to show the world to their daughter.

Jennings flipped the page of the album, expecting to see a small naked dancer in front of a campfire. The picture wasn't there. She dug through the cushions, even moved the couch to look underneath, but she couldn't find it.

Her search was interrupted by ringing.

Grabbing her phone off the counter, she carefully laid the photo album in its place.

Mitch's name lit up the screen and put an immediate smile on her face. "Hey, handsome."

"Miss me yet?"

"Not as much as Norma Jean." The little dog was currently laying in front of the back door, waiting for her favorite person—the one who snuck her food off the table when he thought Jennings wasn't looking. The dog was already under the impression the world revolved around her; Mitch's adoration wasn't helping her inflated ego.

"Aw, I miss that scruffy mutt. But I miss you more. Memphis is a grind without you. Especially Betsy."

She wouldn't mind seeing Betsy again, but she'd have to be dragged back to Memphis kicking and screaming. She may have borne her biggest secret, but she wasn't any closer to wanting to relive it. "Tell your mom I said hi. And Harry." Her gaze landed back on the empty photo album page. "Did you snag the naked picture of me?"

"Busted."

Jennings chuckled, because there wasn't a hint of remorse in his tone. "Don't be flashing that around to your friends. You could get pinched for child pornography."

"Keeping it close to my heart, don't worry. Besides, this isn't really a hanging-out-with-friends trip. Unless you count several hours in a dim sum truck with Harry."

"Dim Sum? Like the dumplings?"

He laughed and the sound sank low into Jennings' gut, temporarily soothing the unsettled feeling that had been there the last two days she'd spent alone surrounded by the past.

"Yes, like the dumplings. We borrowed the truck from a friend to use for surveillance. Both of our vehicles are pretty recognizable around here."

"Did you at least get to eat some?"

"Sum. That's funny."

She rolled her eyes. "You're punchy tonight."

"Hazard of the job. Staking out a bar and all."

"Just stay alert enough to turn down any advances."

"Trust me, you are the only advancer I'm interested in."

"Somehow I don't feel reassured." Part of her wished she was there—to fend off the women who were likely eyeing him at this moment—but why did it have to be Memphis? It was such an odd coincidence that his hometown was the same place that took the last good thing she had in her life. "I don't like you being there."

"I don't like it any more than you do. But Jason has to pay for what he's done."

"How is Carla?" Jennings felt bad that she hadn't even asked how the woman was doing. She may be a skank, but no one deserved to be beaten—especially by the man who had vowed to love her.

"I'm not here for Carla." His playful tone was gone.

"Yeah, I know. It's for Harry." She wasn't jealous of Carla. Jennings believed him when he said he loved her. Because she felt it too.

"No, Jennings. I'm here for you, and every other woman he's hurt over the years."

Light exploded behind her eyes and blinding pain pressed against her skull. "Excuse me?" She braced her hands on the counter, suddenly dizzy.

Mitch mumbled a series of curse words. "Babe, I'm sorry, maybe I have had too much to drink tonight." A thudding noise echoed through the phone, like he was banging his head against something.

Suddenly, she was back in that alley, on that dark night, huddled behind a dumpster, using a heavy velvet curtain she'd found as a blanket. She thought she was well-hidden, but when the man had loomed over her, with a sneer on his face, she knew she'd been sorely mistaken.

She could still picture him, average height for a man, young, but older than her, with dark, vacant eyes and a tattoo of a snake on his neck. She stared at that snake the entire time, focusing on each scale, tracing it with her eyes, determined not to remember what he was doing to her.

When he was done, she considered laying there and just letting the blood drain out of her until she was gone. But she knew if there was any chance of her baby surviving, she had to ask for help. And deal with the consequences later.

So, she'd stumbled out to Beale Street and flagged down a taxi, telling the driver that she fell and needed to go to the hospital.

***

"Jennings, babe. You still there?" He slapped a couple twenties on the bar and hurried outside. "Babe, you're freaking me out. Talk to me." She'd been deathly silent since his drunken revelation.

When she finally spoke, her voice came out as a whisper. "What the hell, Mitch?" Then she hung up.

He'd blown it. Two days of boredom staking out Jason's haunts had led to one too many shots at The Beetle and his fucking loose lips. He tried to call her back, but the phone went straight to voicemail.

He left a pleading message, then as an added measure, shot off a text echoing his sentiments and begging for forgiveness. He climbed into his truck and nearly had the key in the ignition before he realized that he couldn't drive. If he could, he'd go straight to Asheville and try to clean up this mess.

Instead, he dialed Harry.

"Did you find him?" His voice was like dragging a turnip across a grater on a good day, after being woken up, he sounded like death.

"I messed up, Harry. I f'ing blew it." He squeezed the back of his neck, trying to dull the pounding there.

"Explain yourself, kid. I'm not a mind reader." His mentor sounded more alert now and more pissed off.

Leaning his head against the steering wheel, Mitch told Harry about his drunken slip of the tongue.

"Damn, kid. I thought you had blown our op. All this drama over the dame?"

"No, Jason's a no-show. Again." He wanted to make some smart-ass Sam Spade retort, but he curbed himself because he had to ask for a favor. "Can you pick me up at The Beetle? And maybe I can crash at your place?"

Harry barked out a laugh. "What, don't want to incur the wrath of Betsy by showing up drunk?"

"Not particularly." And certainly not on top of the rest of his shitty night.

"You can stay here. But call an Uber. I'm not a damn taxi service."

It was the second time in fifteen minutes someone had hung up on him.

He ordered a ride, then tried Jennings again. He was leaving yet another voicemail when the car pulled up. He opened the back door and slid into the seat. "I love you, babe. Please call me back."

As he tapped to end the call, his eyes landed on the driver. Dread crept up his spine before the man even opened his mouth. "Long time no see, Snitch. Heard you was lookin' for me."

Mitch was too busy berating himself to notice the fist flying toward his face. His last thought before the darkness took over was that Jennings would never forgive him.

Chapter Twenty-Eight

Jennings threw the phone down on the couch and huffed out an aggravated breath. How was she supposed to forgive Mitch when he wouldn't answer the damn phone? She was supposed to be the one holding a grudge.

It'd been two days since he let it slip that Jason was the man who attacked her.

She'd been so overcome by the revelation she spent the night curled under her grandmother's wedding ring quilt racked by memories of the horrific event long ago. She'd lied to the nurse at the hospital, she'd lied to the policeman who showed up to interrogate her, and she'd been lying to herself for twenty-two years.

Shock and fear had made her hang up on Mitch and turn off the phone. But a restless night and a hard look at the truth made her see the light by the time the sun came up. He wasn't the bad guy. He was the man who was trying to defend the honor of a helpless sixteen-year-old girl.

He was the man who was standing up for her.

She'd turned on her phone to find increasingly frantic messages from Mitch, begging for her forgiveness. Then nothing. For over forty-eight hours, it had been radio silence. Was he really going to throw away what they had the moment it got a little hard? Was he really going to abandon her now? Now that he had ripped open the wound she'd covered up years ago?

She and Norma Jean had spent the last two days weeding the garden and the evenings digging through closets and making piles for donations and trash. This afternoon she'd discovered her granny's old Singer and set it up on the kitchen table to see if she could remember anything she'd been taught. And to distract herself from the hurt that lurked in the dark recesses of her mind.

At the back of the master closet, she found two bins chock full of fabric. Most of it was polyester, straight from the 60s, but she also found a lightweight denim she was determined to wrestle into a skirt that would cover more than her Las Vegas wardrobe.

She left the phone stuck between two couch cushions and went back to the kitchen to work on the hem of the skirt. Anything to numb the pain building in her chest.

An hour later, Jennings lifted her foot off the pedal and flipped the presser foot up, then clipped the threads. She turned the skirt right-side out and snapped it into shape. Not too bad for her first effort. No pattern or anything. She rose to press it with an ancient iron before trying it on. The iron hissed and steam shot from the bottom. She used her other hand to spread out the seam, just like her grandmother had shown her too many years ago to count.

Her phone rang, startling her, and she jerked her hand right onto the scorching hot metal plate. "Dammit!" She rushed into the kitchen and ran the water as cold as it would get, while her phone continued to scream "Living La Vida Loca". It wasn't even Mitch calling.

Eventually the welt on her hand stopped pulsing in anger and she turned off the tap. She blew lightly along the mark on her way to the bathroom. Digging through the medicine cabinet, she realized that 90% of the stuff in there was so old it would likely do more harm than good, but she did find an ancient tube of antibiotic ointment. She smeared a dab on, and the ache quieted slightly. She had started chucking expired bottles of aspirin and vitamins in the trash can when Ricky Martin screamed again from the other room. It must be important for Elena to call back so quickly.

She sprinted to the living room and dug the phone out from between the couch cushions. "Elena, what's wrong?"

A stream of jumbled Spanish mixed with wracking sobs.

"Sweetie, calm down. And English, please." Jennings had never heard Elena so anxious, and it hurt her heart to hear her friend in such distress—now that her heart was fully functioning again. Well, mostly.

Elena sucked in a breath and blew it out loudly. "*Chica*," her voice cracked on the familiar nickname, "it's Martin. He had a heart attack. He's in surgery right now." Another sob escaped her lips. "I can't make it without him, Jennings."

"Oh, Elena, I'm so sorry." Jennings remembered the night the two had met, at a staff party for Christmas. The handsome bartender had literally swept Elena off her feet when he moved her out of the way of a crashing Christmas tree. The two had been inseparable since and married almost ten years. Which was a long time, especially when a Liza Minnelli look-alike officiates the wedding.

Elena was distraught and with most of her family in Puerto Rico, she was alone and scared. Jennings mentally counted the remaining money in her bankroll. Between getting her hair done, buying a decent dress for the wedding, and getting supplies for the house, she had already dented it to the point that it would need a complete restoration. But her friend needed her, and her fledging poker career would have to be pushed even further to the back of the stove. It would also be another diversion from Mitch not calling her back. "I'm getting on the next flight. I promise."

"Bless you, Chica, I just don't know what to do. I hate to take you away from Mitch, and your brother, but I could really use a friend."

"No, honestly, it's fine. Mitch ran off on a case and Benny is still in Aruba. It's not a bother at all. I'll call back as soon as I've made the arrangements." She didn't want to burden her already-worried friend with the Mitch drama, plus she wasn't ready to share the sordid tale she'd been keeping secret for all the years they'd known each other.

Jennings disconnected and immediately started searching for a flight. Luckily, even though the Asheville airport was small, they had a direct flight to Vegas leaving in the morning.

She booked the flight and then flew into action, calling boarding kennels to find a place for Norma Jean and tossing garments and cosmetics into a bag. Benny and Aimee would be back on Saturday, so she would drive his car to their place and then get an Uber to the airport. As for Mitch, maybe he'd come to his senses by the time she got back.

Chapter Twenty-Nine

The smell of piss and cigarettes permeated Mitch's awareness, taking him back to his late teens, and hanging out in the alley behind The Beetle waiting for trouble. But when his eyelids finally cracked open, he wasn't outside and there were no dumpsters, just cracked linoleum and a toilet that hadn't been cleaned since Reagan was president.

Ironically, he needed to pee, but his foggy mind couldn't figure how to accomplish the task with his hands behind him and his wrists chained to the pipes under the porcelain wall-mounted sink.

He struggled to remember how he found himself in this predicament and what day it was. There was light coming in the tiny window high up on the opposite wall, but it felt artificial, like a streetlight maybe, so he was guessing it was nighttime. The door to the bathroom was closed, and he couldn't make out any sounds from beyond it.

His stomach cramped, eliciting a gurgle, and he coughed up a mouthful of bile. He gauged the distance to the toilet, then swallowed it back down. If he missed, he'd be smelling the acrid stench for the foreseeable future. He doubted Merry Maids would arrive in the morning.

Closing his eyes, he searched his mind for some clue as to what was happening. He vaguely remembered having breakfast with Harry, eggs and bacon, with a side of smothered hashbrowns. Was that the last time he ate? And how long had it been since then?

He burped, and the taste of tequila (the cheap shit, which he never drank) lingered in his mouth. His brain fog could be caused by too much to drink, but the memory loss was more puzzling. And upsetting.

Sucking in his breath, he tried to remember the breathing exercises that hot yoga teacher was harping on when Benny dragged him to some Relax & Rejuvenate experience at The Grove Park Inn.

"Jennings!" His eyes flew open, and he bucked against his restraints, suddenly desperate to get free, to find her, to figure out what the hell had happened. Was she hurt?

Someone pounded on the door. "Keep it down in there, Snitch. Some of us are trying to sleep out here."

The sound of Jason's voice penetrated the mire inside his brain. He didn't remember it all, but he remembered that bastard's sneer right before someone sucker punched him.

The door slammed open, banging into the opposite wall.

"Guess you need a nightcap, Sleeping Beauty." The depraved gang leader held up a bottle of the cheapest tequila money could buy. From behind him, a tatted-up guy with a ponytail ducked under Jason's arm and knelt beside Mitch.

"Open wide." The minion grabbed Mitch's jaw and squeezed. He struggled, but between the chains and the size of the man's arms, he knew he didn't stand a chance. The muscle dropped several pills in Mitch's mouth and then Jason followed up with half the bottle of liquor.

Mitch choked, trying to spit out the poison, and realized this wasn't the first time they had done this. No wonder he felt drugged. Muscles clamped his hand over Mitch's mouth and glared at him.

Jason took a swig from the bottle. "Damn, that's nasty." He tossed the bottle into the sink. "Don't worry, Snitch. We'll save the rest for breakfast."

Mitch coughed again, which caused most of the contents of his mouth to flow down his throat. *Fuck. Back to oblivion.*

Muscles let go of Mitch's face and left the room.

Jason kicked his captive in the ribs and then spun toward the door. "Now pipe the fuck down. I'm entertaining a lady friend."

Mitch strained to see past Jason through the tears in his eyes. Beyond the door lay a ratty motel room with two double beds. On the one closest to the bathroom, he could see two small, bare feet. They weren't moving, and he'd bet the last few of his brain cells that the person attached to those feet wasn't there of her own accord.

Jason sneered down at him and then slammed the door shut on his way out.

A clearer picture of what had happened emerged, but it was too disturbing to contemplate, so Mitch gave into the alcohol–and-drug-induced stupor.

***

The next time Mitch came to, he was in a mostly empty warehouse, sitting on an old ladderback with his hands zip-tied behind him and his ankles shackled to the chair legs. It was daytime, according to the sun streaming through the windows.

The space had high ceilings, maybe twenty feet, and garage doors on three sides. He was alone and from what he could tell, the building was just one large room. He craned his neck to look behind him, and saw one door, which was open and led to a bathroom.

It looked nicer than the last one he was in, but he was pretty grateful to be out in the open and upright.

He rocked in the chair, trying to determine if he could get to his feet, but instead he crashed forward, banging his face against the concrete floor. Blackness overtook him for a moment, but he didn't pass out. He felt every ounce of the pain radiating from his likely broken nose.

"Taking a nappy, Snitch?" Jason's voice came at him from behind, but he couldn't turn his head to see where he came from.

The chair was jerked off the floor and set on its legs again, Mitch bouncing against the seat and the movement whipping his head back. Stars appeared behind his eyes, but he swallowed a gasp, because he refused to show weakness to the thug.

When he opened his eyes, he was surrounded by a group of men in various degrees of ink, piercings and menacing expressions. Most were packing and Jason stood in the middle of the crowd running a six-inch blade across his thigh. *This is it. I'm going to die. There will be no justice for Jennings. I'll never kiss her luscious lips again, never sweep her hair off her neck and kiss the tender spot behind her ear. Never tell her I love her.*

"Why did you come back to Memphis, Snitch? Did that bitch call you whining?" Jason ran his fingertip along the edge of the silver blade, his eyes glinting with pure evil. He had progressed from a little punk to a straight-up psychopath in the twenty years since Mitch had gone straight.

Straining to focus, he tried to figure a way out of this mess. He couldn't just give up. Not with Jennings waiting for him back in Asheville. Not if there was any chance she would forgive him and let him love her forever. He'd watched his fair share of old movies with Harry and one thing he knew about raving lunatics—at least in Hollywood—they loved to hear themselves talk.

"Which bitch are you referring to? They're all bitches, as far as I'm concerned." Maybe there was a chance he could convince Jason he was on his side.

The gang leader's face scrunched up in confusion. "I'm not in the mood for games. Tell me where Carla is."

So, his end goal was to finish Carla off? Maybe she did have some evidence that could put him away. "I haven't seen her since she married your ass back in Vegas. She's your nightmare now. I'm just in town visiting my mother." Hopefully Harry had the nightmare tucked away somewhere secure.

"You weren't visiting that aging dancer. You were hanging out on my turf."

"I was visiting an old haunt. Hoping to reconnect with some friends. I got no reason to hone in on your business."

Jason slid a familiar phone out of his pocket. "Stop fucking around and unlock your phone so I can prove you're lying to me."

If his phone was on, maybe Harry had tracked it. Mitch wished he knew what day it was. Just how long had the pyscho been holding him? "Fucking untie me and I'll unlock it. I'll even call Harry and ask him where his good-for-nothing niece is."

"Do I look like a moron? Tell me the fucking code."

"It's face ID."

The creep's lip curled into a snarl. "I said stop fucking with me. You think you'd still be alive if I could open the phone with your ugly mug?"

Mitch had seen a lot of bad shit in his lifetime, but the darkness behind Jason's eyes rivaled it all. Had the punk selling stolen stereo equipment in a back alley really graduated to murder? Straining to keep the tremor out of his voice, he kept up the show of strength. "You think I can remember some fucking passcode? Give me the fucking phone." *Come on, Harry. Anytime.*

One of the minions got a call and then crossed the scarred concrete floor to whisper to his boss. Jason's eyes narrowed and he snapped his fingers at the biggest of the thugs. "Marlborough, take your crew to The Beetle. See what's up." Half of the posse sauntered out a door in the corner.

It was down to four underlings and the chief psychopath. Mitch liked those odds much better. Now he just had to get untied. And a weapon would help. "What's wrong, J? Someone actually threatening your corner?"

"The only thing you need to worry about is the code for your phone, Snitch."

Mitch tried to shrug, but it was tough in his position. "I got nowhere to be."

Suddenly, Jason was in his face, and that shiny-ass blade was pressed against his jugular. "Sure sounded like you've got some ho on the hook. 'Love you, babe.'" The last part came out in a saccharine pitch like he was imitating a Barbie doll.

Mitch flashed back to the night Jason had picked him up, and him pleading with Jennings to call him back. He couldn't let this sicko know about Jennings. And certainly not that he was head-over-heels in love with her. Then she'd become another pawn in his demented chess game. "I was just leaving a message for your mama. She's a little older than I usually go for, but at least it's a safe bet you haven't screwed her."

The blade pressed harder and something hot and sticky slid down Mitch's neck. This cat-and-mouse game was going to get him killed. And then Jennings would never forgive him.

"You've got two seconds, Snitch."

Mitch hadn't prayed in a long time, but he was willing to try anything at this point. He'd just closed his eyes when it sounded like every window in the warehouse exploded. Several flashbangs, smoke, and too much gunfire for anyone's health later, he opened his eyes to find Harry standing over him, strapped with a bullet-proof vest and wearing a bored expression.

"In the future, if you say you're going to crash at my place, I'd appreciate a phone call if your plans change."

Chapter Thirty

When Mitch woke up, he was convinced he was back in that warehouse. His ears were still buzzing from the flashbangs, his eyes burned from the smoke, and his throat felt drier than the Sahara. But when he raised his arm to touch the bandage on his neck, he knew he was free.

Panic subsiding, his breathing normalized, and he could hear a steady beep and smell the familiar antiseptic scent of a hospital. Squinting, he tried to take in his surroundings while allowing as little light into his aching eyes as possible.

Yup. Uncomfortable hospital bed, paper gown, tubes running everywhere, and Harry passed out in a visitor's chair, snoring to the rhythm of a snare drum.

His neck felt like he was starring in *The Mummy*, pain radiated from his nose and his head hadn't hurt this bad since he drank three bottles of scotch over a weekend in his twenties. Then he started to remember everything that had happened, and his heart hurt worse than his head. "Jennings..."

Harry stirred, swiping a hand across his chin and coughing like there was an animal stuck in his lung. He grabbed a cheap, plastic pitcher and chugged from it, then slammed it on the table over Mitch's legs. "Well look who decided to wake up."

Mitch was too weak for a comeback. "Jennings?"

His mentor sighed, shaking his head. "Still worried about that dame after all this?"

"Phone."

Grumbling, Harry slid his phone into his hand and left the room.

Mitch tapped in the passcode (no, he wasn't stupid enough to use face ID). He had a series of missed calls and texts, including several from Jennings on Wednesday morning. Her last text simply read "WTF?"

He tapped her contact, praying she would answer, and everything could go back to normal—whatever that looked like. The call went straight to voicemail, and the sound of her voice was like a stab to his aching heart. He called back four times just to listen to her. Finally, he left a message explaining that things had gone south, and he was in the hospital, but as soon as he got out, he was driving straight to Asheville.

He had really fucked up this time, and apparently, he lived to see the misery on the other side of a life without Caroline Jennings Lee.

He closed his eyes, willing himself to slip into the darkness. He must have drifted off, because when the phone rang, he nearly jumped out of the bed. He fumbled with the phone, blindly swiping the screen. "Jennings?"

"I was hoping she was with you. What the heck, Mitch?" That was as close as Benny came to cussing.

His mouth felt like sandpaper, and he wasn't sure how he was going to handle this conversation. He spied the pitcher Harry had drained earlier and luckily there was just enough water left to wet his throat. "Are you calling from Aruba?"

"No, we flew home today. Where are you? And where is my sister?"

How was it Saturday already? It had been almost a week since he'd seen the woman he loved. He hoped like hell he could fix this. "I left her at the Bear

Mountain house. Is she not there?" *And is she ignoring Benny's calls too?* That didn't make any sense.

"She left my car at my house with a note saying she had an emergency and she'd be back soon. What did you do to her?"

There was no way he could explain the whole sordid affair to Benny right now. "Have you tried to call her?"

"Now why didn't I think of that?"

"Things went sideways in Memphis, B. They got Jason, but I'm at Saint Francis. As soon as they let me out of here, I swear I will find her and make this right."

Benny sighed loud enough Mitch swore air rushed out of the phone. "This is exactly why I didn't want you involved with her. I'll talk to you later."

The call ended and Mitch cursed Vegas for once again turning his life upside down.

***

Mitch slid his left leg into his pants, but when he raised the right one, the hospital room titled sideways, and he landed on the floor with a thwack. Undeterred, he stuck his other leg in and wiggled the pants up over his hips. He had the fly zipped and the paper gown over his head when the angry nurse from the night shift appeared.

"Just what do you think you're doing, mister?" From his position on the floor, he could see a black clog tapping the floor in a threatening rhythm.

"I dropped a contact under the bed."

"I knew you were gonna be trouble the moment I laid eyes on you. The good-looking ones always are." She stepped into the hall. "Judy, call an orderly to help me get Mr. Tall Dark and Scruffy back into bed."

Mitch rubbed his hand over his jaw, where he was sporting a week's worth of beard. But there was no time to shave. He had to get out of this place. Holding onto the side rail of the bed, he hoisted himself back to his feet, his vision swimming for only fifteen seconds this time. An improvement, but driving would still be iffy.

He'd spent his awake hours trying to track down Jennings, but he had a pretty good idea where she had to be. Benny was pissed and ignoring his calls and Elena's phone went straight to voicemail like Jennings's. That was her whole world, so if she wasn't in Asheville, she had to be in Vegas. Which meant he had to go back to Sin City. And there was no time to drive.

Nurse Rachet stood in the doorway, blocking his exit, her arms crossed over an ample chest. If she smiled occasionally, she'd probably be attractive.

Charm was his go-to weapon of choice, so Mitch pulled a t-shirt over his head and ran his hand through his hair, hoping to play into her admitted attraction to him. "It's been a terrific visit, five stars all the way. I'll be sure to rate you on Yelp, but I've got an engagement in another venue." He grabbed the plastic "Personal Belongings" bag that would likely become his carry-on, unless he could convince Harry to meet him at the airport with his duffel. Squeezing his eyes shut, he let go of the railing and willed himself to remain upright.

He'd been refusing the pain meds for several hours now, but the lingering effects were messing with his balance.

"The only place you're going is back to bed." She moved forward, as if to grab him, stepping out of the doorway.

He seized the opportunity and shuffled past her and into the hall. He looked both ways. A tall, bald guy in scrubs was coming from the left, so Mitch turned right and staggered down the hall, his plastic luggage clenched to his chest.

"Stop him!" Nurse Frowny-Face screamed at Baldy, who caught up with Mitch in about eight seconds, two doors down from his room. It was the most pathetic chase scene in history.

The orderly, who's nametag read "Marcus," grabbed Mitch to steady him. "Man, what you trying to do? Make a break for it? Have you not met Mattie?" He dropped his voice. "People around here call her Matilda the Hun." Marcus grabbed a wheelchair that was parked near the nurse's station and pushed Mitch down to sit in it.

"I've got to leave. Like yesterday." Mitch slumped in the chair out of defeat. He hadn't even made it off the ward.

"Hospitals suck, dude. No way around it. But you look like a dump truck backed over you." If circumstances were different, Mitch would take Marcus out for a beer. As it was, maybe they could share an apple juice later.

"It's not the hospital. I've got to find someone."

Marcus bobbed that shiny brown head and pointed at him. "Gotcha. It's a woman."

Mitch sighed and nodded.

"Got it bad?"

"So bad."

The Hun appeared and grabbed the handles of the wheelchair. "Back to bed, Rico Suave."

"Hey, Mattie, you know what I saw down in the breakroom on four?"

The chair stopped its forward momentum.

"They got one of those cookie cakes for someone's birthday. Just sitting there with only one slice out of it. Seemed a shame to me."

"Chocolate chip?"

"Is there any other kind?"

Mitch tilted his head discreetly and could see the nurse deliberating.

Marcus took one step toward the chair. "I could get the patient settled back in bed. You know, if you wanted to take a quick break."

She narrowed her eyes. "You sure you can handle him? He's swarmy."

"Phesh. I got this." He waved a hand through the air.

"I have been on my feet for hours." She let go of the handles. "If you don't mind…"

"Not at all." Marcus grabbed the wheelchair and started back toward Mitch's room.

The nurse hightailed it down the hall and passed through a set of double doors.

Mitch appreciated the rescue, but it didn't get him any closer to finding Jennings. Then he realized the orderly had passed his door and they were approaching the elevators at the end of the hall.

"Marcus, man, you're my hero."

"Dude, I'm just taking you out for some fresh air. I don't know nothing about anything."

Mitch nodded, relieved to have found someone who got it. He pulled out his phone and ordered a car. Nothing was going to keep him from finding his girl. Not a cranky nurse. Not a head that spun like the tilt-a-whirl at the carnival. Not even an airplane that could crash into a ball of fire in a cornfield over Kansas.

Chapter Thirty-One

For twenty years, all she'd had to worry about was herself. First, Norma Jean showed up and wormed her way into her heart. Then she woke up one day and realized Elena was basically her best friend.

It was weird how those things crept up on you.

Now, her life seemed full of people who cared about her. At least that's how it felt when she finally got her phone charged back up and turned it on to about a hundred messages from Mitch, Benny and even the gruff Harry. As soon as Martin was out of the woods and Elena seemed okay, Jennings headed back to the airport, back to the life she hadn't expected a few weeks ago.

Vegas had been hot, loud and unappealing. She'd mostly been at the hospital and at Elena's trying to get her friend to eat and sleep and shower. She didn't once consider sneaking off to a casino to play poker. She'd been solely focused on making sure her friend had everything she needed. And it felt good. Really good.

When she realized Benny was worried about her, she felt like the Grinch when his heart grew three sizes that day. Having her brother back in her life made the sun shine brighter, the clouds look fluffier, and the lights of Vegas seem dimmer.

And when Harry told her Mitch was in the hospital after being held captive by Jason, it felt like she had swapped places with Elena and now she was the frantic woman worried about the man she loved.

Because she loved Mitch. As much as it terrified her, she couldn't deny it. She was in love with him. Despite her fears. Despite his insistence on avenging her past, obviously at his own peril. Despite the stubbornness that almost got him killed.

Finally, the row in front of her emptied out and she filed off the plane with the other weary passengers. It had been a rocky flight, and she was glad to be back on the ground.

As soon as she was in the terminal, she dialed Harry. "How is he?"

"A pain in my ass. But he'll survive."

"Has he always been this stubborn?" She ducked between two rows of chairs and bypassed a line of people waiting for a caffeine fix. She briefly considered joining them, but pressed on, not wanting to waste any time.

Harry grunted. "Since the day I met him. That's why I could never shake him. Held on like a spunky rat terrier."

"I can't..." She trailed off as a mirage that looked like a drunk, homeless man appeared in the crowd of people surging her way. "Harry, I gotta call you back."

She blinked to clear her vision, but the bearded, bruised, bandaged man continued to stagger in her direction. He saw her then, and lurched to a stop, angering the people directly behind him. Hand gestures abounded and she could hear a few choice words, even from a distance.

She quickened her pace, her rolling bag bumping along behind her. She zigzagged through throngs of travelers—parents dragging toddlers, corporate types with their phones glued to their ear, an elderly couple that wouldn't make it to their gate before midnight.

Mitch lurched forward, his body swaying. He obviously wasn't well, but here he was in the Memphis airport, clutching a white and blue plastic bag to his chest, having already passed through security, which meant he was planning to get on an airplane. The man who didn't fly. And wasn't a fan of Las Vegas.

They stopped in front of the VIP lounge, a foot and a half separating them. He looked worse up close. Like an MMA fighter who had lost in the first round.

"You going on vacation?" She gestured at the bag he had dropped to the floor. It was one of those bags they give you in the hospital that usually contained grippy socks and a throw-up bucket.

"Thought I'd catch a show, play some craps. I heard the buffets in Vegas are awesome."

She scrunched up her nose and shook her head. "That food sits out for hours. You're better off eating out of a dumpster. Better ambiance, too."

He started to list to the side, so she grabbed him by his biceps. Nice, strong arms. She'd missed those arms.

"I never liked craps anyway. Too much hootin' and hollerin'."

She picked up his bag and wrapped his arm around her shoulders, then led him to a chair. When he sat down, air wheezed out of his lungs like a deflating balloon.

"You should be in a hospital."

He leaned close to her, whispering. "I was. I escaped."

She smiled, her eyes filling with tears. "You were going to get on a plane."

"I told you I'd come find you, no matter what." He tucked a strand of hair behind her ear, then leaned forward, resting his forehead against hers. "But since you're already here, I think I should probably go back to the hospital. I'm seeing two of you."

Epilogue

A week later, everyone gathered on Betsy's deck for another Chef Ghille masterpiece spread. He had roasted an entire hog for the occasion and if Mitch hadn't given her an orgasm about fifteen minutes ago, Jennings would have come just from the smell wafting through the house.

Mitch had spent two more days in the hospital and had been recuperating since at his mother's, with Betsy making a fuss over him and Jennings making sure he didn't lose his mind. The sex served as an excellent distraction. He was still milking his injuries and making her be on top—which she had zero issues with. And if Betsy was around, they just turned the Elvis music up to drown out the burnin' love.

The police had been over more than once, taking statements about the events of twenty years ago and the more recent past. Jason would be behind bars for the rest of his natural life. Mitch had only scratched the surface of his criminal exploits.

The doorbell rang and Betsy greeted Harry and Charter, devouring the attention being hostess afforded her. Benny and Aimee arrived moments later, and introductions were made all around.

Once everyone filled their plates with delicious, artery-clogging food, Harry raised his glass of sweet tea and cleared his throat.

"If y'all will pipe down, I've got something to say."

Mitch placed his plate next to hers on the table, then wrapped his arm around her as he sat down. She was surrounded by people who truly cared about her and had spent the last week in a city that had given her a panic attack on her last visit. She finally felt like she had put the ghosts of her past to rest.

"I got good news, and I got bad news." Harry coughed, then took a swig of his drink. "The good news is I'm retiring."

A cheer went up around the table, but the older man hushed everyone and motioned with his hands to simmer down.

"The bad news is that I heard from the doctor today and the cancer seems to have taken a hike. You folks are stuck with me a little longer." He pointed at Mitch. "I'm going to have lots of time to perfect my golf game, so you better work on your putt."

The group got really loud then, all gathering around Harry and some of them even having the nerve to hug him. He claimed to hate the sappy show of support, but Jennings was certain she saw a smile tug at the lined corners of his mouth. Mitch embraced him tightly, and when they separated, he had tears in his eyes.

Looked like they'd be visiting Memphis on a regular basis. Luckily, these people had helped her make her peace with this place. With her past. With her future.

She felt hopeful, loved, and like she had a family again.

Betsy insisted everyone eat before the food got cold, but just as they all took their seats again, the doorbell rang.

"I'll get it!" Mitch jumped up and raced inside.

She wondered who else would be coming, but Aimee started talking about seeing flamingos in Aruba and she wasn't sure how long Mitch was gone. Everyone around the table talked between bites of macaroni salad, fried green tomatoes and pulled pork.

Jennings had barely put a dent in her plate when she realized how full she was. But not of Chef's Ghille's cooking, instead of Southern hospitality, heritage and love.

She didn't notice Mitch returning, until he was right beside her, a mischievous grin on his handsome face. Paired with his hands behind his back, she figured he was up to something. "Who was at the door?"

His eyes twinkled, and he was practically vibrating with excitement.

Soon, the raucous guests grew silent, and everyone was staring at the two of them.

"Mitch," she said in a low voice, between gritted teeth, "you're freaking me out."

"Nothing to freak out about, but I have something that belongs to you. Well, you and Benny." From behind his back, he pulled out an old, beat-up guitar. Covered in Woodstock stickers.

For a moment, she couldn't breathe. Couldn't comprehend what she was seeing.

"What's that?" Benny's question broke through her stupor, and she tentatively reached out her hand to touch the strings.

"It's Dad's." She met Mitch's eyes over the guitar, hers blurring with tears. "How did you get this?"

"It was Harry and Charter, mostly. They worked their connections through the department so it wouldn't be taken as evidence."

"They had more than enough on Jason, without that guitar." Harry swiped a napkin across his mouth. "Didn't see no sense in it rotting away in an evidence locker."

"I know how much it meant to you." Mitch said the words softly enough, she doubted the others could hear. He pushed the guitar into her hands. "It belongs with you."

"And Benny." She sought her brother's face through her tears.

He grinned broadly. "We'll leave it at your place, maybe I'll take lessons or something."

"Dad would love that."

Everyone went back to eating, while Jennings sat there in stunned silence. She never thought she'd see this last piece of her father again. It was like a final bandage over her wounded, but healing, heart. And she knew she owed that healing to the man beside her.

She slid her hand under the tablecloth, squeezing Mitch's knee, then leaned close to whisper to him.

"I love you."

He swung his head to look at her, eyes wide and a grin spreading across his face. He met her lips, his tasting of savory barbeque sauce and lemonade. "I love you too, CJ."

She knew her smile matched his in that moment. He had started calling her that after they found each other in the airport. He said it was the perfect combination of sweet and sassy, just like her.

For over twenty years, she had run from being Caroline and barely lived as Jennings. Somehow CJ was a chance at who she could be without deserting who got her where she was today—happy and with a heart full of love.

No one at the table seemed to notice the earth-shattering revelations that had passed between them, so Mitch twined their fingers together under the table and they went back to eating the amazing food and enjoying the company of those they loved.

About the author

Tara grew up with her nose buried in a book, and not much has changed. She's a serial entrepreneur – doggie daycare owner, quilt shop owner, maker and, of course, author. Currently, she lives in the mountains of North Carolina with her #1 love, a shichon named Agador Spartacus. Her whole family lives nearby, including her two grown sons, who are inspirations for the "cool" things young people say.

If you enjoyed this book, please consider leaving a review on Goodreads or Amazon.com. Thanks!

Also by

Eastport Beach Romances

Welcome to Heron House (Book 1)

Meet Riley and Ben as they are each starting over and learning to love after loss.

A Heron House Affair (Book 2)

You're invited to the social event of the year! Dance the night away with Trip and Ada.

Something's Brewing at Heron House (Book 3)

Sharkey & Hope navigate an opposites-attract romance in a hilarious and moving way.

Coming Feb 2026

Standalones

Above Average Girl (2022)

This is a sweet romance about a plus-sized girl trying to find her way in the dating world with a little help from her friends.

The Things I Do For Her (2022)

Truly a story of friendship, this sweet romance is about growing up, finding love and moving on.

Ebooks available on Amazon.
Paperbacks available through all major retailers.
For signed paperback copies, go to www.dreamingoftheseafabrics.com.